PHALLIC
PANIC

PHALLIC
PANIC

FILM, HORROR AND THE
PRIMAL UNCANNY

BARBARA CREED

MELBOURNE
UNIVERSITY
PRESS

MELBOURNE UNIVERSITY PRESS
An imprint of Melbourne University Publishing Ltd
187 Grattan Street, Carlton, Victoria 3053, Australia
mup-info@unimelb.edu.au
www.mup.com.au

First published 2005
Text © Barbara Creed 2005
Design and typography © Melbourne University Publishing Ltd 2005

Cover and text design by Nada Backovic Designs
Typeset in Goudy 11.5/13.5 point by Syarikat Seng Teik Sdn. Bhd., Malaysia
Printed in Australia by McPherson's Printing Group
Cover image: Columbia/The Kobal Collection

National Library of Australia Cataloguing-in-Publication entry

Creed, Barbara.
  Phallic panic: Film, horror and the primal uncanny
  Bibliography.
  Includes index.
  ISBN 0 522 85172 X.

  1. Horror films. 2. Horror films—Psychological aspects.
  3. Psychoanalysis and motion pictures. 4. Monsters in
  motion pictures. 5. Men in motion pictures. I. Title.

791.436164

CONTENTS

ACKNOWLEDGEMENTS

I am indebted to Louise Adler, CEO and publisher at Melbourne University Publishing, for her commitment to this book and unfailing good humour. Warm thanks to Elisa Berg, commissioning editor, for her excellent suggestions and amazing patience. I would especially like to thank Sally Moss for her rigor in editing the manuscript and for her acute and always helpful comments; Jo Tayler for her impeccable proofreading; and Catherine Cradwick for her fine editorial work and creative suggestions. A very special thanks to Meredith Martin, research assistant par excellence, whose tireless assistance and amazing powers of organisation were absolutely essential to the completion of this project. And finally, as always, my heartfelt thanks to Jeanette Hoorn for all her support, critical feedback, and lively discussions.

I am also very grateful to the Humanities Research Centre for a three-month fellowship in 2004, which enabled me to complete part of the manuscript.

Thanks to the Kobal Collection, London, for granting permission to reproduce illustrative material from their archive.

INTRODUCTION

What are monsters? What role do monsters fulfil in modern society? What are the differences, if any, between male and female monsters? Is one sex always monstrous in relation to the other? The Hydra, Minotaur, Sphinx, Cyclops, Sirens, Medusa —these fabulous beings all held a central role in the myths, religion and art of classical antiquity and there is no doubt that monsters continue to play an active and important role in the contemporary popular imagination. The newest art form of the twentieth century, the cinema, took over the role of folklore, myth and gothic fiction to become the main vehicle for the telling and re-telling of stories about monstrous beings whose aim is to terrify and thrill a captive audience. Vampire, werewolf, Frankensteinian creature, witch, ghost, mummy, *femme castratrice*, slasher, cannibal and psychopath—the cinema abounds with murderous and monstrous creatures, male and female alike.

According to Freud, those things, persons, events and situations that arouse dread and horror belong to the realm of 'the uncanny'. Freud argued that the uncanny was particularly associated with feelings of horror aroused by the figure of the paternal castrator, neglecting the tropes of woman and animal as a source of the uncanny. He referred to death, but primarily in relation to the return of the dead. Yet the horror aroused by the classic male monster of horror is almost always aligned with what I have termed 'the primal uncanny'—that is, woman, the animal and death. I believe that by placing greater emphasis on woman, the animal and death we can develop a new understanding of the role of the uncanny in horror and of the male monster. Traditional approaches to the male monster have tended to focus on his image as terrifying because of its association with castration, dismemberment and death. These have been influenced by the significance attached to castration in psychoanalytic approaches, such as Freud's, to the cinema.[1] The central aims of this book are to explore the concept of the primal uncanny and to widen our view of the male monster by examining his characteristics in relation to the primal uncanny.[2]

The representation of the male monster—his body, appearance, desires and deadly actions—raises many issues. What is it that contemporary audiences find horrifying about the male monster? What does the image of the uncanny male monster tell us about our own anxieties, desires and deepest fears? How does the male monster undermine the values of patriarchal society? Why do so many of these monsters become cult figures? By drawing on Freud's famous 1919 essay, 'The Uncanny', as well as on critical responses to it, we can construct a theoretical framework for analysing these issues.

The sense of ambivalence that Freud says is central to the uncanny permeates all representations of the classic monster: vampire, wolf–man, mad scientist, ghost, ripper. In particular, this ambivalence underlies the male monster's uncanny alignment with death, the animal and the maternal body—uncanny because the male symbolic order designates these areas as 'other', as being outside the realm of what constitutes proper phallic masculinity. As a result the male monster is familiar yet unfamiliar, a monstrous creature that is male and phallic yet also deeply connected to the domain of the primal uncanny.

The monster is not simply a meaningless beast whose function is to run amok, incite terror, kill indiscriminately and do well at the box office. The identity of the monster, male and female, is inseparable from questions of sex, gender, power and politics. In order to better understand the dark side of our culture and the reasons why the symbolic order creates monsters, consciously or otherwise, we need to ask questions about the monster's origins, nature and functions. Queer theorist Judith Halberstam argues that the representation of the monstrous body 'that scares and appals changes over time, as do the individual characteristics that add up to monstrosity, as do the preferred interpretations of monstrosity'.[3] This is true but it doesn't preclude the fact that the classic monsters of the horror film share certain characteristics which, in my view, can be best understood through the lens of a psychoanalytic interpretation. Halberstam argues that 'monstrosity (and the fear it gives rise to) is historically conditioned rather than a psychological universal'.[4] It is clear that historical factors, as well as technological developments, such as special effects, play key roles in the representation of the classic monster and its appearance. However, the specific nature of its otherness, and the threat it embodies, can be most convincingly explained in relation to the primal uncanny. Although the concept of a primal uncanny offers a universalising account in terms of the monster's own psychology, it does not mean that the monster's appearance, representation and choice of preferred victim cannot and do not change over time.

One of the original meanings of 'monster' is from the Latin *monstrare*, meaning 'to warn' or 'to show'. With its usually horrific features, the monster demands to be seen. In order to generate suspense and a sense of the uncanny, an effective horror film does not immediately put the monster on full display; instead it offers a fleeting glimpse, a quick disturbing glance. The uncanny object, event or sensation is not simply there in the film; it must be produced through the screen–spectator relationship. The monster is, in a sense, veiled or cloaked by shadows and darkness so that a feeling of mounting horror accompanies its revelation, which usually occurs at the end of the narrative. German philosopher Frederich Schelling, in his definition of the uncanny, wrote that the uncanny was the 'name for everything that ought to have remained ... secret and hidden but has come to light'.[5] Thus the meaning of 'monster' (to warn or show) relates directly to the uncanny (to bring into the light what should have remained hidden). The cinema is the perfect medium for the display of the uncanny monster—for bringing into the open what should have been kept out of sight.

To what extent has sexual difference played a role in the traditional display of monsters?[6] Aristotle was one of the first philosophers to grapple with the problem of monsters and their sex. He claimed that anyone who differed from their parents was essentially a monster because, in such instances, 'Nature has in a way strayed from the generic type.'[7] Not noted for endorsing gender equality, Aristotle argued that the first instance of such deviation occurs when a female is formed instead of a male, although he somewhat grudgingly accepts that women are necessary for the perpetuation of the species. Nonetheless, he insists that man is the norm: 'The female is as it were a deformed male.'[8] Centuries later, the Catholic Church advanced a similar view. Women constituted monstrous deviations from the moral/ male norm. *The Malleus Maleficarum* (1484), in use for nearly three centuries, was the official inquisitor's manual for witch prosecution. Its influence extended well into the twentieth century; the 1948 edition praised its authors—two Dominicans, Heinrich Kramer and James Sprenger—as men of 'extraordinary genius' and the book itself as 'supreme' from the point of view of history, psychology and the law.[9] *The Malleus Maleficarum* provided details of the way women differed from men, differences that rendered them not only monstrous, but also more susceptible to becoming a witch—the supernatural female monster par excellence. The witch who could change shape and weave spells was held responsible for natural calamities (such as a bad harvest) as well as supernatural events. Woman is 'an evil of nature, painted with fair colours!'[10] The main reason for her otherness is her lust: 'But the natural reason is that she is more carnal than man, as is clear from her many carnal abominations.'[11] Woman's monstrosity constitutes a moral deviation which leads to monstrous deeds. Whereas Aristotle defined female monstrosity in terms of a variation from the (male) norm, the Church defined female monstrosity in relation to woman's sexual appetites.

Not only is woman by nature monstrous, she also creates monsters. Cultural historian Marie-Hélène Huet, in her fascinating study *Monstrous Imagination*, argues that, from the classical period through to the Enlightenment, people believed that if a woman gave birth to a monstrous child it was because of the destructive power of the maternal imagination: 'Heliodorus of Emusa tells of a queen of Ethiopia who reputedly bore a white child after seeing, on the wall of her bedchamber, a picture of the pale Andromeda.'[12] Huet cites the example of an infant born with the face of a frog. This was attributed to the fact that the mother was holding a frog (thought to be a cure for fever) in her hand the night she conceived. The power of her imagination influenced the facial characteristics of the developing embryo. Woman's more ardent and susceptible imagination was similarly used to explain birth defects, birthmarks and other abnormalities. Huet also cites the case of 'the hairy virgin' of 1560; woman was thought capable of copulating with animals, in which case she would produce an excessively hairy child. Huet refers to the popular Renaissance debate concerning bestiality: 'the author of *Secreta Mulierum* (widely thought to be Albertus Magnus) attributed the birth of monsters either to contempt for nature's laws, that is, human copulation with animals, or to the mother's delinquent imagination at the time of conception'.[13]

In other words, philosophers and theologians of the day believed that woman was so close to nature that she was capable of copulation with animals. If she imagined having sex with animals she would give birth to an excessively hirsute infant. Woman is defined as a monster in her own right or closely aligned with the creation of monsters, either through the power of her imagination or through bestial acts. Woman, it appears, has traditionally been more closely aligned to the production of monsters and monstrous deeds than has man. This changed dramatically with the publication of Mary Shelley's *Frankenstein* (1818), in which man creates his own monster artificially. Although popular film portrays a range of female monsters—from witch and castrator to vampire and womb monster—there are many more films that star male monsters.

One of the most enduring of male monsters is the beast. Novelist and theorist Marina Warner tells us that 'the first Beast was the god of love, Eros', who later developed into the beast of the fairy tale *Beauty and the Beast*.[14] This famous tale has persisted throughout the centuries, its most recent incarnation the enormously popular 1993 Disney version of Jean Cocteau's 1946 masterpiece. The tale has been interpreted as a female rite of passage in which the young girl must learn to love the monstrous animal, who almost always transforms into a handsome young man. In a fascinating article on the many transformations of the tale over the centuries, Warner points out that while in the medieval period animality was associated with the devil and his 'hooved hairiness', in the modern age, 'the wild man has come into his own as an ideal'.[15] Why are so many beasts depicted as animals or as men trapped in the body of an animal? Why in the twenty-first century do we continue to tell stories about male monsters and other terrifying creatures such as aliens, serial killers and cyborgs? Why are so many of these monsters male? From Dracula to Frankenstein's monster and Jack the Ripper, man has been represented as a monster across a range of modern discourses: literature, drama, myth, popular culture and film.

In the main, the classic cinematic monster originated in the Gothic literature of the late eighteenth and early nineteenth centuries. Born of the modern period, monsters have embodied particularly modern fears and anxieties arising from Darwinian debates over human nature, Freudian theories of civilisation and repression, and the results of scientific experimentation such as artificial birth and cloning. These monsters have now assumed modern characteristics. In contemporary films, Dracula is a queer monster (Jordan's *Interview with the Vampire*), the wolf–man appears as an urbane book editor (Nichols's *Wolf*), Frankenstein's monster is a cyborg (Verhoeven's *RoboCop*), the mad doctor a molecular scientist (Cronenberg's *The Fly*), the Jekyll/Hyde double a pair of identical twin gynaecologists (Cronenberg's *Dead Ringers*), the ripper a trans-gendered psychotic (Demme's *The Silence of the Lambs*), the gothic ghost a disfigured male child molester (Craven's *A Nightmare on Elm Street*), and the cannibal a sophisticated, urbane psychoanalyst (Scott's *Hannibal*) who eats his patients—with the correct condiments, of course. The essential nature of these monstrous male figures has remained the same but the external appearance and characterisation of each has been given a contemporary look. What do these uncanny male monsters have in common? How do they signify the primal uncanny? In horror, transformation is represented as a regressive process in which the natural animal world takes over from the civilised, human domain as man regresses into an uncanny beast, familiar yet unfamiliar.

A number of transformative monsters either assume characteristics associated with the maternal body—specifically the womb—or they attempt to usurp the powers of the womb. The male monster's association with the womb demonstrates a powerful instance of the workings of the primal uncanny. When Frankenstein, Dr Jekyll, and Seth Brundle from *The Fly* (1986) attempt to re-create life, or re-birth themselves, they become womb monsters, a fact usually symbolised by the array of tubes, fluids and egg-shaped chambers in their laboratories. In *Altered States* (Ken Russell, 1980) the male scientist, attempting to return to his origins, appears covered in the membrane of a birth sac. With his pointed features, softly spoken words and flowing red and black cape, Count Dracula appears as a feminised creature who on the full moon rises from his grave deep in Mother Earth in order to sate himself with the blood of women. He is not unlike a monstrous unborn infant, dependent on a blood cycle for his existence. The wolf–man, who wears his fur on the inside of his skin, is a savage animal from the natural world who reminds man of the fragile boundary between the civilised and natural worlds. He essentially gives birth to himself, by turning himself inside-out.

The ghost is associated with woman and the womb through its inhabitation of the haunted house. In dreams and phantasy, the haunted house, as Freud argued, functions as an analogue of the human body. As we will see, the haunted house in many horror films is linked to woman and the uncanny womb. As transformative monster, man in general assumes characteristics associated with the primal uncanny—with the feminine and natural worlds. Like woman and the animal he is a fluid and

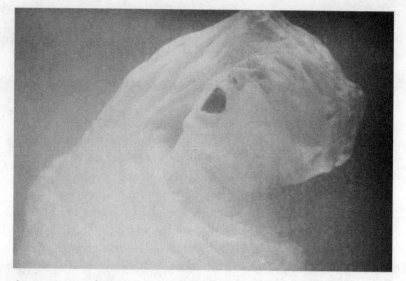

An uncanny transformation—man re-births himself (Altered States, 1980)
(Warner Bros/The Kobal Collection)

An uncanny transformation—man merges with animal (Fright Night, 1985)
(The Kobal Collection)

mutable creature, lacking clear and distinct boundaries, who frequently reminds us that a key aspect of his monstrous nature is bound up with birthing and reproduction.

The uncanny monstrous male is in many instances akin to a folkloric and mythical shape-shifter who, as he transforms from one state to another, uncovers secrets about man that 'ought to have remained ... hidden', specifically his desire to become 'other'. Since the classic male monster, in order to challenge the phallocentric symbolic from within, is aligned with the realm of the feminine, the animal and death, to some spectators he is a repulsive, threatening beast, to others a creature who signifies rebellion and change. One of the main reasons why the male monster is sometimes an immensely sympathetic figure is precisely because he is caught between the opposing forces of culture and nature, the civilised and primitive. These sympathetic brutes include Dracula, who sexually liberates women; the wolf–man, who appeals to us because he is an innocent victim; Frankenstein's monster, who did not ask to be 'born'; King Kong, who is destroyed by the civilised world for money and profit and who dies for love of a woman; and even Hannibal Lecter, whose civilised demeanour renders him more appealing than a number of so-called civilised men from his walk of life. The rules governing behaviour in the urban jungle are often far more brutal and bloody than those of the natural one. Two of the most influential thinkers of the period, Charles Darwin and Sigmund Freud, attested in their writings to man's dual nature, to his origins in the primitive world and to the thin veneer of what man calls civilisation. When these taboos are lifted, the uncanny almost always emerges and 'infiltrates' what feminist theorist Hélène Cixous calls 'the interstices of the narratives', opening up 'gaps we need to explain'.[16]

Through the figure of the male monster, the horror film speaks to us about our origins, our deep-seated anxieties and our debt to woman, nature, the animal and death. Each of the monsters discussed in this book, through its alignment with the primal uncanny, brings to light things 'that ought to have remained ...

secret and hidden'. Dracula, the Prince of Darkness, leads us to question the nature of phallic sexuality. The vampire is an erotic seductive male whose dominant appeal lies with the perverse forms of eroticism he offers—oral sex, bisexual pleasures, necrophilia. The wolf–man signals the failure of civilisation; he reinvigorates man with animal desire and points to the cannibalism that lies at the heart of so-called civilised society. The mad doctor or womb monster, who has debased the ancient ritual of couvade, makes it clear that science cannot control the birth process: when man attempts to create life without woman the source of monstrosity is doubled—he both becomes a monster and brings forth monsters. The ghost points to secrets within the family or group; its presence reveals issues relating to troubled forms of sexual desire and to secret crimes including child abuse. The Ripper (and his recent protégés, the slasher and modern cannibal) reveals the deep-rooted misogyny at the heart of patriarchal society; his brutal acts also point to man's fear of his own death. The various forms assumed by the transformative male monster bring to light different problems signifying different dimensions in this relationship. In addition, man's transformation into the 'other'—whether wolf–man, vampire, mad doctor, slasher or cannibal—strikes at the heart of the symbolic order which requires that masculinity adopts a discrete, complete, phallic form.

Proper masculinity embodies phallic power and asserts masculine qualities of power, rationality, ascendancy and control. By his very existence, the male monster points to the fact that masculinity, as defined by the symbolic economy, is a fragile concept, one that is rarely, if ever, fulfilled. To undermine the symbolic is to create a disturbance around the phallus, to create a sense of phallic panic. The central ideological function of the classic male monster, discussed in this book, is to do precisely that—to undermine the symbolic order by demonstrating its failures, contradictions and inconsistencies. The resulting panic is possibly more acutely felt or visibly registered because the monster is not female but male. The monster signifies the failure of man to achieve a masculine ideal which, of course, French psychoanalyst Jacques Lacan argued was unobtainable in the first place. In this book I argue that man (and woman) is not by definition a rational, coherent, civilised being. Awareness of the impossibility of achieving proper masculinity can lead to a whole constellation of male disorders such as phobias, anxieties and hysteria. What the male monster points to is the *pretence* that the achievement of proper masculinity is possible. It is the creature's monstrous body, as much as its deeds, that symbolises the breakdown of this illusion. Strangely, some monsters are potentially sympathetic figures. This is why there is something attractive and appealing about the creature that is at home in the heart of darkness.

Literary critic Leslie Fiedler has argued that the 'stranger' of patriarchal culture is woman: 'But there remains among us … an unassimilated, perhaps forever unassimilable, stranger, the first other of which the makers of our myths, male as far back as reliable memory runs, ever become aware. And that stranger is, of course, woman.'[17] Yet man too is a stranger in a land of his own creation. To take up his place in the symbolic order, man has repressed desires that would otherwise mark him as female, other or animal. Wearing the mask of monster, man desires to destroy the symbolic economy from within, to test the fragility of the law, through acts of metamorphosis, murder, mutilation, blood letting and cannibalism. In his monstrous appearance, hybrid forms and murderous and abject intentions, the male monster fundamentally signifies the 'ruin of representation'—that is, the ruin of the male symbolic order.

Like Oedipus, the male monster also commits terrible deeds that threaten the foundations of society. In other words, the presence, or excessive presence, of the male monster as a creature of the primal uncanny makes it possible, in the first instance, to raise the very question of the ruin of representation as a male question. What does man want? The ruin of representation and the collapse of the symbolic order? One function or consequence of the existence of the male monster —his ubiquity and power— is to highlight contradictions that exist at the heart of patriarchal culture, particularly in relation to questions of male identity and the actual nature of patriarchal civilisation. For this reason, the monster, for many spectators, has, as Marina Warner argues, 'come into his own as an ideal'.[18] In a different but related context, it is relevant to note how a number of monstrous superheroes, such as Batman, Spiderman, Catwoman and the Phantom, have absorbed elements of the primal uncanny, particularly the animal, to enhance their superhuman powers in their fight against corruption within the symbolic order.

The male monster 'disturbs identity, system, order'. It does not 'respect borders, positions, rules'.[19] He embraces meaninglessness and self-annihilation. There is no concomitant desire for a return to normality or re-affirmation of the symbolic on the part of the monster. He is the point where meaning collapses. This gives rise to a sense of meaningless horror, sometimes registered by the cry not of the victim but of the monster himself. Psychoanalytic theorist Slavoj Žižek, who is critical of ideological interpretations of the monster, argues that 'The analysis that focuses on the "ideological meaning" of monsters overlooks the fact that, before signifying something, before serving as a vessel of meaning, monsters embody enjoyment qua the limit of interpretation, that is to say, *nonmeaning as such*'.[20]

Although I agree with Žižek, I would also argue that the male monster embodies 'the limit of interpretation' or nonmeaning within the system of signification; nonmeaning and enjoyment can also have ideological significance. In other words, if inscription in language—in the symbolic—is almost always phallocentric and designed to shore up the power and authority of the symbolic, then the monster's nonmeaning, which includes enjoyment, is designed to unsettle the symbolic order and as such is ideological.

Insofar as the monster is constructed by and within the phallocentric symbolic order, it is important to ask: how nihilistic is the monster? Are we talking about the complete disintegration of meaning or are we referring to a controlled space that only threatens disintegration? The former would suggest a place of meaninglessness such as death, annihilation and the end of narrative; the latter suggests a space that might be taken up by the monster within narrative, a point of resistance and rebellion. Of course monsters may signify both at different places in the narrative. Perhaps the threat that the monster offers is ultimately designed to recuperate or reinforce the symbolic. Does the presence of the monster signify a kind of carnivalesque means of allowing for a controlled 'return of the repressed'? Does horror offer a kind of Bakhtian social safety valve? Or does the male monster signify a desire for the collapse of patriarchal civilisation?

In this book I argue that, through the figure of the male monster, the horror film speaks to us about the nature of masculinity and man's ambiguous relationship with the realms of woman, the animal and death, and the symbolic order of law, civilisation and language. The various forms assumed by the transformative male monster signify different problems at the heart of man's relationship to the imaginary and symbolic orders —particularly the latter. As the architect of both orders, man is at home in neither. With its universal narrative forms and sophisticated array of special effects, the cinema has created a modern mythical space in which to tell and re-tell stories old and new about the 'thing' in the forest and monsters that walk by night. The uncanny male monster arouses dread and horror in order to raise questions about the symbolic order and to problematise the belief that civilisation represents progress. In many horror films this knowledge—that civilisation is a myth—has generated an uncanny form of anxiety that I have termed 'phallic panic'.[21]

FILM, HORROR AND THE PRIMAL UNCANNY

Dismembered limbs, a severed head, a hand cut off at the wrists ... all these have something peculiarly uncanny about them ... being buried alive ... intra-uterine existence ... the female genital organs ...

SIGMUND FREUD[1]

Doubles, automata, ghosts, witches, vampires, waxwork figures, haunted houses, severed body parts, women's genitalia, the undead—according to Sigmund Freud, all of these and more constitute the domain of the uncanny. The uncanny evokes fear, unease, disquiet and gloom; it 'is undoubtedly related to what is frightening—to what arouses dread and horror'.[2] These images and emotions also characterise a great deal of popular cinema, particularly films belonging to the categories of horror, science fiction and the surreal. Over recent years there has been a renewed interest in the uncanny and a number of important studies have appeared across a range of disciplines—from literature to feminist theory, architecture and film.[3]

In his famous essay 'The Uncanny' (1919), Freud developed a substantial theory of the uncanny. In the first section of the essay he considers a range of etymological sources of the uncanny as well as the writings of Jentsch and Schelling on the meaning of the uncanny. Next he offers an interpretation of 'The Sandman', an important short story by E. T. A. Hoffman, whom he describes as 'the unrivalled master of the uncanny in literature'. In 'The Sandman', Freud argues, 'the feeling of something uncanny is directly attached to the figure of the Sandman, that is, to the idea of being robbed of one's eyes'.[4] 'The Sandman' tells the story of Nathaniel, who as a boy develops an unnatural fear of a certain lawyer, Coppelius, who he believes is the dreaded sandman. The sandman steals the eyes of children who won't go to sleep. He 'throws handfuls of sand in their eyes so that they jump out of their heads all bleeding'.[5] Coppelius is a friend of Nathaniel's father—the two men appear to be engaged in a mysterious experiment that suggests they are trying to create artificial life.

As a young man, Nathaniel, who has never resolved his infantile fears, becomes engaged to Clara, a distant relative, who along with her brother came to live with Nathaniel and his mother when they were orphaned. Nathaniel also falls in love with a mysterious lifelike doll, Olympia, who he fails to realise is not human. He believes that the doll is actually the daughter of his neighbour, Professor Spalanzani. At the same time, he believes the local clockmaker, Coppola, is none other than the terrible Coppelius, or the sandman. Coppelius and Professor Spalanzani have created Olympia together. Nathaniel learns the truth about Olympia when he sees her eyes fall from her head, leaving gaping holes. In the end he commits suicide by jumping from a parapet.

Freud argues that the sandman, who he equates with the castrating father, is the true source of the uncanny. He disagreed with Ernst Jentsch who, in his 1906 essay 'On the Psychology of the Uncanny', argued that a powerful source of the uncanny is 'intellectual uncertainty whether an object is alive or not and when an inanimate object becomes too much like an animate one'.[6] After discussing Hoffman's story, Freud presents a series of objects, events and sensations that he argues are uncanny. Freud places much importance on the threat of loss and castration—the threatening father figure, severed limbs, loss of eyes, death.

In conclusion, he discusses the representation of the uncanny in literature and other forms of the creative arts.

In his essay, Freud turned to a neglected area belonging to the field of aesthetics because he believed that psychoanalytic theory could help to illuminate this issue. He was interested not in the theory of beauty but in 'the theory of the qualities of feeling'. He pointed out that academic treatises usually prefer to explore the question of which 'circumstances and objects' call forth 'feelings of a positive nature' that are associated with 'the beautiful, attractive and sublime'.[7] He was interested in a related but opposite question. What is it about frightening people, things, impressions and events that arouse 'dread and horror', 'repulsion and distress'?[8] 'One is curious to know what is this common core that allows us to distinguish as "uncanny" certain things that lie within the field of what is frightening.'[9] The uncanny, however, is not necessarily reducible to the general emotion of fear. '[The uncanny] is not always used in a clearly definable sense, so that it tends to coincide with what excites fear in general. Yet we may expect that a special core of feeling is present which justifies the use of a special conceptual term.'[10]

From the outset Freud defined the uncanny as 'that class of the frightening which leads us back to what is known of old and long familiar'.[11] His aim was to demonstrate the circumstances in which 'the familiar can become uncanny and frightening'.[12] He was particularly interested in the secret side of the uncanny, and noted with interest Schelling's definition of *unheimlich* as 'the name for everything that ought to have remained ... secret and hidden but has come to light'.

Freud traced the meaning of the uncanny through many languages. The definition of what is frightening relates to what is unfamiliar and derives from the German word *unheimlich*:

> *The German word* 'unheimlich' *is obviously the opposite of* 'heimlich' *['homely'],* 'heimisch' *['native']—the opposite of what is familiar; and we are tempted to conclude what is*

'uncanny' is frightening precisely because it is not known and familiar ... Something has to be added to what is novel and unfamiliar in order to make it uncanny.[13]

For the unfamiliar to be rendered uncanny it needs to be something, as Schelling put it, that should have remained out of sight. Theorist Rosemary Jackson has argued that this definition gives an ideological or 'counter cultural' edge to the uncanny.[14] In other words, the uncanny has the power to undermine the social and cultural prohibitions that help to create order and stability.

Freud was particularly interested in the relationship of the uncanny to the 'home'—an important connection for this study, as so much horror originates in the home. *Heimlich* is used to refer to places such as the home, a friendly room, a pleasant country scene, a person who is friendly, or a family. It can also refer to a secret place or action, an act of betrayal (behind someone's back), to someone unscrupulous. Freud points out that one of the most important things about the term *heimlich* is that it contains a double meaning: *heimlich* also signifies its opposite meaning and is used to signify *unheimlich*.

In general we are reminded that the word *heimlich* is not unambiguous but belongs to two sets of ideas, which, without being contradictory, are yet very different: on the one hand it means what is familiar and agreeable; on the other, what is concealed and kept out of sight. *Unheimlich* is customarily used, we are told, as the contrary only of the first signification of *heimlich* and not the second.[15]

So, *heimlich* can signify its opposite, it can come to have the meaning usually given to *unheimlich*. It can mean 'that which is obscure, inaccessible to knowledge'.[16] Thus the term itself has a double meaning: '*heimlich* is a word the meaning of which develops in the direction of ambivalence, until it finally coincides with its opposite *unheimlich*. *Unheimlich* is in some way or other a subspecies of *heimlich*'.[17]

The double meaning of *heimlich* is important to a discussion of the uncanny as it underlines the close association between these two concepts: homely/unhomely; clear/obscure; knowable/ unknowable. When referring to the familiar/unfamiliar nexus I have used the terms *heimlich* and *unheimlich* throughout the book; otherwise I use the term 'uncanny'. One can easily turn into the other. This double semantic meaning is important for a discussion of the workings of the uncanny in film as the latter is often produced at the border, at the point of ambivalence, when for instance the friendly inviting place of refuge suddenly becomes hostile and uninviting, or the cheerful welcoming host becomes cold and frightening. *Unheimlich* can be used as the opposite of *heimlich* only when the latter signifies the homely. When used as a separate term, *unheimlich* means 'eerie, weird, arousing gruesome fear'. It signifies the 'fearful hours of night', a 'mist called hill-fog', everything 'secret and hidden'.[18]

It was Schelling's statement—that the uncanny is that which ought to have remained hidden but has come to light— that gave Freud the insight he needed to elaborate an aesthetic theory of the uncanny and its effects. Freud states that Schelling 'throws quite a new light on the concept', in that *heimlich* can also refer to the act of concealing. Freud includes a biblical reference (1 Samuel, v 12) that refers to '*Heimlich* parts of the human body, *pudenda*'.[19] This aspect of the uncanny no doubt influenced Freud's final definition, in which he includes a category relating to the female genital.

The key to the uncanny, Freud argued, is repression. The uncanny is that which should have remained repressed (a different meaning from 'secret' or 'hidden') but which has come to light. As mentioned, Freud disagreed with Jentsch, who argued that the major feature in the creation of an uncanny feeling is intellectual uncertainty. In his analysis of the Hoffman short story 'The Sandman', Freud concluded that repression, in relation to the boy's castration anxiety, was a more important source of the uncanny than intellectual uncertainty about whether an object, such as the doll Olympia, is animate or inanimate.

Freud argued that the uncanny signifies the return of an earlier state of mind associated either with infantile narcissism or primitive animism. He concluded that there are two classes of the uncanny: one associated with psychical reality, which is most likely to occur in relation to repressed infantile complexes such as the castration complex and womb phantasies; and the other relating to the 'omnipotence of thoughts' grouping and associated with physical reality. The two groups, however, are not necessarily easily distinguished.

> *Our conclusion could then be stated thus: an uncanny experience occurs either when infantile complexes which have been repressed are once more revived by some impression, or when primitive beliefs which have been surmounted seem once more to be confirmed.*[20]

Freud points out that events associated with the 'omnipotence of thoughts' category are not always uncanny. While the strongest forms of the uncanny relate to infantile complexes such as castration complexes and womb phantasies, 'experiences which arouse this kind of uncanny feeling are not of very frequent occurrence in real life' in comparison with fiction and other creative practices.[21]

Freud concluded that the uncanny as it is represented in creative works deserves a separate discussion for it is 'a much more fertile province than the uncanny in real life'.[22] In the creative arts, the subject matter is not necessarily exposed to reality testing, and there are many more ways of creating uncanny effects. When the author moves into the world of reality—as distinct from fantasy—he or she has the power to create, increase and enhance anything that might lead to an uncanny effect, even creating 'events which never or very rarely happen in fact'.[23]

The cinema, particularly the horror film, offers a particularly rich medium for an analysis of contemporary representations of the uncanny. In his book *The Uncanny*, Nicholas Royle rightly points out that the uncanny is not necessarily associated with strange objects, events and sensations that terrify. 'The uncanny can be a matter of something gruesome and terrible ... But it can also be a matter of something strangely beautiful, bordering on ecstasy ("too good to be true"), or eerily reminding of something like *déjà vu*.'[24]

In his discussion, Freud establishes a series of categories of the uncanny—all of which will provide a basis for analysis of the uncanny effects of the films discussed in the following chapters. These are: castration anxieties represented through dismembered limbs, a severed head or hand, being robbed of the eyes, fear of going blind or a fear of the female genitals; uncertainty as to whether an object is alive or dead, animate or inanimate— as in dolls and automata; those things that signify a double: a twin, a cyborg, a doppelgänger, a ghost or spirit, a multiplied object, an involuntary repetition of an act; a fear of return of the dead, spirits and ghosts or a haunted house; erasure of the distinction between imagination and reality, when something thought to be imaginary appears in reality; a feeling associated with a familiar/unfamiliar place, a place that seems known yet unknown; a womb-like space that represents repressed uterine memories, intra-uterine existence, being buried alive, the female genital organs, the mother's genitals, entrance to the former home or the womb; an animistic belief in omnipotence of thoughts (killing someone with a mere wish), dread of the evil eye, demons, magic, special injurious powers, the coincidence of wish and fulfilment, repetition of similar experiences, the experience of a double (this area of the uncanny is a matter of 'reality testing' because it proceeds from actual experience); and a situation in which primitive beliefs, that the individual thought he or she had overcome, rise to the surface and are confirmed.

These forms of the uncanny describe the metamorphosis of the familiar into the unfamiliar, of bringing to light what should have remained hidden, of the dissolution of boundaries between the real and imagined—and all are mainstays of the horror film. Many films that explore the uncanny represent the eye as a signifier of horror. Even in post-modern horror films such as *Evil Dead II* (Sam Raimi, 1987), which play with black humour, uncanny images of the eye disturb boundaries. The male monster

Uncanny staring eyes—the somnambulist from The Cabinet of Dr Caligari, *1919*
(Decla-Bioscop/The Kobal Collection)

of horror is an uncanny surreal creature invoking a strong emotional response in the viewer, who is threatened by the dissolution of established boundaries necessary for the perpetuation of culture and society.

CRITICISM OF FREUD'S ESSAY 'THE UNCANNY'

I. *Olympia & Clara*

A number of theorists have criticised Freud's interpretation of Hoffman's short story 'The Sandman'. They argue that he concentrated almost exclusively on the theme of castration while underplaying, even ignoring, the key role of the feminine played out in relation to the doll, Olympia. Jane Marie Todd claims Freud neglected the figure of the doll and the questions raised by

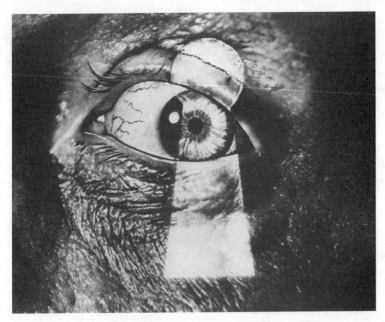

In the eye of horror—Peeping Tom, *1960*
(*Anglo Amalgamated/The Kobal Collection*)

Black humour in the post-modern uncanny—Evil Dead II, *1987*
(*Rosebud/Renaissance/The Kobal Collection*)

its presence in relation to castration.[25] Like the sandman, who tears out the eyes of children who will not go to sleep, the doll Olympia is equally terrifying in that it is not clear whether she is animate or inanimate. Todd argues that the doll's gaze is uncanny in that it exposes the male gaze as unreliable and without substance; that is, Nathaniel, who thinks Olympia is alive, sees what is simply not there. In terms of Freud's theory of castration, this suggests that Nathaniel finds the doll beautiful and non-threatening because he fails to see she is not phallic. He also fails to see that Olympia's gaze does not convey innocence but rather the nothingness or emptiness associated with non-being.

Hélène Cixous criticises Freud for focusing on castration and not paying enough attention to the doll, which she argues is uncanny in the extreme, in that it collapses the border between animate and inanimate. Thus Olympia uncannily undermines the border between life and death. Olympia signifies what cannot be represented directly—that is, death: the lifeless state of being to which we all return. Cixous argues that Freud displaces 'the *Unheimliche* of the doll with the Sand-Man'[26] and further that 'he minimizes the uncertainty revolving around Olympia, thus pushing Olympia toward the group of the *Heimliche* and clearly diminishing the texture of the story'.[27]

In his article 'Freud's Uncanny Women', Phillip McCaffrey argues that Freud, in a number of texts, fails to draw attention to the presence of the 'Uncanny Woman'. 'If we connect these ideas we arrive at the concept of a female figure who embodies sexuality and castration and death, a figure I would like to call the Uncanny Woman.'[28] McCaffrey discusses a number of variations of the 'Uncanny Woman', including automaton, double, castrator and castrated (victim). He concludes that the two main versions are those of victim and castrator.

It is clear that Freud does ignore woman's uncanniness in his analysis of 'The Sandman'. We find this is also true of his approach to the case histories of Little Hans and the Wolf Man. In both of these the mother or Nanya, respectively, appears as the uncanny castrating parent, yet Freud assimilates her role to the father's. The main reason for this appears to be Freud's determination to align the castrating parent with the father, not the mother.

In my view, the presence of the female uncanny is central to Freud's essay. She is there in the figure of Olympia. She is also there in other signifiers of the uncanny that Freud lists: the *unheimlich* female genital organs; the uterus; the phantasy of being buried alive; womb phantasies; the evil eye; the threat of castration; death and ghosts; and repression of primitive, animal desires. The uncanny feminine is also present in 'The Sandman' in relation to male womb phantasies, which Freud ignores completely in his analysis.

Freud states that the uncanniness of the story is directly associated with the sandman and fear of losing one's eyes, which he interprets as a fear of castration: 'fears about the eye and castration ... become intelligible as soon as we replace the Sand-Man by the dreaded father at whose hands castration is expected'.[29] He argues that this is a 'more striking instance of uncanniness' than the one attached to the figure of the doll, Olympia, who is uncanny in that Nathaniel cannot tell whether she is animate or inanimate.[30] Not all critics agree.

II. Male mothers: Professor Spalanzani & the sandman

There is a further omission in Freud's interpretation of 'The Sandman'. Olympia can be seen as a central figure of uncanniness because, like Frankenstein's monster, she has been created by two men: her 'father', Professor Spalanzani, and Coppelius, the sandman. Thus she signifies artificial life and the fragility of the boundary between animate and inanimate. The two men have given birth to a monstrous doll whose uncanny lifelike appearance ends up destroying Nathaniel. Given that there is a double scenario of the phantasy of the male mother in 'The Sandman' it is even more surprising that Freud chose to ignore this motif. The doubling occurs in relation to two sets of men: Nathaniel's own father and Coppelius; and the Professor and Coppelius. Their actions result in a further play of doubling. The two men evoke their own womb and their own creation.

Through a play of presence and absence, their artificial womb/ laboratory evokes a phantom image of the original womb, the maternal home. The doll itself, through its artificiality, similarly points to its prototype, the original living woman. The entire scenario brings the uncanny into play through the overarching presence of an invisible or phantom womb, the disembodied sets of eyes, and the maniacal behaviour of the two pairs of male midwives. The motif of the uncanny phantom womb hovers over almost all horror films that depict narratives of womb envy and couvade.

In his original story, Hoffman describes how Nathaniel, when a boy, decides to hide in his father's study so that he can catch a glimpse of his father's mysterious visitor whom he is convinced is the sandman. When the boy peers out he sees the 'repulsive Coppelius'. He 'stood as if rooted to the spot' as he observed the scenes before him. What he had thought was a wall cupboard is in fact 'a black cavern' in which there is a small hearth. There are all kinds of 'strange implements', glowing tongs, a hammer and 'brightly gleaming substances'. Like Frankenstein and his servant, the two men appear to be creating life. Nathaniel notices that his father's face has become like 'a repulsive devil-mask'. As Coppelius hammers away he sees 'human faces appearing all around, but without eyes—instead of eyes there were hideous black cavities'. Coppelius calls for eyes: 'Eyes, bring eyes!' the monster cries in 'a dull hollow voice'.[31] This scene of creation is echoed later in the description of the creation scene between the Professor and Coppelius who, like a pair of male midwives, have successfully given birth to the uncanny doll, Olympia.

The 'black cavern' appears to be a small laboratory; it cotains strange instruments, substances and body parts, such as the eyes, used by the men in their attempt to create life. It also emits a 'strange-smelling vapour'.[32] In discounting Olympia's creation and the figures of the male mothers, Freud also ignored the representation of the primal scene, a perverse scene of origins, at play in 'The Sandman'. The presence of the two men—the professor and optician—coming together to give birth to a beautiful lifelike doll, it can be argued, is also uncanny. It brings to light man's monstrous set of desires: the desire to usurp the female generative role, to create his own (mechanical) version of female beauty and to fetishise a woman who is neither living nor dead. An underlying theme of this strange tale is of a displaced maternal womb, that first home which Freud described as one of the most uncanny of all things.

III. *The animal*

The image of the animal also appears in 'The Sandman' but Freud, in his desire to emphasise the role of the castrating father, ignored the animal as a source of uncanniness. Intimations of the animal are there in relation to the sandman himself and his children. Nathaniel describes the sandman as a bestial figure—half-human and half-animal. The boy is terrified of his hideous presence, his 'green cat's eyes', 'mis-shapen head', and the growling and hissing sounds he makes.[33] But the most 'repugnant above all were his great knotty, hair-covered hands'. When he seizes Nathaniel he calls him a 'Little beast!' and bares his teeth as he drags him towards the fire, singeing his hair.[34] The sandman lives in an owl's nest in the moon. He feeds the 'bloody' eyes of the human children to his bird-like offspring. The sandman 'carries them to the crescent moon as food for his little children, who have their nest up there and who have crooked beaks like owls'.[35]

The human/creature hybrid is particularly uncanny. The image of the sandman's children eating 'bloody' eyes with their 'crooked beaks' is particularly uncanny. Figures such as werewolves and vampires, who can change shape and form, bring to light what should have remained hidden—the animal at the heart of the human. When the sandman seizes Nathaniel the boy fears he will roast him in the flames, giving rise to a hint of cannibalism and the primeval father. Cannibalism is also a key signifier of abject animal behaviour. Royle makes this point about the underlying suggestion of cannibalism in the story.

'Doesn't the sandman evoke an uncanny trace or tang of cannibalism right from the start?'[36]

THE PRIMAL UNCANNY

Although Freud focuses on the sandman as a central source of the uncanny, his essay presents a large number of objects, persons, events and situations that can give rise to a feeling of the uncanny. However, as Royle explains, the uncanny

> is not 'out there', in any simple sense: as a crisis of the proper and natural, it disturbs any straightforward sense of what is inside and what is outside. The uncanny has to do with a strangeness of framing and borders, an experience of liminality.[37]

Insofar as everything that is subject to repression is uncanny, it constitutes a vast field. 'The world is uncanny,' Royle says at one point.[38] He also correctly emphasises that every individual may 'experience it differently, and each time with a different sense of what is familiar and unfamiliar, surprising and strange'.[39]

If the uncanny signifies a disturbance of 'any straightforward sense of what is inside and outside', then the primal uncanny offers an understanding of the nature of that disturbance; it is related to woman, death and the animal—elements that the male symbolic order represents as 'unfamiliar' and 'strange' in its attempt to normalise masculinity as familiar, proper and natural. These elements are also fundamental in that they suggest the possibility that the symbolic order may have been founded not on the figure of the paternal castrator but on rituals and prohibitions attached to the primal worlds or figures of woman, death and the animal. The variety of taboos invoked in relation to these figures (incest, cannibalism, bestiality, the corpse) suggests that the uncanny will emerge when these taboos are lifted. As Rosemary Jackson argues, the uncanny 'functions to subvert and undermine cultural stability' by giving rise to 'fantasies of violating these taboos'.[40] This transgressive power belongs to the male monster who, in his destructive rampages against society, challenges the authority of the phallic order. In so doing the male monster frequently emerges as a sympathetic figure.

The sense of horror pertaining to the primal uncanny permeates representations of the male monster. This horror underlies the male monster's uncanny alignment with death, nature and the maternal body—uncanny because the male symbolic order designates these three main areas as 'other' and as outside the realm of what constitutes proper phallic masculinity. As a result the male monster is familiar yet unfamiliar, a monstrous body that is phallic yet also linked to death, nature and the maternal/feminine body. By way of understanding the horror film as a most propitious site for the representation of the primal uncanny, let's look at these characteristics and how they relate to each other as well as their defining features.

Woman

In the signifying practices of patriarchal ideology, woman is associated with key areas of the primal uncanny—birth, nature, the animal and death. In his writings, Freud related woman and her sexual and reproductive functions and organs with the uncanny and also linked woman to death and the uncanny, but in his essay on the uncanny he focuses on the castrating father/sandman as the central source of the uncanny. Yet surely birth, nature, mortality, death—these things which should have remained hidden—are brought to life in the body of woman.

In my book The Monstrous-Feminine, I argue that woman is represented as monstrous primarily because of her close association with the world of the body and nature.[41] This is brought about because of her reproductive and procreative functions. Like the animal body, woman's body is unstable; it changes shape in pregnancy and it exudes bodily fluids such as milk during lactation and blood during menstruation. Woman's body is also penetrable, able to be dominated and taken by force. Because of her close alignment with nature and the body, woman as monster threatens the male symbolic order of law, civilisation and language. Man defines woman as 'other' and attempts to exclude her from the symbolic order of law, language and religion, but such expulsion is always only partial. The primal uncanny lives inside and alongside all forms of human subjectivity and signification. In the horror film it gives voice to its hidden and troubling presence through the body and being of the male monster, who is essentially a creature of the primal uncanny.

Drawing on the concept of abjection, I argued that patriarchal ideology represents woman's reproductive functions as abject in order to produce her as monstrous. In the horror film she is represented as primeval mother (Scott's *Alien*), menstrual monster (De Palma's *Carrie*), womb monster (Cronenberg's *The Brood*), bleeding wound (Hitchcock's *Psycho*), menopausal monster (Aldrich's *What Ever Happened to Baby Jane?*), *femme castratrice* (Zarchi's *I Spit on Your Grave*, Verhoeven's *Basic Instinct*) and castrating *vagina dentata* (Scott's *Alien*, Spielberg's *Jaws*). The monstrous-feminine is also aligned with death. She gives life, the infant enters the world from her womb, and in her role as Mother Earth she takes life back. In her role as femme fatale or the fatal, castrating woman, she is also associated with death. Freud explored this association between woman and death in relation to the ancient images of the Death Goddesses. The monstrous-feminine signifies the primal uncanny in that through her body everything that 'ought to have remained secret and hidden ... has come to light'. Those things that patriarchal culture seeks to keep hidden involve man's relationship to the animal world, the world of nature, woman, life, birth, decay and death. Although horrifying, the monstrous-feminine also offers a great deal of pleasure to spectators encouraged to identify with her wildly excessive, anarchic, deadly behaviour.

Woman's monstrosity is derived from her physical, sexual and biological identity. Unlike woman, man does not give birth, lactate or menstruate and hence is not signified as monstrous through his reproductive functions or parenting functions. He becomes monstrous, however, when he is aligned with the world of the primal uncanny that the symbolic order has so strongly repudiated. The male monster is made monstrous when he enters the domain of woman, animal and nature.[42] He transforms into a menstrual or blood monster (vampire), a womb monster (mad doctor), a cannibalistic animal (werewolf), a blood beast (slasher) or a woman (transgendered monster). He becomes monstrous because he seeks to destroy woman and her reproductive identity (the ripper) or deny woman as the origin of life and one who reminds him of his debt to the feminine and animal worlds (the mad doctor).

Freud placed special emphasis on the uncanniness of the female body, of woman's genital organs and womb, 'the former *Heim* [home] of all human beings'.[43] Freud stated that the 'uncanny is that class of the frightening which leads back to what is known of old and long familiar'.[44] This suggests that the notion common to all aspects of the uncanny is that of origins. This 'uncanny is in reality nothing new or alien, but something which is familiar and old-established in the mind and which has become alienated from it if only through the process of repression'.[45]

There is a strong sense in which the male monster of many horror films attempts to return to his origins, to re-create himself, and other life forms. The vampire and werewolf, for instance, re-create themselves without recourse to the other. The scientist who attempts to play God creates life while the scientist who re-births himself (*The Fly, Altered States*, Robertson's and Mamoulian's *Dr Jekyll and Mr Hyde*) is attempting both to usurp the female role and to play God. The scientist becomes monstrous in the act of giving birth to monsters—usually female monsters who represent a particularly potent sign of the primal uncanny. The Ripper sets out to obliterate altogether his first home, the womb, which reminds him of his debt to woman and nature. The ghost, who inhabits the haunted house, reminds us of our troubled relation to the maternal body. Freddy, the ghost of the *Elm Street* films, attempts to transform his spectral body into a haunted womb in which he imprisons the souls of dead children.

Generally, critical writings emphasise the fear aroused by castration anxiety in Freud's theory of the uncanny. But Freud does not simply refer to the external genitals of woman; he allocates a central place to the subject's 'former home', the womb. The uncanny is that place which is 'known of old, and long familiar', the place from which the individual has become alienated through repression. It is in fact this feeling of something 'known of old' that is central to the uncanny.

Freud points out that in some languages the German term 'an *unheimlich* house' is only translatable as 'a haunted house'.[46] The ghost transforms the home—what Freud describes as our first home or the womb—into an uncanny place in which everything that was once familiar is rendered strange, eerie and terrifying. When the spectre is male, it almost always assumes characteristics of the primal uncanny. The uncanny house of many horror films is often haunted by the ghost or trace of a memory of women—wives, mothers, sisters. The presence of the ghost points to family secrets and troubled sexuality.

The haunted house, the family home, is horrifying precisely because it contains cruel secrets and has witnessed terrible deeds committed by family members against each other. The origin of these deeds almost always takes us back to the monster's quest for his own origins. The house becomes the symbolic space—the place of beginnings, the womb—where the drama is played out. Michael Myers of John Carpenter's *Halloween* films is transformed into a masked monster after he witnesses his sister having illicit sex in the house; on his release from prison he sets out to murder other teenagers, particularly women, who also engage in pre-marital sex in the family home. He seems to live undetected in the nooks and crannies of houses, waiting to enact his terrible vengeance on the innocent. In *Psycho* (Alfred Hitchcock, 1960), Norman Bates's murdered mother dies in her bed and Norman hides her mummified corpse in the cellar, yet her presence continues to haunt the house. Jack transforms the hotel in *The Shining* (Stanley Kubrick, 1980) into a blood bath in his attempt to cut up the family he believes is sucking dry his life-blood. One of the most uncanny cinematic scenes depicts the ghosts of murdered twin sisters, victims of another demented father, awash in waves of blood that crash through the hotel corridors. Here the hotel is literally the body of horror, the place of the uncanny, where the failure of desire is transformed into waves of blood and death.

Death

The monster signifies death; it offers the viewing subject what Rosemary Jackson describes as 'a rehearsal for death'. It is the border, the gap, or in-between space that divides life and death that is uncanny. Death is the repressed other of life, 'the void', the 'impossible representation'.[47] The monster, in all of its forms, signals that border, brings on the possibility of death, undoes the structures that preserve the individual's sense of unity and coherence. Woman is associated with death, that other domain of the uncanny that Freud stated was associated with the uncanny in the highest degree. Insofar as woman and the maternal body are linked to the earth and death, the monster, the 'void', takes on an uncanny feminine form. As Jackson points out, death cannot be portrayed directly; 'it appears in literature either as figura (emblem) such as the medieval *memento mori* skeletons, or as mere space … *Das Unheimlich* is at its purest here, when we discover out latent deaths, our hidden lack of being'.[48] Cixous states that the ghost signifies 'the fiction of our relation to death made concrete'.[49]

Freud refers to death in his essay 'The Uncanny', but he does not discuss the death drive. Royle states that the death drive may well signify the most uncanny thing of all. The 'death drive comes to figure uncanniness better than anything that is actually discussed in Freud's essay', but this 'most uncanny example of uncanniness is eerily not in "The Uncanny"'.[50] Hoffman also associates woman with death in 'The Sandman' but Freud does not refer to this important source of uncanniness. Olympia signifies death in that she hovers at the border between the two states of life and death. She is so lifelike that she appears to be animate but in reality is inanimate. She reminds Nathaniel of the 'legend of the dead bride' and when he touches her he feels 'a coldness as of death thrill through him'.[51]

It is Nathaniel's failure to recognise this that ultimately leads to his own death. The other figure of uncanniness is Clara, Nathaniel's fiancée. Hoffman clearly links her to death. 'Nathaniel looked into Clara's eyes, but it was death which gazed at him.'[52]

Woman is also represented in the horror film to signify what Cixous described (and Freud ignored) as 'the fiction of our relation to death made concrete'. Theorists and critics of horror regularly remark on the fact that the monster invariably pursues and murders women. In horror, women are the victims of 'rape, mutilation and murder'.[53] Some have argued that the 'only thing better than one beautiful woman being gruesomely murdered was a whole series of beautiful women being gruesomely murdered'.[54] As Andrew Tudor points out, 'The threat articulated here, then, is that of the omnipotent human predator, seen at its most intense (though not exclusively) in situations of male-upon-female pursuit'.[55] Woman, not man, is predominantly the monster's victim, her death screened in much more intricate detail than that of the male. Her terrified expression, screams of horror, violated body—all of these are used to make the 'fiction of our relation to death concrete'. Michael Powell explored this very issue—woman as the bearer of death—in *Peeping Tom* (Michael Powell, 1960). The psychopathic killer stalks young women, mainly prostitutes, films them with his movie camera, then stabs them to death with a sharp blade mounted on his camera's tripod leg. In conclusion he films their death, focusing on the look of abject horror on their faces as they realise they are about to die. He wants to capture the look of death. He then watches the film of their deaths in his private cinema. In a misogynistic culture, woman becomes the bearer of death, a cinematic equivalent of the medieval *memento mori*. As the 'fiction of our relation to death [made] concrete', woman gives her form and shape to the primal uncanny.

In his other writings, Freud saw woman and death as related. He viewed death as something that separates and castrates as well as something that offers stasis and a desirable sense of inanimation. Death is not something that exists apart from life, inhabiting a separate space of its own; death is an integral part of life. Several of Freud's own dreams corroborated for him the belief that it is the mother who not only gives but also takes life. In his dream of 'The Three Fates', he states that he could not accept the view that 'we were all made on earth and must therefore return to earth':

> This did not suit me and I expressed doubts of the doctrine. My mother thereupon rubbed the palms of her hands together —just as she did in making dumplings, except that there was no dough between them, and showed me the blackish scales of epidermis produced by the friction as proof that we were made of earth. My astonishment at this ocular demonstration knew no bounds and I acquiesced in the belief which I was later to hear expressed in the words: 'Du bist der Natur einen Tod schuldig' [which is translated in a footnote as: 'Thou owest Nature a death'].[56]

The belief that it is the mother who understands the workings of death and teaches the child to accept the necessity of death occurs again in Freud's 'The Theme of the Three Caskets'. Here he refers to the mother's three aspects as she appears 'in the course of a man's life: the mother herself, the beloved one who is chosen after the pattern, and lastly Mother Earth who received him once more'.[57] The mother herself absorbs the infant's body into her own yet also confers independence; she gives life and takes life away insofar as life contains within itself its own end.

Literary historian Elizabeth Bronfen argues that in Western culture the tropes of 'death' and 'woman' function 'as privileged tropes for the enigmatic and for alterity'.[58] She sees a close analogy between woman and the death drive. Just as death inhabits life, femininity is not constructed in clear opposition to masculinity but rather inhabits the masculine as its own otherness.

> As manifestations of such a force of oscillation, both death and femininity not only call into question rigid categories, but also mark the absence of a fixed place within culture. They function as the foundation and condition of culture's representational systems, as telos and origin, yet themselves exist nowhere as reference for this representation.[59]

Bronfen points out that 'woman functions as a privileged trope for the uncanniness of unity and loss, of independent identity and self-dissolution, of the pleasure of the body and its decay'.[60] The culture confers upon woman a close association with life and death; cultural practices similarly reflect these roles. In the horror film, woman signifies the primal uncanny and its abject relationship to death.

Animal

Nature and her prime signifier, the animal, constitutes another border that produces the uncanny, the line between civilised and uncivilised, the self and the non-self. In patriarchal cultures woman is aligned with the animal. Like the animal, woman also has a blood cycle, becomes pregnant, gives birth, sheds afterbirth, lactates, and suckles her young. Many societies erect taboos and cultural prohibitions in relation to the maternal procreative body. Unlike the idealised male body, the female body is not taut, discrete and classical; the female body is unstable. Because of her close alignment with nature and the animal, woman as monster threatens the male symbolic order of law, civilisation and language. In the founding myth of Christianity, woman is depicted as aligned to the animal world. Because woman listened to the serpent, she was responsible for the destruction of man's Eden.

Classical mythology offers a number of potent images of the primal uncanny. Woman as Sphinx is an uncanny human/

animal hybrid. She has the face and chest of a woman, a dragon's tail and the body of a lion with wings. The Sphinx destroyed all male heroes who passed her way and failed to solve the riddle she posed. She signified the ruin of representation and of male civilisation. Similarly, Medusa turned men to stone because she presented such a horrifying sight; she had an enormous head, with serpent hair, excessively long teeth that resembled a boar's snout, and golden wings. According to cultural historian Barbara Walker, another meaning of her 'dangerous face was the menstrual taboo'.[61] Primitive peoples believed that 'the look of a menstruating woman can turn men to stone'.[62] Another interpretation of her horrifying appearance was that she represented death itself; to lift the veil that covered her and look upon her face was to die. Medusa represents a classic instance of the primal uncanny in which woman, animal and death become one.

In his study of western art, *Idols of Perversity*, Bram Dijkstra argues that woman is much more closely aligned to the animal and natural worlds. In classical art a beautiful woman was often depicted next to an animal companion with gaping jaws and sharp teeth. Dijkstra analyses a series of paintings that represent women with tigers, lions, large cats and grizzly bears. The wild beasts, teeth bared, are usually placed alongside the woman's genital area, signifying the threat of her mythical *vagina dentata*. Dijkstra writes that snarling 'jaws suggested the *vagina dentata* which turn-of-the-century men feared they might find hidden beneath' women's gowns.[63] He also analyses the popular paintings of nymphs and satyrs in which women cavort with hairy-hoofed beast men in forests and jungles. He argues that these did not simply signify mythical themes but pointed to the fact that it was believed women were so closely aligned with nature that they were able to cross the border between civilisation and wilderness without any difficulty. Dijkstra also points out that the satyr is frequently represented with Negroid or Semitic features, suggesting that woman also cavorted with the man who was stereotyped as less than human, a beast. Debased Darwinian ideas held that people were in danger of devolving and that woman was much more likely to devolve to a more primitive animal form than man.

When man becomes animal, as in werewolf and apeman films, the primal uncanny is invoked. By aligning himself with the side of the feminine and the animal, man sheds his *heimlich* countenance and rapidly becomes *unheimlich*. The male beast signifies the horror of not being able to distinguish self from other. This aspect of the uncanny—of becoming animal, of being unable to distinguish the human self from the animal self—is explored in narratives of metamorphosis and cannibalism, particularly the werewolf film. The monstrous human/animal beast is inherently uncanny and points to a relationship that should have remained hidden, not brought into the light. This is because the animal has always functioned as a signifier of the non-human. In his important essay on the subjection of the animal, French theorist Jacques Derrida refers to the primal uncanny when he discusses the 'bottomless gaze' of the animal:

> As with every bottomless gaze, as with the eyes of the other, the gaze called animal offers to my sight the abyssal limit of the human: the inhuman or the ahuman, the ends of man, that is to say the bordercrossing from which vantage man dares to announce himself to himself.[64]

Derrida is critical of all philosophers, 'from Aristotle to Lacan, and including Descartes, Kant, Heidegger, and Levinas', who all say the same thing: 'the animal is without language. Or more precisely unable to respond'.[65] The animal signifies the 'abyssal limit of the human'—the edge of the primal uncanny. Like woman, the animal has been designated 'other', existing in a troubled relationship to the rule of law and language.

The horror invoked by the primal uncanny relates specifically to the proximity between familiar and unfamiliar, the ability of one to become the other, to invoke a sense of strangeness and fear. The three essential features of the primal uncanny—woman, nature, death—are inherently familiar, yet capable of a sudden transformation into the unfamiliar. They are familiar because of their place within the symbolic order, but they accrue a degree of unfamiliarity through their status as 'other' in relation to the male symbolic order of law and language. Hence the primal uncanny, through the image of the monster, is always threatening to make its presence felt, to bring what should have been kept hidden and secret into the light. When the forbidden emerges its appearance generates an uncanny disturbance, a sense of phallic panic.

Freud downplayed the figure of woman while ignoring the animal altogether. The primal uncanny draws together the configurations—woman, animal, death—in order to reveal how they are inextricably linked. The concept of the primal uncanny offers a new way of thinking about the uncanny and the representation of male monstrosity in the horror film and other cultural practices. It argues that while male monsters may assume variable forms, and that aspects of their meaning and significance may change from one film to another, there are also certain fundamental characteristics that have informed and shaped the representation of male monstrosity in the cinema. The concept of the primal uncanny emphasises the key roles played by woman, death and the animal in the construction of the uncanny. What an examination of Freud's uncanny reveals is that there is another uncanny—a primal uncanny—that a study of the horror film brings into the light of day. Cultural theorist Elizabeth Wright has argued that if the uncanny is to be considered truly subversive, it must ask new questions and create new meaning, rather than simply represent a return of the repressed.[66] In subsequent chapters we will see that the horror film, in its representation of the primal uncanny, does ask new questions about the nature and function of the male monster and the role of the primal uncanny in cinematic representation and other cultural forms. The uncanny reveals the ways in which we can recognise the strangeness in ourselves and in the world around us, particularly the everyday world. The primal uncanny offers a way of understanding how that strangeness, when aligned with the frightening figure of the male monster, is constructed from 'otherness'—that otherness which the male symbolic order has aligned with the uncanny tropes of woman, death and the animal.

2

FILM AND THE UNCANNY GAZE

Film haunts Freud's work. It is there in the essay on the uncanny, for example, flickering allusively, elusively, illusively at the edge of the textual screen.

NICHOLAS ROYLE[1]

The uncanny gaze is central to the horror film. As we have seen, Freud drew on Schelling's definition of the uncanny as 'that which ought to have remained secret and hidden but has come to light'.[2] The kinds of objects, person, events and sensations that 'come to light' include dead bodies, ghosts, spirits, a double, dismembered limbs, a severed head, the female genital organs, the grave, fear of castration, of losing one's eyes or limbs, and fear of the deadly castrator, the monster who threatens the individual with dismemberment and death. The uncanny gaze also brings to light things that ought to have remained hidden about the nature of the male symbolic order. The vampire questions the nature of phallic sexuality, the wolf–man the supremacy of civilisation; the mad doctor uncovers the failure of science; the ghost exposes secrets within the family; and the ripper brings to light man's fear of death and woman. However, these things on their own are not necessarily uncanny. The uncanny sensation must be produced by the text itself, through the methods it adopts to uncover the uncanny.

In terms of Schelling's and Freud's definitions, uncanniness is produced through the act of revelation, of bringing something horrific into view. To arouse a maximum response of 'dread and horror' in the viewer the uncanny object or event must be represented as familiar yet strangely unfamiliar. In this way the uncanny gaze is constructed in relation to the revelation, the bringing into the light, of something that is familiar yet unfamiliar. 'Thus *heimlich* is a word the meaning of which develops in the direction of ambivalence, until it finally coincides with its opposite, *unheimlich*'.[3] There is a gradual development, an ambivalence, a difficulty in at first seeing clearly the nature of the uncanny thing or event. Nicholas Royle argues that the uncanny 'comes above all, perhaps, in the uncertainties of silence, solitude and darkness'.[4] These conditions suggest that the uncanny gaze is produced in a strangely atmospheric situation. Perhaps the object or event is shrouded or covered over by a veil or mist. Freud offers a number of examples that emphasise concealment: 'The *unheimlich* mist called hill-fog'[5]; 'The *unheimlich*, fearful hours of the night'[6]. Also the *unheimlich* female genital is 'concealed'.[7] The monster invariably appears at night when shadows shroud everything. The vampire and werewolf strike at night, when the moon is full. The ripper and ghost are also creatures of the shadowy night. 'But it is also impossible to conceive of the uncanny without a sense of ghostliness, a sense of strangeness given to dissolving all assurances about the identity of the self'.[8]

In his essay 'The Uncanny', Freud relates, in a footnote, his own uncanny experience of not recognising himself. He was travelling by train and alone in his compartment when 'a more than usually violent jolt of the train swung back the door of the adjoining washing-cabinet and an elderly gentleman in a dressing-gown and a traveling cap came in … I can still recollect that I thoroughly disliked his appearance'.[9]

The elderly gentleman was, of course, Freud himself. He interpreted this event as a failure to recognise his double and his dislike of himself as 'a vestigal trace of the archaic reaction which feels the "double" to be something uncanny'.[10] The other reason for Freud's negative response to his own image is that the reflection revealed to him is the strangeness that dwells in us all. The conditions in the train (the 'violent jolt', an unexpected 'reflection in the looking-glass', the darker atmosphere of a '*wagon-lit* compartment') all converged to create an optimum situation for the play of an uncanny gaze. The structure of the uncanny gaze places the beholder in an unexpected, often frightening, position in relation to the object of the gaze. The uncanny gaze in this instance revealed to Freud what was normally kept hidden—that is, the uncanniness that resides within, which makes us all strangers to ourselves. The uncanny, Derrida states, involves the sense of 'a stranger who is already found within'.[11] Freud emphasised the reflection as a 'double' but I would emphasise the uncanniness evoked by what the image revealed to the startled man—that we do not always know ourselves, that the estrangement of the self from itself is a fundamental condition of being human.

In the cinema, the uncanny gaze is created through a process of concealment and revelation and often in a context of shadow and light. As the horrified spectator focuses on the scenario unfolding on the screen, the uncanny gaze is constructed at that point at which the familiar becomes unfamiliar. The identity of the character on the screen becomes troubled. The spectator experiences a sense of fractured identity, of the self in 'bits and pieces'. The uncanny undermines the notion of the Cartesian *cogito, ergo sum* ('I think, therefore I am') that proposes the subject as coherent and cohesive. The uncanny warns that the subject's sense of wholeness is illusory and that the familiar self is always in danger of not knowing itself. The uncanny image of the cinema is nurtured by the idea that the subject is unknown to itself. Many films that explore the uncanny do so in relation to a reflected image of the self in which the character, like Freud, is startled by his or her own reflection. There are very effective examples of this moment in Hitchcock's *Psycho* and *The Haunting*

(Robert Wise, 1963), for example, when the leading female character, alone in a haunted house, frightens herself by unexpectedly glimpsing her own image in a mirror. The uncanny gaze is structured in relation to the uncanny object, sensation or event in order to intensify the spectator's inner sense of foreignness, strangeness and doubleness. As French psychoanalyst Julia Kristeva says, 'With Freud indeed, foreignness, an uncanny one, creeps into the tranquillity of reason itself.'[12]

As Nicholas Royle points out in relation to literature, the 'uncanny is a reading-effect': 'The uncanny is a ghostly feeling that arises (or doesn't arise), an experience that comes about (or doesn't), as an effect of reading.'[13] The same is true of the cinema. It is not a matter of 'spot the uncanny', to use Royle's phrase; the uncanny must be created by the film text, by lighting and sound and the structures of looking. The uncanny in film is produced most often as an effect of looking, specifically in relation to the uncanny gaze. The uncanny is also created in relation to sound (a creaking door, noises in the night, the howl of wolves), a particularly important vehicle for the production of eerie events and sensations.

There is a particularly uncanny moment in *The Shining* when the young boy, Danny, is riding his tricycle along the seemingly endless corridors of the Overlook Hotel. We have accompanied him on this ride before. We are familiar with the long winding halls, the geometric pattern on the carpet, the sense of isolation. All of this is very *heimlich*, although the familiar atmosphere is accompanied by a growing sense of unease as it becomes clear that there is something very sinister about the hotel. Suddenly two identical twin girls who are about Danny's age appear, blocking his passageway. Like ghosts, they invite him to come and play with them 'forever and ever'. The *unheimlich* may appear suddenly as long as there is a sense of transformation of the ordinary or familiar. This is a particularly uncanny moment because Stanley Kubrick, the director, has expended time and effort in creating a familiar scene in order to transform it into the unfamiliar. The fact that the two girls are identical twins as well as

Eerie girl ghosts from Kubrick's The Shining, *1980*
(Warner Bros/The Kobal Collection)

ghosts renders the scene even more uncanny. Then the uncanniness intensifies as the girls re-appear, this time as corpses, their bodies cut up and bleeding. This latter scene also constructs the uncanny by rendering the familiar unfamiliar. Just as we have adjusted to the sight of the ghostly twins, they suddenly re-appear in another, unfamiliar context. Their clean and whole bodies are cut up and covered in blood. Thus the viewer is required to hold at least two impressions together in a moment of terror, as the *heimlich* becomes *unheimlich*.

Later in the film the twins appear again, this time as two hideous hags. They rise from the bath waters of the 'forbidden' room of the hotel where presumably they were murdered by their father. One initially appears as a beautiful young woman who rises from the bath and embraces Danny's demented father (Jack Nicholson) who has wandered into the forbidden room. At first he is overjoyed as he imagines the pleasure of sex that the woman seems to hold out to him. Then, in one uncanny moment, the scene is rendered horrific. The already slightly strange but not unfamiliar scene (a beautiful naked woman offering sex) is suddenly rendered uncanny—the girl changes before his eyes into a monstrous hag whose decaying skin falls apart in the man's hands. The moment when the woman's whole and beautiful body transforms into a rotting scabrous one is horrifyingly uncanny. The spectatorial gaze, already troubled by the appearance of the ghostly but beautiful woman, is suddenly fractured through the film's use of mirrors, reflections and doubles to convey the uncanny nature of her bodily metamorphosis.

How horrific is the uncanny moment? At this point—when the viewer absorbs the full horror of the uncanny transformation—he or she might turn away, choose not to look. In *The Monstrous-Feminine* I have argued that the abject gaze—that is, when the viewer looks away in horror—fulfils the criterion of a 'fifth look' of the cinema.[14] The uncanny gaze, however, is not always abject. Because, as Kristeva argues, there is nothing familiar about the abject, the abject gaze always occurs when the spectator looks away. 'Essentially different from "uncanniness", more violent, too, abjection is elaborated through a failure to recognize its kin; nothing is familiar, not even the shadow of a memory.'[15]

The so-called splatter film does not invoke an uncanny gaze because in the excess of blood and gore there is nothing that transforms from the familiar into the unfamiliar. Everything is unfamiliar. Excess is the enemy of the uncanny. The uncanny gaze is more likely to hold the spectator in its grip because the scene always invokes something that remains familiar. There is no failure of recognition. Thus the uncanny gaze is one of ambivalence and transformation in which one state of looking (the *heimlich*) merges into its opposite (the *unheimlich*) but each form of looking is never entirely free of the traces of its other. The *heimlich* gaze becomes an *unheimlich* gaze at that moment when the uncanny inserts itself into what Cixous describes as the interstices of the narrative; the uncanny gaze uncovers what should have remained hidden—it creates a gap. This is not the same as the distance required for the controlling voyeuristic look; rather, it constructs a disunity, a contradiction. The uncanny gaze is not a controlling look but one that surrenders all power through its contemplation of that which is secret and forbidden. This moment registers shock on the spectator's body—eyes fill with horror, goosebumps prickle the skin, hairs stand on end, flesh creeps, the body shivers. The uncanny gaze, whose uncanniness spreads over the body, both repels and lures. There is always something attractive in looking at the frightening or forbidden, such as the human male (or female) in one of its monstrous guises. The appearance of the monster always renders the familiar setting unfamiliar, particularly when the setting is the family home or the familiar suburb, town or city.

The uncanny gaze is central to the horror film. The representation of the uncanny in film, however, does not just terrify the viewer. Here it is important to point out that the uncanny, as with the representation of the abject in film, can be terrifying yet also hold a strange lure for the viewer. Perversely, the viewer wants to be terrified, to experience a range of feelings associated with horror and the uncanny—anxiety, fear, astonishment, dread. The viewer may also experience pleasure in watching that which has been repressed brought into view, may enjoy the opening up of taboo areas. In the cinema, the uncanny has the power both to repel and attract viewers secure in the knowledge that they are watching from the safety of their cinema seats.

Freud's choice of Hoffman's 'The Sandman' to illustrate the powerful effects of the uncanny is of particular relevance to an understanding of the structures of the uncanny gaze. As psycho-analytic critic and film theorist Joan Copjec points out, 'Freud, influenced by the literary works on which he drew, underlined the privileged relation uncanniness maintained with the gaze.'[16] This is true, but—although he doesn't use the term—it is Hoffman who describes the power of the uncanny gaze in 'The Sandman'. With its emphasis on voyeurism, the objectification of woman, disembodied eyes and loss of sight, 'The Sandman' can be interpreted as an allegory about looking and the cinema. The sandman himself is like the film director in that he controls the gaze throughout the story, from the moment when Nathaniel first develops a fear of him coming to tear out his 'occe' (eyes) at night, to the moment when he jumps to his death from the tower, calling out: 'Ha! Lov-ely occe! Lov-ely occe!'[17] Hoffman creates an uncanny gaze by juxtaposing the familiar with the unfamiliar, bringing to light things that should have remained hidden, particularly the power of the inner eye, the imagination, to create images of the sublime, filled with awe and dread.

The most uncanny moment in the story is like a scene from a horror film. It is when the old woman tells Nathaniel that the sandman causes children's eyes to 'jump out of their heads all "bloody"' then feeds them to his children who have their nest in the crescent moon. From this moment on, Nathaniel never sees clearly again. Hoffman charts Nathaniel's loss of vision with the sandman's power to orchestrate the increasingly uncanny events that befall him. It is as if Nathaniel had entered a cinema and let his vision be directed and changed by the director/sandman himself—except that Nathaniel is literally driven insane. His image of the 'cruel sandman now assumed hideous detail within' him.[18] When he sees Coppelius he sees a 'fearsome apparition' and a 'dreadful spectre'.[19]

His greatest failure of vision occurs in relation to Olympia the mechanical doll with whom he falls in love. Like the lover of countless films, he only sees what his imagination wants to see. To him, Olympia is a living woman, although he is aware that something is wrong with her own eyes.

> She seemed not to notice me, and her eyes had in general something fixed and staring about them, I could almost say she was sightless, as if she were sleeping with her eyes open. It made me feel quite uncanny.[20]

Nonetheless he sees her as 'a heavenly woman', 'a beam of light', his 'glorious star of love'.[21] He even dances joyously with her at a party, yet still does not realise she is an automaton. His inability to see clearly affects his relationship with Clara. When he writes a poem about Clara, his betrothed, he imagines that on their wedding day Coppelius 'appeared and touched Clara's lovely eyes, which sprang out like blood-red sparks, singeing and burning, on to Nathaniel's breast'.[22] Her eyes become like nipples imbedded in his breast. The spectacle maker, Coppola, who is actually Coppelius/the sandman, sells him a pocket telescope that brings objects into focus more sharply than any other. Through the window of her house, he spies on the beautiful Olympia; he is even less able than before to detect that she is an automaton. He imagines that he sees her eyes 'full of desire' when she looks at him. Like the cinema, the telescope in fact renders everything more clearly but causes him to project only his own inner feelings onto everything he sees in relation to the beautiful Olympia, the clockwork doll. He is obsessed with his vision of her. Like the enraptured film fan, he falls in love with an image, a ghost inside a frame.

When Nathaniel discovers the truth, the professor this time throws Olympia's 'blood-flecked eyes' at him and they strike him in the chest—again appearing to form nipples on his breast.[23] In his deranged mind the bloody eyes that the sandman feeds to his children are like a mother's nipples with one difference—the milk is blood. It is the revelation that Olympia is an uncanny automaton that unsettles his mind. In other words it is when he sees the uncanny clearly for the first time that he is driven insane.

In his essay on the uncanny, Freud states: 'fiction presents more opportunities for creating uncanny feelings than are possible in real life'.[24] Although Freud does not refer to the cinema, his comment is perhaps more relevant to the modern art form. His reference to the writer pretending 'to move into the world of common reality' has important implications for the representation of the uncanny in film. With its unique ability to capture or construct an image of reality, film is particularly well equipped to represent the uncanny—'to increase [the] effect' of the uncanny and 'multiply it'.[25] It is that class of the uncanny 'which proceeds from repressed complexes' rather than from 'forms of thought that have been surmounted' that is 'more resistant and remains as powerful in fiction as in real experience'.[26]

> The storyteller has a peculiarly *directive power over us;* by means of moods he can put us into, he is able to guide the current of our emotions, to dam it up in one direction and make it flow in another, and he often obtains a great variety of effects from the same material.[27]

In this statement, Freud could well have been referring to the medium of film: all the hallmarks that he applies to the storyteller could equally apply to the film director. As Nicholas Royle states, 'Film haunts Freud's work. It is there on the essay on the uncanny, for example, flickering allusively, elusively, illusively at the edge of the textual screen.'[28]

Themes that in any way evoke the monstrous and strange are almost always associated with the uncanny. The uncanny, however, is not necessarily something that always remains the same or manifests itself in the same degree. It has been argued that the uncanny may appear in response to an era that is outwardly dominated by the principles of control, regulation and order. In her fascinating study of culture, Terry Castle argues that the eighteenth century, which glorified reason, actually produced or invented the uncanny. She claims that:

> The very psychic and cultural transformations that led to the subsequent glorification of the period as an age of reason or enlightenment—the aggressively rationalist imperatives of the epoch—also produced, like a kind of toxic side effect, a new human experience of strangeness, anxiety, bafflement, and intellectual impasse.[29]

Philosopher Mladen Dolar similarly argues:

> There was an irruption of the uncanny strictly parallel with bourgeois (and industrial) revolutions and the rise of scientific rationality … Ghosts, vampires, monsters, the undead dead, etc., flourish in an era when you might expect them to be dead and buried, without a place. They are something brought about by modernity itself.[30]

The first films appeared at a time of great social, cultural and economic change, which was accompanied by an irruption of the uncanny in popular culture. Film, born in the twentieth century, recorded the anxieties of a fin-de-siècle culture and the beginnings of a new century of extraordinary change accompanied by an all-pervasive sense of anxiety and strangeness. The emerging twentieth century proved to be an age of progress, marked by new inventions in science, technology and communication systems; it was also an epoch marked by wars, mass death, weapons of mass destruction, morbidity, genocide, paranoia and political repression. These disruptions brought with them a new form of the uncanny, one represented graphically in the new art form of cinema. They also offered viewers a way of reconciling the familiar, more stable rhythms of the past with the unfamiliar patterns and sensations of modernity. The cinema created an uncanny gaze that enabled the modern spectator to deal with shocks and jolts of an uncanny new world. The modern uncanny also responded to the very real terrors of the age, representing these terrors in narratives of horror, fantasy and science fiction.[31]

The cinema, as an institutional form, itself constituted a form of the uncanny. It created a kind of uncanny space— a dream factory—where audiences could sit alongside complete strangers, in the dark, and watch strange images of the human face and form flicker across the screen. The phantasmagoria of the twentieth century—uncanny images of human life on a white screen—offered viewers a new way of seeing the world.

The method by which a film tells its story is itself uncanny in that a film animates a series of inanimate images in order to create an illusion of movement and life. As Lesley Stern argues:

> We do not have to look very far for examples of the uncanny in cinema (figures of doubling and dismemberment, for instance, abound), but beyond isolated examples it might be the case that the fascination that cinema, as an aesthetic phenomenon, exerts ... is intimately implicated in uncanny procedures. Cinema, as we know it, systematically plays upon (though not always interestingly) a slide between the familiar and the unfamiliar (the Unheimlich).[32]

In other words, cinema portrays images that are already, in a sense, doubles. Film is uncanny in that its moving images are what Kittler has described as the 'celluloid ghosts' of already absent 'actor's bodies', actions and events. [33] The cinematic image also takes on the intimation of a ghostly world in that the projector animates the inanimate, bringing before the spectator's eyes moving images that were once still. When these are projected in slow motion, particularly images of moving bodies, they can appear particularly uncanny. This is because the familiar pace of bodily movements has been slowed down and rendered unfamiliar. The same is potentially true for images projected in fast motion. These devices offer a powerful means of creating an uncanny gaze. Drawing on 'the trope of the somersault', Lesley Stern presents a fascinating discussion of what she sees as 'two inflections of the cinematic uncanny: "the fateful" and the "euphoric"'. [34] Her discussion provides a compelling instance of the argument that the uncanny is not simply there in the text but must be produced.

The cinema also created a modern bestiary, a collection of cinematic monsters, old and new, who, over the decades came to embody or represent different forms of the uncanny. The male monster appears in various guises: vampire, wolf–man, mad doctor, slasher, cannibal, mummy, zombie and ghost. When the dominant, familiar patriarchal order is made strange or unfamiliar through the presence of the male monster—as distinct from the female—a feeling of utmost 'dread or horror' is aroused, leading to a sense of phallic panic. [35] The dominant order cannot endorse a de-familiarising of the phallic signifier—that is, a deconstruction of masculinity via masculinity. The female monster also wears a range of faces: archaic maternal body, menstrual monster, womb monster, *vagina dentata*, witch, ghost, vampire, *femme castratrice*. She unsettles the phallic signifier in different ways. [36]

Castle argues that one of the hallmarks of the uncanny is 'masquerade and sexual impersonation'. [37] The cinematic uncanny draws on the idea of masquerade in a wide sense, applying it to the idea of the monster that is capable of assuming various forms and guises. The male monster assumes feminine and bestial qualities in a number of his forms: the vampire can be described as a menstrual monster; the mad scientist or doctor, a womb monster; the werewolf, an innocent man; the ghost, a child killer, a theatrical spectre with a preference for impersonation. The slasher, who has virtually no redeeming features, is a blood beast and/or cannibal; he is a creature aligned with nature and the primitive: a monster who creates a sense of phallic panic not because he signifies 'otherness' but because he is not 'other' enough. When the male monster is rendered feminine or aligned with the animal or death, his monstrousness is shaped by the primal uncanny. Male monsters offer a critique of the dominant phallocentric order, transforming the familiar and homely into the unfamiliar and strange through the power of the uncanny gaze.

3

MAN AS WOMB MONSTER: FRANKENSTEIN, COUVADE AND THE POST-HUMAN

Why is it that the maternal landscape, the heimisch, *and the familiar become so disquieting?*

HÉLÈNE CIXOUS[1]

For some, 'the most uncanny thing of all', said Freud, 'is the idea of being buried alive by mistake', which is really a transformation of another phantasy—that 'of intra-uterine existence'.[2] From its inception, the cinema has represented phantasies that explore the uncanny intra-uterine landscape. This is particularly true of Frankensteinian narratives that feature a male scientist or doctor attempting to give birth to new life without the agency of woman. The central theme of these films is that when man creates life he gives birth to monsters. In his attempt to appropriate the power of woman he almost always fails. Although he creates a monster, many of these films argue that the true monster is the mad doctor or scientist himself. Thus, there are twin sources of monstrosity at work in which the relationship between one monster (the creator) and the other (the created) is often extremely complex, particularly when the created monster is female, as in *Metropolis* (Fritz Lang, 1921) and *The Bride of Frankenstein* (James Whale, 1935). These films argue that science cannot or should not attempt to take the place of woman.

Horror films have explored this theme through the phantasy of man creating life (Whale's *Frankenstein*), re-birthing himself (Russell's *Altered States*), giving birth after an alien rape (Scott's *Alien*), manufacturing mechanical life (Lang's *Metropolis*), creating life through new reproductive technologies such as cloning (Jeunet's *Alien Resurrection*), or trying to control the maternal landscape: the uterus itself (Cronenberg's *Dead Ringers*). Films that represent male mothers and uterine themes include the many versions of the Frankenstein and Dr Jekyll and Mr Hyde films: *The Bride of Frankenstein*, *The Stepford Wives* (Bryan Forbes, 1975), *Demon Seed* (Donald Cammell, 1977), *The Manitou* (William Girdler, 1978), *It's Alive* (Larry Cohen, 1974), *The Fly* (David Cronenberg, 1986), *Altered States* (Ken Russell, 1980), *The Boys from Brazil* (Franklin J. Schaffner, 1978), *Total Recall* (Paul Verhoeven, 1990), *Species* (Roger Donaldson, 1995) and *Gattaca* (Andrew Niccol, 1997). Horror films that explore the theme of artificial creation usually feature an uncanny uterine landscape that points to man's desire to assume woman's generative powers, to imagine himself as the source of life in that landscape.

Almost all cultures have myths and rituals about men giving birth. The phenomenon of couvade, in which men in some societies simulate the act of giving birth (they experience pain, squat or lie in a birthing position, thus simulating labour), reveals the extent to which men hold women's birth-giving power in the highest regard. It is an awe-inspiring practice that has been incorporated into religious and ritual practices. In some non-western societies couvade continues to play a pivotal role, thus ensuring the involvement of fathers in childbirth. As the power to give birth was regarded most highly this became an important activity of the earliest male divinities. According to Barbara Walker, as male gods lacked a uterus they frequently gave birth from their mouths.[3] The classical god Zeus gave birth from his head. All of the mystery cults of the early Christian period involved a baptismal re-birth through male blood. According to

Walker, the male birth myth is universal. This myth is central to the horror film, although the majority of these films reveal that modern couvade rituals have debased ancient practices. In his attempt to create new life, the male womb monster of the horror film re-creates an intra-uterine mise en scène, a maternal landscape, which is symbolically his womb, his birth-giving place. He gives physical form to an unconscious memory of his first home. He wants to live in the uncanny moment and in an uncanny space. This dynamic is particularly evident in David Cronenberg's two films *The Fly* (1986) and *Dead Ringers* (1988) as well as in classic films about the male womb monster, such as Whale's *Frankenstein* (1931) and the Freddie Francis film *The Evil of Frankenstein* (1964). Films that explore cloning and post-human reproductive technologies, such as *Demon Seed* and *Alien Resurrection*, construct elaborate birthing fantasies against an intra-uterine landscape that is grotesque in the extreme.

Many of these films, particularly *Frankenstein* and *Altered States*, offer a fascinating study of male hysteria as a symptom of the failure of its male protagonists to create life. The doctor or scientist who sets out to usurp the role of woman often becomes increasingly disturbed, his behaviour indicating an hysterical obsession, suggesting he is the true monster. Although Freud wrote primarily about female hysterics, he always maintained that hysteria was not simply a female malady.[4] In one sense, hysteria is specific to women in that historically it was associated with problems of the womb. (The word 'hysteria' comes from the Greek *hysteros*, meaning 'womb'.) The Egyptians believed the origin of hysteria was associated with abnormal movements of the uterus, which they thought could actually travel around the body. Plato described the womb as similar to an animal or creature that enjoyed an independent existence in the body. When the wandering womb rose in the body it created a condition known as 'globus hystericus'—that is, the sensation that 'a ball was rising in the oesophagus, producing a feeling of choking or suffocation'.[5] According to Hippocrates, if the uterus:

Uncanny man-made wombs—The Evil of Frankenstein, *1964*
(Hammer/The Kobal Collection)

Uncanny man-made wombs—The Fly, *1986*
(20th Century Fox/The Kobal Collection)

attached itself to the heart, the patient would feel anxiety and oppression and begin to vomit. If it fastened to her liver, the woman would lose her voice and grit her teeth and her complexion would turn ashen. If it lodged in the loins, she would feel a hard ball or lump in her side.[6]

Hysteria was once viewed as a quintessentially female illness primarily because its symptoms almost always involved an emotional outpouring. Showalter lists these as 'fits, fainting, vomiting, choking, sobbing, laughing, paralysis'.[7] The years between 1870 and World War I were known as the 'golden age' of hysteria because of a rise in the number of cases officially reported. Then with the advent of the war, the illness assumed a new form. Large numbers of men were reported as suffering from hysteria. Their symptoms, initially described as 'shell shock', included paralysis, blindness, disorientation, nightmares and depression.

As in the case of women, Freud also argued that the cause of hysteria in men was a failure to take up the designated gender role. Using the female reproductive system as a guide, he drew connections between the symptoms of hysteria in women and men. He drew a parallel between the 'abdominal cavity' in men and the 'site of the "ovaralgia"' in women.[8] If the cause of hysteria in men is a consequence of their failure, for whatever reason, to adopt the proper masculine role, then it is clear why the incidence of male hysteria would have risen in war time when men not only witness horrific scenes of death and destruction but are also expected to maim and kill other men.

Men who desire to give birth may also exhibit hysterical symptoms. In the case study of Little Hans, Freud noted that Hans wanted to have a baby, to give birth to a little girl, and that he didn't want his mother to have one.[9] In the Wolf Man case history Freud proposes that his patient, when a boy, entertained a fantasy about having a child with his father: 'In his identification with women (that is, with his mother) he was ready to give his father a baby, and was jealous of his mother, who had already done so and would perhaps do so again.'[10]

It was Melanie Klein who developed Freud's ideas and proposed a theory of womb envy in men as a counterpart to Freud's theory of penis envy in women. Klein argued that both boys and girls experience an early femininity phase in which both sexes identify with the mother and take pleasure in the feminine. During this period the boy desires to possess a womb so that he might have a baby. In some men, the failure to have this capacity can lead, as Claire Kahane points out, to frustration at best and at worst to 'envy, rivalry and even hatred of women'.[11] This failure may well lead to hysteria, mainly brought on by a man's failure to fulfil his proper gender role as a father.

Although films that explore man's desire to give birth to new life tend to fall into the category of horror, the subject is also suited to comedy. In *Junior*, for instance (Ivan Reitman, 1994), Arnold Schwarzenegger plays Dr Alex Hesse, who is inseminated with a fertilised egg that grows to full term in the cavity next to his stomach. The infant is born by caesarian section. Overcome with maternal devotion, Dr Hesse symbolically transforms his hard masculine body into a soft feminine one as he morphs into the realm of the maternal. Determined to keep his baby, the man of muscle dresses as a woman, even sporting breasts instead of biceps. Although not a horror film, *Junior's* portrayal of Schwarzenegger in maternal drag does endow the monstrous mother with a new face. The originating story of all these films, including *Junior*, is Mary Shelley's novel *Frankenstein* in which Dr Frankenstein creates a monster of his own. In almost all these films, the male scientist succeeds only in creating monsters. This theme is explored with graphic realism in the early and later versions of *The Fly* in which the scientist transforms himself into his own monster.

THE UNCANNY WOMB

Of all the bodily organs, Freud sees the uterus, or womb, as particularly uncanny. This is because the womb is the most *heimlich*

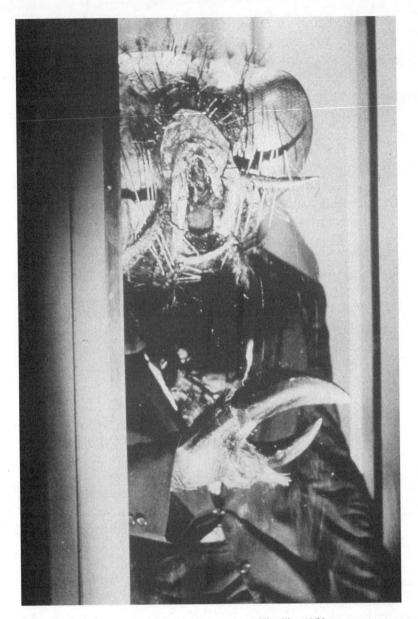

When man usurps woman's role he creates monsters—The Fly, *1958*
(20th Century Fox/The Kobal Collection)

yet *unheimlich* place of all. It is our first home, the memory of which haunts our unconscious, sometimes rising to consciousness in particularly uncanny moments. This is most likely to occur with 'neurotic men'. Freud states that the response of these men to their former home offers 'a beautiful confirmation of the uncanny':

> It often happens that neurotic men declare that they feel there is something uncanny about the female genital organs. This unheimlich *place, however, is the entrance to the former* Heim [home] *of all human beings, to the place where each one of us lived once upon a time and in the beginning.*[12]

Freud then broadens his argument to potentially include all men. Jokes and dreams are not the province of neurotic men only:

> There is a joke saying that 'Love is home-sickness'; and whenever a man dreams of a place or a country and says to himself, while he is still dreaming: 'this place is familiar to me, I've been here before', we may interpret this place as being his mother's genitals or her body.[13]

In this instance the man experiences the uncanny through a dream. He associates a place or country with a yearning for home that Freud says is also a desire for his first familiar home. Presumably he seeks the comfort of a familiar place, which in his dream is an amalgam of place/country/maternal body. The uncanniness expressed here is not linked to fear, as in the first instance, but to a phantasy of yearning. The sight of the female genital organs evokes a repressed memory of another experience, that of intra-uterine existence. This memory 'ought to have remained hidden but has come to light'. Presumably something fearful was associated with this memory but we have to search elsewhere in Freud's text to discover what this is. The answer to the fearful memory attached to the female genital appears earlier in the essay, when Freud associates the uterus with another, quite different, uncanny experience—a phantasy that is central to many horror films, particularly the mummy films:

> To some people the idea of being buried alive by mistake is the most uncanny thing of all. And yet psychoanalysis has taught us that this terrifying phantasy is only a transformation of another phantasy that originally had nothing terrifying about it at all, but was qualified by a certain lasciviousness—the phantasy, I mean, of intra-uterine existence.[14]

Here is one explanation as to why some 'neurotic men' experience the female genital organs as uncanny. This is the entrance to their former home, which evokes an uncanny feeling of having been buried alive by mistake. Originally, Freud tells us, this phantasy was not terrifying; rather it 'was qualified by a certain lasciviousness'. Here the editor of the essay refers the reader to Freud's analysis of the Wolf Man and his discussion of intra-uterine phantasies: the womb phantasy and the phantasy of re-birth. Both invoke incestuous desires: the womb phantasy a wish for sexual intercourse with the father, the phantasy of re-birth a wish for intercourse with the mother. As previously mentioned, Freud also discussed womb envy in the Little Hans case history. Little Hans desired to give birth to a baby of his own in which his own mother would be the father. It is curious that Freud neglected phantasies of womb envy in his interpretation of 'The Sandman', particularly as Hoffman's story features two sets of male mothers whose activities are associated with a pervasive atmosphere of uncanniness. The reason appears to be that Freud wanted to assert the central importance of castration anxiety and the role of the father as castrator rather than phantasies of womb envy that are linked directly to the maternal figure and the primal uncanny. Freud always held that the father, not the mother, played the key role in the institution of the family.

In the horror film man is made monstrous when he attempts to usurp the primary functions of woman, particularly in relation to reproduction, sexuality and birth. The scientist who attempts to create life becomes monstrous—usually more monstrous than his creation—and the monster itself is by definition monstrous. Thus, these films represent a doubled form of monstrosity. The monster itself, when female, can be seen as an expression of the scientist's feminine self. This is true of films such as *Metropolis* (1921), *The Bride of Frankenstein* (1935), *Dr Jekyll and Sister Hyde* (1971) and *The Stepford Wives* (1975). Or the monster can signify the male mother's dark self, his displaced desire to reproduce. In films that explore the monstrous male mother, un-canniness is associated with the depiction of uterine landscapes and phantasies of birth. It is the maternal figure who reminds man of his debt to nature and of the inevitability of death. As I argued in *The Monstrous-Feminine*, woman is represented in horror films (*The Brood*, 1979, *Alien*, 1979) as the original uncanny womb monster.[15] She is keeper of the womb, the point of origin and source of all life. Man becomes a womb monster because of his unnatural desire to create new life without woman, to usurp her place. In these films the familiar generative mater-nal body is represented symbolically and appears unfamiliar and terrifying. As discussed in Chapter 1, when man attempts to assume woman's powers he also becomes uncanny through association with her primal uncanniness—that is, her womb—which Freud argued was to some men the most uncanny thing of all.

'FRANKENSTEIN' (1931)

James Whale's *Frankenstein* is alive with images of the uncanny: disembodied eyes, a skeleton, graveyards, a living/dead monster, a ghost, eerie landscapes, artificially created life-forms and magic. An adaptation of Mary Shelley's 1818 Gothic novel, *Frankenstein or The Modern Prometheus*, the film deviates in a number of key respects from the literary text. The film begins with a man addressing the audience:

> We are about to unfold the story of Frankenstein, a man of science, who sought to create a man after his own image, without reckoning upon God. It is one of the strangest tales ever told. It deals with the two great mysteries of creation: life and death.

Whale's film became a landmark of popular culture and its monster, played by Boris Karloff, a cultural icon. One of the great early horror films, *Frankenstein* created a series of disturbing screen images and motifs that still retain their power. *Frankenstein* tells the story of Dr Frankenstein, a hysteric who is obsessed with creating life. His method is to assemble body parts, stolen from graves, and to imbue them with life by causing electricity from bolts of lightning to surge through their veins. His scheme works except for one fatal flaw: he inadvertently implants the brain of a criminal into his creation, thus giving birth to a monster. The other mistake he makes is to attempt to create life without woman. *Frankenstein* explores the primal uncanny through the illicit activities of its male mothers, presenting a disturbing picture of debased couvade practices. There is a pervasive sense of monstrosity duplicating itself through the double figures of the mad doctor as monster, as well as his monstrous creation.

The film's uncanny atmosphere starts with the credit sequence in which we glimpse a man's face ringed around by a set of staring eyes. This sequence cuts to an equally uncanny scene, set in a cemetery, in which two men are robbing a grave. A skeleton fixed to a pole—a life-size *memento mori*—intensifies the pervasive sense of unease. *Frankenstein* attempts to portray death through various illusions. In a later scene a skeleton dangling on a rope, which is used for illustration in a lecture theatre, dances in an eerie fashion when accidentally knocked. In this film the dead are presented as skeletons, ghosts, body parts.

When the latter combine in the form of the monster, they create a creature who is literally one of the walking dead.

Frankenstein is locked away, working compulsively in his laboratory with Fritz, his hunchbacked partner, who 'becomes Frankenstein's surrogate wife'.[16] He refuses to see anyone, even his beautiful fiancée. He is more interested in his project than in his betrothed. The various characters we meet all refer to his 'mad dream' and 'insane ambition' to create life. When they force their way into his secret workshop, or phantom womb, we see how its design suggests the rounded, uterine shapes of that first home. The laboratory is literally and symbolically charged with electricity as Frankenstein and Fritz capture the energy from the bolts of lightning that pierce the night sky. The scene is marked by a perverse kind of sexual excitement. Frankenstein pulls various levers and the strange cone-shaped machine shoots up through the roof. The music swells. He is more animated and excited than at any time before or after. All of his energies, creative and sexual, have been sublimated into this moment of creation. As cultural critic James Twitchell points out: 'In fact in all the *Frankensteins* both at Universal and at Hammer, the creation scene is always played very close to a scene of sexual arousal'.[17] When Frankenstein finally brings life to the inert body on his worktable (we see its eyelids flutter) he becomes hysterical with joy. 'It's alive! It's alive!' he screams to the heavens. 'I made that body with my own hands. I took from graves, from the gallows, from anywhere.' It is clear from this moment— when we learn that the monster has been assembled from the dead—that nothing good will come of the experiment. An impassive, hulking brute, the monster is part-human, part-creature, and part-automaton. It hovers in a dark zone between the living and the dead, which recalls Freud's contention that 'apparent death and the re-animation of the dead have been represented as the most uncanny themes'.[18]

Just before the reappearance of the monster, Frankenstein's fiancée, Elizabeth, is overcome with an uncanny feeling: 'I'm afraid. Terribly afraid something is going to happen. I've felt it all day. Something is coming between us. If I could just get it out of my mind.' What is most uncanny about *Frankenstein* is the way in which Whale has created a sense of an uncanny place: the dark womb. He plays on the motifs of water, cellars and graveyards. The uterine spaces of the film are intensely uncanny because they give birth to death—to a monster on the side of death. The monster accidentally kills a young girl, who drowns in the lake. This scene, which was initially censored, then restored in 1987, illustrates perfectly how James Whale intensifies the film's uncanny atmosphere by transforming the *heimlich* into the *unheimlich*. When the monster stumbles upon the little girl, she is playing beside the lake in a scene of pastoral beauty. Unafraid of the monster, she takes his huge hand in her small one and leads him to the edge of the water, saying, 'Will you play with me?' She shows him how to throw daisy petals into the water. Overjoyed, the monster unthinkingly picks her up and throws her into the lake, assuming she will float like a daisy. The bright, happy mood is suddenly filled with darkness and despair. Whenever the monster appears, the familiar becomes unfamiliar and the scene fills with a sense of uncanny disquiet. We see the same *unheimlich* structure in other scenes, particularly the joyous wedding celebrations over which the monster soon casts his shadow.

When Frankenstein, who virtually abandons his 'son' at birth, finally comes face to face with his creation inside a burning windmill, the film focuses on the response of the monster. Realising that his 'father' did not create him whole, nor even nurture him properly, the monster decides that Frankenstein should pay for his cruelty and neglect. He throws Frankenstein from the top of the windmill just as the walls collapse. In James Whale's *The Bride of Frankenstein* (1935), however, we learn that he did not perish. The monster's rage is a rage against life itself; it is clear he wishes he had never been 'born'. In *The Bride of Frankenstein*, in which Frankenstein and his teacher, Dr

Praetorius, attempt to create a mate for the monster, the brute screams out loud: 'I love dead. Hate living.'

Frankenstein was not just a huge box office success; it became the prototype for all subsequent films about the uncanny male mother. In almost all versions of this theme, man creates only monsters. Ironically, in most versions it is almost always the monster that is the sympathetic figure. The source of the horror is the scientist and the abject scene of generation, in which he attempts to create life from death. This brings together three particularly uncanny motifs: death, dismemberment and the intra-uterine landscape. Unable to control the scene of reproduction, the obsessed scientist succumbs to hysterical outpourings of emotion—similar to those in 'The Sandman'. These things, of course, are to be expected in the horror genre; what is fascinating, though, is the many films that associate the male desire to create life with hysteria and the uncanny uterine or maternal landscape. These uncanny scenes comment ironically on the failure of the scientific endeavour to create life. They expose the phantasy of phallic omnipotence and the true source of monstrosity in the film: the scientist as a failed maternal creator.

In Mary Shelley's novel, Frankenstein will not permit his monster to have a mate. At first, when the monster demands a partner, Frankenstein acquiesces. The monster says:

> *I am alone and miserable; man will not associate with me; but one as deformed and horrible as myself would not deny herself to me. My companion must be of the same species and have the same defects. This being you must create.*[19]

He tells Frankenstein that he and his mate will both be cut off from the world but at least they will be monsters together. Frankenstein sets about the process of creation once more but is tormented by the prospect that the bride 'might become ten thousand times more malignant than her mate, and delight, for its own sake, in murder and wretchedness.'[20] This speech clearly demonstrates that Frankenstein did see himself as taking the place of the Christian God who created Eve, a mate more deadly than her companion. Frankenstein, 'trembling with passion, tore to pieces the thing' he was creating.[21] When the monster leaves, devastated by his creator's betrayal, he threatens Frankenstein. 'I will go; but remember, I shall be with you on your wedding night.'

The above sequence of events from the novel inspired the source material for the follow-up film, *The Bride of Frankenstein.* Strangely the title implied that the bride belonged to Franken-stein, not his monster—further compounding the confusion in the popular imagination between master and monster, as many people think Frankenstein is the monster's name. The birth scene in *The Bride of Frankenstein* has a completely different focus from that of the novel. Played by Elsa Lanchester, the bride is actually created; she is a tall, imperious, strangely beautiful figure. Frankenstein and Dr Praetorius are proud of their achieve-ment. As the bride steps from her birth chamber, a bolt of light-ning adorning her hair like a strange ornament, Dr Praetorius speaks her name as if announcing a famous dignitary: 'The bride of Frankenstein!' Of course, the bride is intended for the mon-ster but the clear suggestion is that she is also the doctor's mate. Like Olympia, the beautiful doll from the Hoffman tale, the bride is an exotic woman created by two men.

In the 1998 film *Gods and Monsters* (Bill Condon), the sexual/creative relationship of Frankenstein and his male part-ner are brought into the open. *Gods and Monsters* is a fictional re-creation of the last days of James Whale (played by Ian McKellen), the director of *Frankenstein* and *The Bride of Frank-enstein.* He is now living the life of a Hollywood recluse. With its camp sensibility, it presents an ironic comment on the cycle of *Frankenstein* films. Whale has suffered a stroke whose after-effects mean he is unexpectedly deluged with images from the past. These flash before him, like unwanted phantoms, trans-forming the *heimlich* routines of the daily into an *unheimlich* phantasmogoria. Having watched a re-run on television of *The Bride of Frankenstein*, he recalls a pivotal moment on the set during the filming of the creation scene. James Whale and the actors playing Frankenstein (Matt McKenzie), the bride (Rosalind Ayres) and Dr Praetorius (Arthur Dignam) are on stage, joking before filming starts. The tone is deliberately campy. The 'bride' says, 'Only a mad scientist could have done this to a woman', referring to her make-up and the lightning bolt in her hair. 'Dr Praetorius' says to 'Frankenstein': 'I gather we not only did her hair but dressed her. What a couple of queens we are, Colin'. Whale then interjects: 'That's right—a couple of flaming queens! Praetorius is a little bit in love with Dr Frankenstein, you know.' This comment was no doubt true, but it also points to the homosocial bonds that exist between the male couple (typical of many such films) who desire to produce life. The actors take up their positions. The filming begins. The two scientists stand on either side of the bride, each one holding a fold of her gown. They stand back to admire their creation, their gift to each other. Although uncanny, the scene is also strangely touching; the bride appears to signify the feminine in each of the two men.

Gods and Monsters argues that two men have sublimated their creative and sexual desires into a scientific experiment, which has produced the bride. She is their gift to the monster. Like Professor Spalanzani and Coppelius, Frankenstein and Dr Praetorius have also created an exotic but monstrous woman. The bride has been made from the body parts of the dead and animated by lightning; Olympia is a beautiful automaton that has been brought to life through the precision of clockwork and stolen human eyes. There are further parallels. In each instance a monstrous man (Frankenstein's monster/the deranged student, Nathaniel) falls in love with the uncanny woman. Each monster is destroyed by the creature/woman he cannot possess. In *Gods and Monsters*, the ageing Whale falls in love with a handsome young gardener who, with his square jaw and sculptured head, looks amazingly like Frankenstein's monster. Whale is fully aware of the irony of his situation. The hideous monster he created on film has returned in living form, as a handsome young man, to haunt his dreams.

'ALIEN RESURRECTION' (1997)

The four *Alien* films are particularly uncanny; the mise en scène is haunted by images of birth, uterine shapes, the female reproductive system, doubles and death. Jean-Pierre Jeunet's *Alien Resurrection* is the last in the series that makes up the *Alien* quartet; they constitute a remarkable series of films dominated by an eerie uncanny maternal landscape. In *Alien* (Ridley Scott, 1979), the first in the series, the crew of a spaceship, the *Nostromo*, unwittingly take on board an alien creature that appears indestructible; it can change shape, has acid for blood and is diabolically clever. Its presence is signalled by images associated with excessive fecundity, ominous egg-shaped objects, strange births and violent deaths. It impregnates its human victims while alive and its offspring grow undetected in the chest cavity until they eat their way out, at which point the victim, essentially a nest, dies in agony. The heroine, Ripley (Sigourney Weaver), pits her sharp intelligence against the creature and appears to win the battle. The other monster in the film is the Company, which will commit all kinds of unethical deeds in order to capture the alien for science. This is made clear when it is revealed that the ship's medical officer, Ash, is a cyborg whose mission is to bring back alien life forms, if necessary at the expense of the crew.

In the second film of the quartet, *Aliens* (James Cameron, 1986), the narrative remains essentially the same: a group of space-travellers, again led by Ripley (Sigourney Weaver), must destroy the aliens or die. This film, for the first time, reveals the monstrous Alien Mother in her underground hatchery laying her large fleshy and deadly eggs. In the first two versions the primal uncanny is constantly associated with the primordial alien queen—even when she is not present. In the third film, *Alien 3* (David Fincher, 1992), the landscape is masculinised, bereft of the grotesque egg chambers and the all-pervading sense of gestation and birth. There are no huge slimy eggs, cavernous underground incubators or scenes of oral impregnation. The setting is a bleak, sterile planet, Fiorina 161, in which the androgynous

Ripley is the only woman left. (By *Alien Resurrection* she is not even a 'woman' but a clone.) The series had intentionally or otherwise worked towards the gradual elimination of woman as such. The planet is an abandoned maximum-security prison for the world's most hardened male criminals, who are members of a devout religious sect. The men, all with shaved heads, wear the same prisoners' uniforms. Ripley crash-lands on the planet. She brings an alien queen with her, growing secretly inside her body. In the final sequence she deliberately throws herself into a fiery furnace in order to kill the creature as it bursts from her chest.

In the final film, *Alien Resurrection*, two hundred years have passed. Ripley's DNA (all that remains since her immolation) has been used by a secret scientific group, Doctors Wren and Gediman, to create a clone of Ripley who they regard as 'a meat by-product', making it clear that she has no civil or ethical rights. As the narrative progresses it becomes clear that the scientists signify the true source of monstrosity in the film. They want to make military use of the DNA of the alien growing inside her when she died. Similarly, the alien queen, created from Ripley, incorporates some of Ripley's DNA. The cloned woman and alien queen have become one—an *unheimlich* combination compared to their predecessors. The other aliens are now extinct—Ripley offers them the only chance of re-creating the species. The seven earlier experiments to clone Ripley have failed; the successful clone is Ripley number eight.

Alien Resurrection revisits the monstrous birth chambers of the first two films. However, the uncanny maternal landscape is dramatically altered. Science has now taken over. Whereas the earlier films represented birth as a terrifying act of nature, *Alien Resurrection* presents birth as a perverse act of science; this change is presented most powerfully in the scene where Ripley enters the secret room housing the failed experiments and encounters herself as monster.[22] Because Ripley's DNA has been mixed with that of the alien she possesses super-human strength; she also has acid for blood. Once again Ripley finds herself fighting the aliens; the difference is that she is now, in part, one of them.

The opening sequence of *Alien Resurrection* focuses on flowing movements, shiny surfaces and the suggestion of cellular organisms pulsating into multifarious shapes. In contrast to the previous films, this one emphasises the cell, the very beginning of life and of the source of monstrosity. As in *Frankenstein*, the opening credits sequence of *Alien Resurrection* unfolds against a background that focuses on uncanny eyes. In the former, a circle of eyes rotates around the image of a face; in the latter the credits unfold against images of fleshy, pulsating body parts in which the only recognisable organ is an eye. The opening scene is set on the USM *Auriga*, a medical research vessel belonging to United Systems Military. Science is no longer an individual endeavour but has been corporatised and nationalised. Two immense doors open and a slow tracking shot delivers us to the foot of a cylindrical vessel—similar in conception to the one in *Frankenstein*—which is pushed upwards by jets of steam. The outer casing opens to reveal a glass cylinder. Inside we see a naked female figure. It is Ripley, who died at the end of the third film. We hear her familiar voice introducing us to the narrative as if a fairy story: 'My mommy always said there were no monsters, no real monsters. But there are!' The camera tracks back to reveal a group of male scientists (joined later by two female scientists) in white coats who are involved in an operation—Ripley's 'real monsters'. We see mechanical arms performing robotic surgery. A knife cuts open an abdomen. 'She's perfect!' one of the scientists exclaims. Another stretches his arms through a protective shield to use a pair of forceps to extract a bloody creature. We recognise it from the previous films as a deadly baby alien. It opens its mouth to reveal a retractable jaw and razor-sharp teeth. The scientists are horrified by Ripley's baby, carefully sealing it in a container. They congratulate themselves on having successfully cloned Ripley and the alien queen growing inside her body. The scientists of *Alien Resurrection* not only give birth to a female monster, Ripley, but also to an alien queen whom they use to create a new breed of aliens with superior powers.

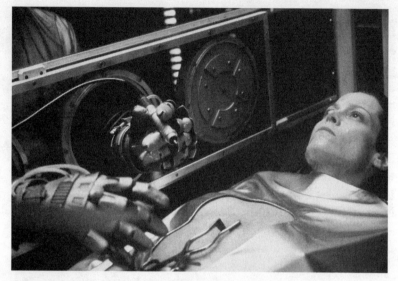

An uncanny double—the cloning of Ripley in Alien Resurrection, *1997*
(20th Century Fox/The Kobal Collection)

When we first see Ripley she conveys an uncanny aura; is she alive or dead, human or non-human? A scientist leans in close to her and says: 'You're going to make us all proud!' Like Frankenstein's monster she rejects her creators; she wraps her legs in a vice-like grip around his body, her hands on his neck. A soldier rushes in with a stun gun and she is securely hand-cuffed. Next we see Ripley tied to a chair, learning the meaning of words in order to construct her as a 'human' subject—something denied to Frankenstein. The scientists are astonished at her capabilities, her immense strength and the fact that she has memories. One of the group explains that her memories have been passed down 'generationally at a genetic level by the aliens'. She also has their strength and 'a highly evolved form of instinct'. They decide to keep her alive for the time being. 'She's a freak!' one of the scientists exclaims. It soon becomes clear, however, that it is the scientists who are the freaks, representing the civilised savagery of science and technology.

One of the most compelling scenes occurs when Ripley enters the chamber that houses the failed attempts to create her clone. The monstrous bodies of her dead clones have been put on exhibition in giant test tubes. Ripley walks among the display, looking at her deformed selves, creatures that are familiar yet unfamiliar. The scene is like an uncanny Darwinian journey back through time into Ripley's/humanity's devolutionary history. She touches the containers as if to acknowledge her dead selves and the suffering each has undergone in the name of scientific progress.[23] When she approaches number seven she realises that the creature is still alive. This clone is the most advanced and clearly resembles Ripley. Chained and hooked up to medical machines, number seven testifies to the horrors of scientific attempts to create life. She begs Ripley to kill her. This scene clearly demonstrates that the price of cloning is the production of many, many monsters. It also represents a bizarre futuristic scene of couvade in which the male mother is essentially more monstrous than any of his creations. *Alien Resurrection* offers a fantastic instance of what feminist philosopher Rosi Braidotti, in her work on genetic engineering and cyber culture, has called the 'teratological imagination'.[24]

Although Ripley herself is actually a clone and therefore monstrous by definition, she demonstrates that she is more ethical, and hence human, than the men and women who represent civilisation and science. Ripley is prepared to sacrifice herself to fight the threatening, unethical power of scientific endeavour. Ripley is neither human nor monstrous—she is an uncanny configuration of the two. As transgenic clone she also points to the *relative* nature of the abject; that is, the fact that the boundary separating self from other can shift. This demonstrates the lure of the abject which, as Kristeva argues, is always ambiguous. 'We may call it a border; abjection is above all ambiguity'.[25] In this instance, Ripley as *unheimlich* clone is far more *heimlich* than the men who have created her. The film also suggests that there is no such thing as a perfectly identical clone or a cloned double—the double offering a dominant source of the uncanny in horror. If memory can be inherited through DNA (as in Ripley's case) it is probable that science cannot control what kinds of memories are passed on and in what form. Given that the material conditions of creation would also vary from one creation to another, it is possible that clones, as they are being created, may experience different dreams and nightmares. Although a clone, Ripley is still determined to destroy her nightmare.

Every individual has an 'eerie double', said Otto Rank.[26] In the *Alien* films Ripley's eerie double is the Alien Mother. She haunts Ripley throughout the series. Rank, who begins his essay on 'The Double' with a reference to the silent film classic *The Student of Prague* (Hans Ewers, 1913), says: 'a person's past inescapably clings to him and … it becomes his fate as soon as he tries to get rid of it'.[27] As the series progresses, the alien queen comes closer and closer to being absorbed by/absorbing Ripley. Not glimpsed in *Alien*, the first of the four films, the queen nonetheless haunts the mise en scène. In *Aliens*, the queen is brought into the light from her shadowy egg chamber to do battle with Ripley. Seen briefly in *Alien 3*, having secretly impregnated Ripley, she dies when Ripley throws herself into a fiery inferno. Again the queen is glimpsed in the shadows of the final film, *Alien Resurrection*, but here she has become a part of Ripley's own flesh and blood; Ripley, now a clone of herself, has been merged with the queen, who was in her body when she perished in the inferno. The uncanniness intensifies with each new film; the alien queen is omnipresent, unshakeable, and monstrous. From the moment Ripley tries to destroy the queen she becomes 'her fate'. This is the nature of the uncanny double.

The alien queen represents death as a supremely uncanny event: death through insemination and death through birth. Secretly she invades the human body, plants her seed, disappears; the embryo silently grows in the body, finally bursting forth from the stomach cavity, ripping apart its human incubator in a nightmarish primal scene. This is Ripley's fate. The shared image of the four *Alien* films, if thought of as one work, is of woman running—running to escape her double, the obscenely fertile, indestructible Alien Mother. The faster she moves away, the more inextricably she is linked to her nemesis until (two centuries later) their DNA is mixed in the same body—the eighth clone of Ripley, a female monster that has been created by a group of male scientists working in the national interest. Like Frankenstein's monster before her, Ripley, who did not ask to be born, loathes Science, her creator. There is no doubt that Science is the true monster in the film. This is why our sympathies in *Alien Resurrection* are more clearly on the side of the actual monsters: Ripley; her cloned selves; Call; the alien queen; her monstrous son, whom Ripley is eventually forced to destroy. In contrast to *Frankenstein*, *Alien Resurrection* does not suggest that creator and monster are doubles of each other. Sympathy is now completely with the monster. The other shared image of the four *Alien* films is of woman running to escape the men who represent the new science that desires to control the all-powerful reproductive alien queen, the source of the primal uncanny.

'DEAD RINGERS' (1988)

David Cronenberg's *Dead Ringers* presents a version of man as womb monster that is very different from the classic Frankenstein myth.[28] At first, *Dead Ringers* seems to be grounded in the real world in which the monster is human. However, we soon discover that central to the narrative is a female figure who possesses a triple-headed uterus and as such is essentially a monster, a source of extreme uncanniness. Like Dr Frankenstein, Dr Praetorius and the anonymous scientists of *Alien Resurrection*, the other protagonists, the Mantle twins, are also obsessed by their female monster—their obsession is a hysterical response to her extreme uncanniness. As in his films *The Fly* (1986) and *The*

Brood (1979), Cronenberg represents his monstrous figures within a convincingly real world.

Dead Ringers offers a fascinating study of male hysteria as a defence against the failure of its male protagonists to control the female reproductive system, which they both envy and despise.[29] It reverberates with signs of the uncanny. The two male characters, Beverly and Elliot Mantle, are identical twin gynaecologists, each one played by the same actor, Jeremy Irons. The heroine, Clare Niveau (Genevieve Bujold), with whom they become romantically involved, has a triple cervix. The uncanny motifs of the double and triple run throughout the film: known by everyone as 'the fabulous Mantle twins', Beverly and Elliot form two halves of a whole; each complements the other. Beverly is introverted, Elliot extroverted; Beverly conducts their research out of the public eye, Elliot gives lectures in the public eye; Beverly is awkward and shy with women, Elliot is urbane and sophisticated. No one can tell them apart—not even their women friends. When Elliot hands over his unsuspecting dates to his 'baby brother', he says: 'If we didn't share women, you'd still be a virgin.' Inseparable since birth, the twins live in complete harmony until the day Claire Niveau enters their surgery for fertility treatment. From this moment, the film returns almost compulsively to re-enactments of the primal phantasy of giving birth. As with many horror films about the monstrous male mother, the mise en scène is crowded with intra-uterine motifs and references.

There are at least three key scenes of this nature in *Dead Ringers*. The first occurs when Beverly examines Claire Niveau. To his amazement he discovers she has a triple cervix. Astonished, Elliot—pretending to be Beverly—examines her next. 'That's fantastic!' he says, launching into a discussion of inner beauty. He raises the possibility of holding beauty contests for the insides of bodies, to discover the best liver, or best spleen. Elliot's bizarre suggestion is one of the first intimations of the horror that gradually builds as the narrative progresses. Over dinner that night, Claire asks Elliot about the nature of her uterus. 'It has three doorways, three cervixes, leading into three separate compartments. That is fabulously rare!' Like the Mantle twins, Claire is also a fabulous/monstrous figure. Claire asks Elliot if she could have triplets, 'one in each compartment'.

Not only is Claire's reproductive system 'fabulously rare', it is a physical impossibility. Thus Claire Niveau is a complete deviation from the norm, a fabulous monster, who is both familiar yet unfamiliar. She is a woman whose potential fecundity is both fantastic and terrifying. She symbolises the excessive generative power of the maternal body and as such she threatens to overwhelm the twin gynaecologists whose life work has been dedicated to controlling and regulating women's bodies and their fertility. At first she fascinates them, particularly Beverly, who falls desperately in love.

The second uncanny uterine scenario occurs one night when Beverly awakes from a terrifying nightmare in which he imagines that he and Elliot are joined at the stomach like Siamese twins. As if she is the mother who has just given birth to the twins, Claire bends over and begins to gnaw through the chord in order to separate them. Beverly wakes up screaming in terror; he then huddles into her body in a foetal position. The scene is a horrific primal phantasy, a re-enactment of birth in which the infants, now adults, are still conjoined. The fabulous Mantle twins are also monstrous and uncanny in that they are separate yet joined, single yet double. Soon after, Beverly begins to suffer delusions, imagining that women are mutants. He designs a set of horrific gynaecological instruments, which he plans to use in operations on mutant women. In other words, he creates equipment to match what he now sees as Claire's monstrous reproductive system. Claire has become another of Cronenberg's uncanny maternal freaks whose monstrosity is defined in relation to her reproductive system. In Cronenberg's film *Rabid* (1977), the heroine develops a growth under her armpits which becomes a penis with which she rapes her victims;

and in his later film *The Brood* (1979) she grows a repulsive uterine sac on the outside of her body from which she gives birth to mutant babies.

Claire's presence in the lives of the twins starts to undermine their harmonious self-sufficient universe and to force the brothers to separate (temporarily) from each other. In the end, they abandon Claire and reunite, but at a terrible cost. Aware they cannot ever live separate lives and unable to resolve the problem of Claire, the twins, now addicted to drugs, regress to an infantile state. Together they have transformed themselves into an uncanny monster—two separate beings sharing a psychotic nightmare. In the final uterine scenario, they assume the positions of gynaecologist and female patient. Elliot lies on the examination table, his legs outstretched as if in stirrups. Beverly takes a surgical knife and cuts open his abdomen, in the place where his uterus would be if he were a woman. The death scene is reminiscent of a strange couvade ritual, in which Elliot assumes the position of a woman undergoing a gynaecological operation. In a bizarre twist of fate, he plays the role of the 'mutant woman' while Beverly takes up the position of surgeon. Beverly then ends his own life. The twins are united in death, their bodies intertwined beneath a bloody sheet that hides their terrible wounds.

The archaic maternal figure is the one who reminds man of his debt to the primal uncanny—death, nature and the womb. She is 'fabulously rare'—an impossible creature—and as such is essentially a monster, a source of extreme uncanniness. The texts discussed above all feature male couples and/or groups who attempt to create life, usually a woman: Dr Frankenstein and Dr Praetorius; Professor Spalanzani and Coppelius; the anonymous scientists of *Alien Resurrection*; the fabulous Mantle twins —all are obsessed by their female monster. Frankenstein's monster is the original monster, created from the perverse desire of man to give birth without woman. The bride has been designed as a mate for Frankenstein's monster, for copulation and presumably children. Olympia is a perfect woman, the epitome of female beauty and manners; she is created to be an object of male worship, a figure that reflects back to man whatever he wishes to see. Claire Niveau cannot have children but she is unique in that she possesses a triple-headed uterus. Ripley is a clone, created to produce a monstrous alien queen that will be used in the world's military and defence systems. All of these female creations are, strictly speaking, monsters—but not necessarily abject. They do not threaten annihilation of the self. They are all 'fabulously rare'—even Ripley, with her inherited memories, is strangely unique. The secret that the uncanny has brought to light concerns the true nature of monstrosity.

Cixous asks: 'Why is it that the maternal landscape, the *heimisch*, and the familiar become so disquieting?' It has become so *unheimlich* because the male is revealed as the source of monstrosity, thus suggesting that the rational face of science and civilisation is not necessarily a sane one. This knowledge generates a form of male hysteria that could also be described as phallic panic. These films point to the fact that masculinity is a fragile concept; they reveal a lack in the male who desires to assume the procreative role of woman, which the symbolic order defiles, in order to enable him to feel whole. Unlike other male monsters, such as Dracula and the wolf–man, he is not at home in this role. He has attempted to take over the act of creation, has tried to usurp the role of woman and instead given birth to the uncanny Hydra herself. In the process, he has rendered himself an uncanny monster in thrall to a phantom womb.

4

MAN AS MENSTRUAL MONSTER: DRACULA AND HIS UNCANNY BRIDES

Hence, the horror: You could be dead while living ... The Unheimliche *has no end.*

HÉLÈNE CIXOUS[1]

More than any other male monster, Dracula—the undead monster of the primal uncanny—represents a strange commingling of the familiar and unfamiliar. He is alive and dead, male and female, human and animal, seductive and repulsive, civilised and primitive. During the daylight hours, he lies sated in his coffin like a sleeping foetus; at night he walks abroad, a ravenous sexual monster in search of fresh female blood. Embodying so many contrary meanings, he is a quintessentially uncanny figure, undermining all rational signification. His extreme uncanniness lies in his strong association with an excessive number of uncanny events and objects and desires: death, doubling, blood, metamorphosis, intra-uterine phantasies, the feminine and animal worlds, as well as the vampiric motifs associated with the compulsion to repeat, and the collapse of boundaries between imaginary and real, male and female, living and dead.

The eerie uncanniness of the cinematic vampire has been most strongly captured by F. W. Murnau in his famous silent classic *Nosferatu* (1922), in which he is not the seductive erotic

Count Dracula but a repulsive, frightening vampire infected with the plague. Murnau's Nosferatu is much closer to Stoker's Dracula than Hollywood's charming Byronic bloodsucker. In Bram Stoker's 1897 novel *Dracula*, on which the film is based, when Jonathan Harker first meets the Count he notes that he is a tall, thin, elderly man dressed in black with a strong aquiline face, arched nostrils, massive eyebrows, a cruel mouth, sharp white teeth, pointed ears and broad hands with 'hairs in the centre of the palm'.[2] He always experiences a sense of uneasiness when the Count is near him. His feelings 'change to repulsion and terror' when he sees 'the whole man slowly emerge from the window and begin to crawl down the castle wall over that dreadful abyss, *face down*, with his cloak spreading out around him like great wings'.[3]

Apart from the devil, Dracula is probably the best known of all male monsters. Dracula's brides are also figures of extreme uncanniness; they too are undead and almost always represented as simulacra of each other. Jonathan Harker notices these uncanny similarities when he first encounters Dracula's three beauties: 'All three had long flowing hair, brilliant white teeth ... voluptuous lips'; all three laughed together with the same 'silvery' sound; and all three 'threw no shadow on the floor'.[4] He falls into a 'languorous ecstasy' when one brushes his throat with a 'soft, shivering touch of the lips' but is soon filled with horror when he realises that all three are waiting to suck his blood.[5]

In reality there are three kinds of vampire: the Nosferatu, or the anonymous creature of folklore; the aristocratic seductive figures, male and female, from nineteenth-century gothic fiction; and the erotic, sexual cinematic vampire who has been variously represented as male and female, gay and straight, black and white. While the cinematic vampire may have begun life in an earlier century as a demon or figure of great evil, it has become, in nineteenth-, twentieth- and early twenty-first-century popular culture, a figure of perverse sexuality and a changing symbol for the sexual problems of the age. In the early nineteenth century, John Polidori wrote a tale, *The Vampyre* (1918), about an innocent woman violated by a vampire. At the close of the nine-teenth century Bram Stoker's famous novel used the vampire myth to explore female sexual desire and the changing role of women. In the late twentieth century the vampire, and the idea of contamination through blood, was represented in films as a metaphor for anxiety about AIDS. Amy Taubin argues that, in AIDS-anxiety movies such as *Bram Stoker's Dracula* (Francis Ford Coppola, 1992) and *Interview with the Vampire* (Neil Jordan, 1994), 'blood functions as the medium for a network of contam-ination. It means death from without, even as it circulates within living bodies'.[6]

Literary historian Franco Moretti argues that Dracula, and Frankenstein, are 'unlike previous monsters, dynamic, *totalizing* monsters'.[7] They desire to possess everything, to live forever, and 'to conquer the world'.[8] On another level, monsters such as Dracula are totalising in that they are able to assume different forms. Dracula has appeared on the screen as a classic figure of sadism and male heterosexuality (Fisher's *Dracula*); Dracula has also been represented as stereotyped Jew (Murnau's *Nosferatu*), lesbian vampire (Scott's *The Hunger*), black bloodsucker (Crain's *Blacula*) and as a gay and homoerotic fiend (Jordan's *Interview with the Vampire*). Judith Halberstam extends Moretti's definition of Dracula and Frankenstein to argue that 'totalized monstrosity allows for a whole range of specific monstrosities to coalesce in the same form'.[9] In other words, the 'chameleonic nature of this monster makes it a symbol of multiplicity and indeed invites multiple interpretations'. Halberstam regards the totalising monster as 'a modern invention'.[10]

The modern vampire's totalising nature also links him to the primal uncanny and, significantly, this is the source of his extreme uncanniness. His fluid, multi-faceted nature signifies a feminine quality, one that enables him to cross boundaries and appear in different guises. Such a monster eschews the idea of a stable, set identity, qualities endorsed by the patriarchal form of masculinity. In this sense, Dracula's sexuality is uncanny because it encompasses all desire, thus undermining the play of sexual and gender opposites on which so-called proper sexual identity is founded.

FEATURES OF THE VAMPIRE

The vampire has a number of key defining characteristics: the vampire is one of the undead—that is, he or she has returned from the grave and exists in a liminal state between life and death; the vampire possesses an enviable pair of snake-like fangs which it plunges into the flesh of its victims in order to drink fresh blood, preferably the blood of virgins; the vampire can transform into other creatures such as a wolf, a rat or a bat; the vampire reproduces itself endlessly through its victims—that is, the person who is bitten by a vampire becomes one; and the vampire can only be killed by following carefully prescribed procedures such as plunging a stake through its heart and/or decapitation. Although the vampire can be traced back to classical times, it gained ascendancy with the rise of Christianity. Portraying the vampire as the Antichrist, the Catholic Church made much of its deadly powers. Vampires could prey on the bodies of those who were sinners in the eyes of the Church because they had committed suicide or had not been baptised. It was also believed that religious items such as a cross or holy water could weaken a vampire's powers.

It is easy to see why, as James Twitchell convincingly argues, the vampire of folklore might have been seen as the Antichrist.[11] The vampire was a creature of darkness, not light; it drank blood to enslave the soul of its victim, not to save souls as in the ritual of communion; it signified a body without a soul; it also enjoyed life everlasting, not in heaven but on earth. Vampire mythology received public notoriety in the popular imagination in the seventeenth century when the plague swept through Europe and the vampire was believed to be the source of contamination. Many classic vampire films have drawn on this opposition between the forces of God and Satan, light and darkness, good and evil, and life and death, as a framework for their narratives. More recent films such as *Interview with the Vampire*, in which the two main vampires are in a homoerotic relationship, have deliberately dropped such motifs in order to explore contemporary issues such as gay male relationships.

The most distinctive feature of the vampire—central to all of the various sources—is that he is a consummate sexual initiator. In the classic vampire films of Bela Lugosi and Christopher Lee, Dracula is a sensual, elegant, aristocratic figure, immaculately dressed, with a touch of grey at his temples. In his black satin cloak, usually lined with red silk, complete with dark good looks, sonorous accent and impeccable manners, Dracula is irresistible. Compared with rugged, masculine vampire slayers such as Van Helsing, Dracula is a strangely feminised creature whose victims cannot resist him. It is this characteristic that seems to make him even more seductive and coldly charming to his virginal brides. He is a sensualist, a creature of the flesh whose conquests represent a triumph of body over conscience and of sex over death. His female victims experience extreme orgasmic pleasure. Dracula offers total sexual and sensual gratification, nothing more or less.

Dracula is monstrous because he is the preferred lover, all women who come under his spell desire sex with him and rush to join the ranks of his undead, uncanny brides. He represents desire par excellence while simultaneously signifying—in a Lacanian sense—that desire can never be fulfilled.[12] His monstrous oral sexuality threatens the very basis of phallic patriarchal civilisation. Vampires do not have sex—that is, genital penetration—yet remain the most potent and sexual of all creatures.

LITERARY ORIGINS

A number of nineteenth-century works of fiction exerted a strong influence on the cinematic image of the Count. The first was John Polidori's *The Vampyre* (1819). Polidori wrote the story that was initially devised by Lord Bryon. The two men were members of the famous gathering at the Villa Diodati on the shores of Lake Geneva in 1816. Other members of the party included Percy Bysshe Shelley, and Mary Shelley who also wrote her famous Gothic novel *Frankenstein* (1818) during the sojourn at the lake. Byron, who deliberately cultivated an image of a notorious rake, intended the story as a comment on his own nature—charismatic, moody, sensual. Polidori sent the story to a magazine but it was initially published under Bryon's name.[13] For the first time, the vampire is represented as an attractive but decadent aristocrat who lives on the blood of virtuous young women. It is the seductive character of the vampire that has

Dracula as uncanny blood monster—Dracula AD 1972, 1972
(Hammer/Warner Bros/The Kobal Collection)

exerted such a powerful influence on the cinematic Draculas, from Bela Lugosi to Christopher Lee. The theme of the vampire's erotic power was central to a highly popular romance of 1847 called *Varney the Vampire, or The Feast of Blood*. According to Twitchell, Varney was first published in the late 1840s as a penny dreadful and was so popular it soon entered book form. 'Varney kept returning month after month, always doing the same thing—only the necks changed.'[14]

The second story of influence is Sheridan Le Fanu's *Carmilla* (1872), in which the vampire is female, a lesbian countess who moves among middle-class families of Europe and vampirises young girls. Apart from Stoker's *Dracula*, *Carmilla* has enjoyed the greatest number of screen adaptations. It appears to have been Le Fanu's ability to endow his story with a sensual atmosphere that held such strong appeal for later film-makers. One of the most evocative filmic renditions of *Carmilla* is *The Vampire Lovers* (1970) starring Ingrid Pitt. It is possible that these earlier versions influenced Bram Stoker's landmark 1897 novel; it is also possible that Stoker was writing a different but parallel version of the vampire, adapting the myth to his own design.

Regardless, Bram Stoker's *Dracula* exerted the most important influence on the cinematic vampire. Here the Count is supposedly based on the notoriously sadistic historical figure, Vlad the Impaler, from the race of Dracula, a war-like people from Europe who fought off the Magyar and the Turk. Stoker's Count is a fascinating, ambiguous figure who poses a real threat to society. Charming and beautifully mannered, the Count easily draws his visitors to him. He is also demonic. Not only does he drink the blood of women, he compels them to drink his own. In one scene in the novel, the male characters enter to see the Count with Mina,

> *forcing her face down on his bosom. Her white nightdress was smeared with blood, and a thin stream trickled down the man's bare breast … As we burst into the room, the Count*

turned his face, and the hellish look I had heard described seemed to leap into it. His eyes flamed red with devilish passion; the great nostrils of the white aquiline nose opened wide and quivered at the edges ...[15]

Mina drinks from his bosom as if he were a nursing mother. Some critics argue that the scene is a metaphor for oral sex; it also serves to feminise Dracula, to represent his breasts as erogenous zones, to transform him into a strange maternal figure. The Count's female victims quickly learn to adopt a sexually predatory role themselves. Once bitten, they become sexually alive and active. Mina, however, was a respectable married woman, not the stereotyped voluptuous virgin who found herself in deadly embrace with the cinematic Dracula. Despite the fact that Mina is forced/raped by the Count to suck blood/milk from his wound, she nonetheless expresses guilt. 'Unclean, unclean!' she cries, realising she cannot touch Jonathan again.[16]

Hollywood could not afford to depict the Count's sexual activities in such a sexually confronting way. Tod Browning's *Dracula* (1931), which starred Bela Lugosi, represents the Count's evil demeanour and sexual menace but all erotic moments are enacted off screen. Lugosi's vampire also lacks the subtle ambiguities of Stoker's Dracula. The enormous appeal of Hollywood's Dracula may well be due to the combined influence of Stoker's novel and two other vampire tales in which the monster is represented very differently from Stoker's monster.

In his book *Dracula was a Woman: In Search of the Blood Countess of Transylvania*, Dracula historian Raymond T. McNally posits another major source for Bram Stoker's novel. He argues that Stoker based Dracula not on Vlad the Impaler but on the Transylvanian countess Elizabeth Báthory. Apparently Stoker's unpublished papers include many references to the Countess, who was tried and imprisoned for murdering hundreds of young women and bathing in their blood. It was said that she believed the blood of virgins ensured eternal youth. Perhaps Stoker's emphasis on Dracula's non-phallic sexuality is linked to the vampire's possible origins in the figure of the Countess, a noble-woman who owned many castles and who, unlike Vlad the Impaler, did come from Transylvania.

DRACULA AS SEXUAL INITIATOR

Vampirism as represented in popular film is interpreted or depicted as a rite of initiation and Dracula is the sexual initiator par excellence. Women find themselves unable to resist his erotic bite and sensual caresses. They in turn are sexually energised. This is the main reason why Bram Stoker's novel was so contro-versial and popular; it set the scene for the liberation of women in Victorian England at the very moment when the suffragette movement began to demand equality for women. Cultural critic Martin Tropp argues that Stoker's novel provided 'an enduring vehicle to explore the unease that accompanied the New Woman, and, in fact, to replace the Victorian image of woman with one more suited to a new century'.[17]

The one thing that all of these vampiric monsters share is their main role as sexual initiator. This is particularly true of the classic vampire film. There are of course comic and post-modern films in which Dracula's role is more parodic and less restricted by convention, but even in these texts Dracula remains the sexual initiator of myth and literature. When the full moon appears in the heavens, Dracula stalks his (read also her) victims who are almost always beautiful young women. Once Dracula has plunged his sharp fangs—very much like those of a snake—into the woman's neck and her blood flows, the victim is trans-formed. In taking her blood, Dracula in turn inseminates her with his own hunger, his own perverse desires and taboo obses-sions. The victim is changed in two ways: she is sexually energised, also desiring what is taboo; and she joins the ranks of the undead. If she is a virgin, the implication is that the blood that flows from her neck is symbolic of blood from her hymen. Dracula is not unlike the medieval lord of the manor who, by virtue of his

Dracula, sexual initiator par excellence—Dracula, 1931
(Universal/The Kobal Collection)

Bram Stoker's Dracula, *1992*
(*Zoetrope/Columbia Tri-Star/The Kobal Collection*)

position and power, exercised the rights of the lord on the *jus primae noctis*—that is, he customarily deflowered the brides, or young women on his estates, on the night before their marriage. He initiated the virgin into her first sexual experience.

Freud gives a number of reasons for this practice, one of which is man's fear of woman's blood. In 'The Taboo of Virginity', Freud attempts to explain why earlier, primitive societies—in contrast to so-called civilised societies—made the defloration of virgins subject to a taboo.[18] This dangerous act was to be carried out by an experienced member of the group such as the bride's father or a religious figure. Dracula is a demonic figure precisely because he not only has no fear of women's blood but he actually relishes it, particularly the blood of virgins.

THE PRIMAL UNCANNY AND THE VAMPIRE MYTH

The other key features of the Dracula/vampire myth that deserve further elucidation, particularly because of the prominent role they play in most cinematic representations, come from folklore and relate to his nature as a feminised blood monster. Most importantly, these further define his relationship to the primal uncanny: woman, death and nature.

The first characteristic is the vampire's connection to the earth. Born at the end of the nineteenth century, a creation of Gothic fiction, Dracula soon began to haunt the nightmares of the modern twentieth-century subject. While the world testified to the power of patriarchy and progress, symbolised by new arcades and other soaring architectural triumphs, Dracula remained underground, a creature linked to decay, death and the maternal body—privileged signifier of the primal uncanny. In contrast to the wolf–man, who erodes boundaries between city and forest, the vampire erodes borders that run between whatever lies above ground and what lies beneath. In his essay on the uncanny, Freud emphasised the role of the maternal body. The symbolism of the undead vampire who is nourished on blood and sleeps in his coffin, buried deep in the earth, links him directly with the uncanny archaic mother. When he travels, he often keeps a handful of earth in the bottom of his coffin to keep his 'mother' country close. In the classic vampire movie, the vampire's resting place is depicted as a vault or crypt, a place of winding stairs, cobwebs, rats, spiders and other familiars associated with the witch. It is here that he keeps his lustful brides. Philosopher and psychoanalyst Roger Dadoun argues that 'this is an arched, dark, enveloping space, as uterine as you could possibly imagine'.[19] This is what haunts the dreams of Dracula. After feeding on the blood of his victims, the vampire returns compulsively to the 'maternal' body, a familiar haven, yet unfamiliar

Dracula's uncanny brides wander the caverns of the undead—Dracula, *1931*
(Universal/The Kobal Collection)

because of its links to decay and death. The womb is the source of new life, yet here it harbours the undead; the marked reversal of its natural function renders it uncanny in the extreme.

The second characteristic is his function as a moon monster, a creature of the night whose bloodsucking symbolises much more than his own primeval hunger. The third characteristic is almost always referred to in passing—but again rarely analysed—and that is the vampire's bestiality and his links to the animal world, particularly his power to transform into a werewolf. Because the vampire embraces the abject feminine (blood, suckling, orality) and the animal (his shape-shifting into wolf, rat, bat, spider), he embodies a series of taboo and/or perverse forms of sexual desire: oral sex, blood sex, bestiality, queer sex, and necrophilia. His sexuality is feminised and animalised. Moon monster and beast, it is these characteristics that contribute to and confirm his identity and status as an animalised and feminised monster whose representation draws on the primal uncanny.

One of the most important elements of the vampire myth is its oral–sadistic character. Because the vampire is undead—that is, not-born—he is doomed to repeat the actions of the unborn. Like a suckling foetus he must lie during the daylight in a coffin/womb in Mother Earth and during the night of the full moon (every twenty-eight days) he must feed on woman's (menstrual) blood, release her blood flow, to secure the nourishment he cannot secure in the womb/coffin. He is a strange, uncanny, undead monster. Although he might assume a phallic appearance, Dracula is an oral–sadistic monster, one who sucks blood from the neck of his virginal bride rather than penetrate her. Even if we interpret this act as symbolic of genital (the plunging teeth) or oral sex (the sucking mouth), the act itself is genderless. Dracula can be male or female and the vampire's victim can be of the opposite or the same sex. In folklore the vampire never confines him/herself to attacking members of the opposite sex. It is the de-phallicisation of the myth, and its consequent appeal to bisexual desire, that helps to feminise Dracula and to make him such an erotic uncanny figure. In this context the male vampire signifies a breakdown of boundaries between sex and gender. Once bitten, the wan, pale virgin becomes herself an active, predatory, sexual vampire. Dracula (male or female) thus liberates women from the dictates of a misogynistic patriarchal culture that prefers its women to remain passive and pure.

As I have argued in *The Monstrous-Feminine*, the vampire narrative contains many mythic and symbolic elements that refer to woman's menstrual flow.[20] It is Dracula's indebtedness to these elements that make him—among other things—an uncanny sexualised blood monster, assimilating him to the primal uncanny. The image of Dracula may change dramatically from film to film but one thing remains constant: his origin as a blood creature. How do the full moon, bite marks and blood flow relate to the vampire? In their study of the history and myths of menstruation, Penelope Shuttle and Peter Redgrove argue that the vampire myth was used by early societies to explain what was once the bewildering phenomenon of menarche, or first menstruation.[21] Primitive societies explained a girl's first blood flow in terms of spirits or demons. It was believed that the spirit of a biting creature, such as a vampire bat, lived in a girl's womb and that when the creature bit her, causing her blood to flow, she entered womanhood. During the period of her menarche, and subsequently her monthly menstruation, she was thought to be dangerous and was confined to a menstrual hut located at some distance from the village. This was a dangerous time because the spirit of the biting animal was awake and active. Menstruating women were taboo and men were forbidden any contact with them, particularly sexual intercourse. Fear of woman's menstrual blood persists in some religions such as Hinduism and Orthodox Judaism.

In one sense Dracula could be seen as the biting creature— often thought to be a vampire bat or snake—who bites the woman's flesh and releases her blood flow. He himself also has the power to transform into a creature such as a bat, wolf or rat. He is active on the full moon, which appears every twenty-eight days, the average length of the menstrual cycle. He possesses a pair of snake-like fangs; in fact he glides through the night like a snake. He plunges his teeth into the woman's neck, which, as Shuttle and Redgrove argue, could be seen as symbolic of the neck of the uterus: 'it is always from the *neck*; as we say neck or cervix of the womb'.[22] At a subliminal level, Dracula is a menstrual monster, a creature of the night who revels in woman's blood flow. This uncanny power to move between the two states of male and female places him dangerously close to the feminine and to the natural world.

Although contemporary vampire films depict Dracula as a queer monster initiating members of both sexes, the potent symbolism of the earlier forms of the myth persist. According to Julia Kristeva, blood enjoys a special relationship with abjection and the feminine. Blood, which signifies the 'animal' and its propensity for blood, as well as woman, represents the coming together of 'death and femininity': 'But blood, as a vital element, also refers to women, fertility, and the assurance of fecundation. It thus becomes a fascinating semantic crossroads, the propitious place for abjection.'[23] In this context his bloodletting is also linked to death. When his victims become vampires they join the undead. Thus Dracula's sexuality invokes a mix of sex and death, of perverse necrophiliac desires.

This scenario is also associated with a perverse or bizarre form of incest. Dracula does not procreate in the proper manner. He gives birth through vampirism—that is, the virgins that he vampirises or engages with in sexual activity are both his lovers and his offspring in that at this very moment they are re-born as the undead. Insofar as the vampire has the power to metamorphose, it creates or reproduces itself. There is—as with all of the monsters discussed—a sense of self-creation, of what Marie-Hélène Huet refers to as 'the dark desire to reproduce without the other'.[24] Insofar as the monster–vampire metamorphoses and transforms, he/she is engaged in an act of 'self-making', a 'self-generation' brought about by seemingly endless sexual encounters. In recent vampire films such as *Blade* (Stephen Norrington,

1998), the world is in danger of being taken over by the undead, whose numbers are growing exponentially. Blade is both vampire slayer and part-vampire, so widespread is the contagion. This is also true of other male monsters such as the werewolf and the zombie, who not only metamorphose or re-create themselves but also create others just like themselves through biting and blood flow. Re-creation or re-birth of the undead offers a sterile immortality.

Dracula signifies the primal uncanny through his relationship to the maternal body, to Mother Earth, to death, to woman's blood, and to the mythic association with menstrual rites. He also represents the animal world through his power to metamorphose into a werewolf, bat, rat and other creatures of the night. The vampire is associated with the gruesome and perverse side of the uncanny: the undead, corpses, blood sucking and cannibalism. Freud stated that many perceive as uncanny the compulsion to repeat, but perhaps not so uncanny as being buried alive, which is really a transformation of another phantasy, that of 'intra-uterine existence'.[25] Dracula as a monstrous figure of death is caught up with these two uncanny motifs; he returns again and again to draw blood from the necks of his victims and, once sated, retreats again into his coffin, safely secured in Mother Earth. He is his own prisoner of repeated performances. The uncanny itself, Freud argues, signifies a return of the repressed, a bringing to light of that which should have remained hidden—that his erotic oral sexuality is more seductive than the phallic sexuality of proper upright men. It is the feminine and animalistic nature of the uncanny male vampire that is abhorrent to patriarchal civilisation. Dracula not only desires woman's blood (taboo in so many cultures), he also desires to take woman as if she were an animal—that is, through biting, tearing flesh and drinking blood. For Dracula, sex is a cannibalistic act. Society, despite its stated desires about sexual prowess, in fact does not endorse sex in excess, for women or men. The culture represents such excess as perverse, animalistic and feminine.

UNCANNY FEARS

In his collection of essays, *Signs Taken for Wonders*, Franco Moretti argues that fear of the monster 'cannot be explained wholly in historical and economic terms'. 'On the contrary, it is very likely that its deepest root is to be found elsewhere: in the eros, above all in sex.'[26] In that the monster signifies perverse forms of sexual excess, it both repels and attracts; hence the protagonist (the desire of the text) also desires what he/she fears. As an abject thing, the monster is a supremely ambivalent sexualised figure. The monster also functions as a disguise or mask for the perverse desires of the protagonist and the spectator. Moretti refers to Francesco Orlando, who uses the notion of filtering to describe this masking or covering process. He argues that 'perverse desire could not have been acceptable as content in the literary work without the latter's also accepting *the formal model capable of filtering it*'.[27] Such filters make desires and fears bearable: 'The literary formalization, the rhetorical figure, therefore has a double function: it *expresses* the unconscious content and at the same time *hides* it.'[28] The monster signifies at least two unacceptable desires—one more taboo (and uncanny) than the other. The monster is represented in such a way that it hides or disguises the idea 'that is socially more illicit', while allowing the other less perverse—more acceptable—idea to surface.[29] These two functions are always contained within the figure of the monster, hence his extreme uncanniness.

Moretti refers to the figure of Dracula to demonstrate his argument. Drawing on the work of the psychoanalyst, Marie Bonaparte, he argues that the vampire represents the ambivalent feelings of the child towards its mother, developed during breastfeeding. At first the infant suckles at the breast but when it grows teeth it learns to bite. The mother usually reprimands the infant in some way and it ceases biting but still desires to bite the mother's breast, even though fearing 'retaliation for his "cannibalism"'.[30] Moretti argues that if Dracula were represented in popular culture as female, then this socially unacceptable attitude, involving oral sadism, would be more apparent: 'The conscious mind can rest easy: all that remains of the original fear is a word, "Dracula"'.[31] To further support his argument Moretti points out that the sex of vampires is fluid, interchangeable. He claims that popular culture has in the main transformed Dracula into a man in order to disguise the less acceptable meaning of the vampire. Dracula still evokes uncertainty and horror attached to the act of vampirism and the creation of the undead, but this horror is not as unacceptable as the horror evoked by the act of cannibalism and the threat of punishment. Moretti's argument, in the main, works—although there are now more female vampires in popular culture.

While I agree with Moretti's argument about the symbolic function of the vampire, I think he might have drawn upon a more perverse notion, one that brings to light something even more taboo and uncanny than the motif of oral sadism. This notion also associates the vampire more directly with the primal uncanny. The long quotation that Moretti uses from Marie Bonaparte's writings on Edgar Allen Poe includes reference to the mythical *vagina dentata*, the 'strange' notion that the vagina is 'furnished with teeth, and thus a source of danger in being able to bite and castrate'. Bonaparte writes that 'Mouth and vagina are equated in the unconscious'.[32] Strangely, Moretti does not utilise the earlier section of Bonaparte's argument about the *vagina dentata*. Perhaps this idea was too perverse, even for Moretti! In my view, Dracula's fanged mouth represents both a mouth with teeth and a vagina with teeth. Dracula himself—as a male—does not obviously signify the *vagina dentata* (although the association is there) but the so-called brides of Dracula—the countless young women he converts to bloodsucking—signify the original or archetypal vampire as female. Their fanged mouths may well be equated in the unconscious mind of the spectator with the *vagina dentata*. Hence the uncanniness of the female and male vampire's fanged mouth, smeared with blood. It signifies the familiar mouth and the unfamiliar *vagina dentata*,

the hidden mouth of myth and superstition, whose representation warns man about the dangers of female sexuality that is not
brought under strict control and regulation.

'BRAM STOKER'S DRACULA' (1992)

Since the publication of Bram Stoker's novel *Dracula*, in 1897,
over two hundred film versions have appeared around the world,
including adaptations, remakes, parodies and pastiches. Very few
of these adhere faithfully to Stoker's original. Dracula himself
changes from film to film, primarily to enable his monstrosity to
function as a shifting signifier for changing definitions of what
constitutes monstrosity from one decade to the next. Francis
Ford Coppola, in his version, *Bram Stoker's Dracula*, has chosen
to return to the original but with one key difference. Dracula is
now a romantic hero, a tragic lover, who has become a vampire
out of his uncontrollable sense of loss and desolation. He is very
different from the Count of Bram Stoker's novel, in which he is
described as remorseless and selfish with no redeeming features
at all.

Coppola's Dracula, played beautifully by Gary Oldman, is a
sympathetic figure, a doomed romantic who suffers unbearable
pain because of the death of his beloved. When he finds her
centuries later, in the figure of Mina, he is ecstatic. In representing Dracula as a creature rent by unfulfilled passion, Coppola
brings out and illuminates—for the first time—the strangely
beautiful aspects of the uncanny that are present in the vampire
myth. This is a classic story of *l'amour fou*, also much loved by
the surrealists. Coppola's *Dracula* argues against the possibility of
the fulfilment of desire. The individual subject (given that the
vampire is in all of us) remains a prisoner of his/her unsatisfied
desires, yet continues to believe that desire can be fulfilled. In
his endless, compulsive search for new blood (for an eternal
companion), Dracula believes his innermost, secret desires can

be realised. The theme of failed desire is also central to *Interview with the Vampire*, in which the two male vampires, Lestat (Tom Cruise) and Armand (Antonio Banderas) desire the lover they cannot have, Louis de Pointe du Lac (Brad Pitt), who rejects them both because he desires only what he has already lost: his dead wife and the undead girl vampire. As well as exploring the uncanny side of doomed romantic love, Coppola represents Dracula as tied to the dark side of the primal uncanny.

Coppola's *Dracula* re-creates the King Vampire as a brave and dashing prince who, through grief over the death of his beloved wife, Elisabeta, is transformed into a monster. Apart from this inclusion of a tragic love story, Coppola's *Dracula* follows the original story in most respects. The film begins in the year 1462 with Gary Oldman as Dracula's original incarnation, Prince Vlad of Roumania, later known as Vlad the Impaler. The Prince has left his new wife to fight an invading army. When Elisabeta hears a false rumour that her beloved has been killed in battle, she hurls herself from a parapet onto the stones below. When the high priests tell the Prince that she has committed suicide and will be damned for all eternity, he falls into a terrible rage, renouncing the Christian religion and vowing revenge on the God who has forsaken him. Thrusting his blade into the cross, he causes it to bleed. Waves of blood flow across the floor to where Elisabeta's body lies. The Prince fills a goblet with the cascading blood and drinks. 'The blood is the life and it shall be mine,' he vows. Only by finding his beloved again—in the form of Mina—will Dracula re-experience love and achieve redemption.

Four hundred years later, Dracula still lives in his Castle on his estate in Transylvania. The modern story begins when Jonathan Harker, a London real estate agent, played by Keanu Reeves, visits the Count to settle a number of legal transactions. Jonathan's journey is filled with signs of the uncanny: Dracula's animal eyes fill the night sky; wolves howl; skeletons appear; a blue fire swirls like mist; the coachman has claw-like hands, scales and a hooked beak. Like the novel, the film emphasises Harker's unease on approaching the castle: 'This was all so strange and uncanny that a dreadful fear came upon me.' When Dracula accidentally sees a photograph of Harker's fiancée, Mina (Winona Ryder) he believes it is his beloved Elisabeta to whom Mina bears an uncanny resemblance. The Count immediately plans his departure for London.

Coppola takes great care to represent Dracula as a sexually ambiguous character whose feminine characteristics link him to the primal uncanny. In the scene where Jonathan Harker first meets the Count, the former is dressed like a man, the latter like a woman. The ancient Count cuts an uncanny figure; like a dowager Empress, he flashes long pointed nails and speaks with a strange throaty accent; his face is covered with white make-up, he wears an overblown feminine wig and a long red train that flows behind him like a river of blood. Film theorist Pam Cook notes that he is represented in the film as a 'distinctly feminised' figure and that 'emphasis is on his orality'.[33]

In London, where Dracula is re-energised and youthful again, he introduces himself to Mina as Prince Vlad. The exotic foreigner has taken great care over his appearance, with his hair tied and flowing down his back, his clothes fashionable and appealing. Mina is immediately attracted to him and together they watch erotic scenes from one of the century's newest inventions, the cinematograph. This 'chance' meeting has all the hallmarks of the uncanny; there is a strong sense that this encounter should never have happened. In trying to reverse the tide of history by bringing his dead wife back to life, Dracula brings only tragedy. Yet perhaps this is better for Mina than the alternative of never experiencing a grand passion. At the end of the story, where the action has moved to Dracula's castle in Transylvania, the Count, weakened from lack of blood and his journey across the seas, has changed back into a grotesque wreck with wrinkled flesh and trembling limbs. Yet, Mina still loves him passionately. She never responds to the Count with horror or revulsion— even when he lies in her arms, an abject thing on the verge of death. Only when she plunges the sword into his chest and he begins to die does he revert to his youthful self. Coppola's tale is similar to Cocteau's *Beauty and the Beast*, except that Dracula, who has committed terrible deeds, is far from an innocent beast.

Many scenes highlight female eroticism and female sexual desire. When Jonathan stumbles upon Dracula's three uncanny brides, he is immediately overwhelmed by the feminine. He is engulfed by a bed whose surface dissolves into voluptuous folds from which Dracula's uncanny brides emerge. As the three women caress his body, touch his flesh and draw blood from his skin, he falls into an erotic swoon that is unexpectedly interrupted by the appearance of the Count. The three vampires fall back, two of them momentarily joined together, one attached to the pudenda of the other, like a monstrous classical hydra. They signify the uncanny in bringing to light what should have remained hidden—the hero's willingness to succumb to perverse pleasures, specifically the lure of non-procreative oral sex. The image of their red lips and bloody fangs also recalls a primitive fear of the terrifying *vagina dentata*. Parallels are drawn later between the three vampires and Lucy, whose dresses similarly suggest erotic desire, particularly the red nightgown she wears when she is orally ravaged by the beast/Dracula on the gravestone.

A close analysis of the scene in which Dracula and Mina declare their undying mutual love reveals the extent to which Dracula is a feminised monster. His sexuality is oral, not phallic. After a passionate kiss, Mina asks her lover to reveal his true identity. He tells her that he is Dracula, the Monster. She responds by telling him he is her life. He replies that he will give her life eternal. He bends over her and plunges his teeth into her neck. He then cuts his chest and asks her to drink his blood. There is another close-up, depicting the gash on his breast. He is like a woman who offers his blood as the 'milk of life'. This scene evokes an even more archaic relationship, as discussed by Moretti, that is the embryo *in utero* feeding on its mother's blood, and hence parallels are drawn between the vampire and the nursing mother and blood-sucking foetus. Dracula fills the roles of foetus, mother and lover: he needs to drink blood to live, he offers his own blood to suckle the newly born vampire, he transforms the act of vampirism into one of sexual seduction in which pleasure is dependent on an exchange of masochism and oral sadism.

In the novel, Mina tells the band of men how she was forced to carry out Dracula's perverse desires:

> With that he pulled open his shirt, and with his long sharp nails opened a vein in his breast. When the blood began to spurt out, he took my hands in one of his, holding them tight, and with the other seized my neck and pressed my mouth to the wound, so that I must either suffocate or swallow some of the—Oh, my God, my God! what have I done?[34]

In the film, Dracula is torn between his desire to make Mina one of the undead and his feelings for her. He hesitates, and tells Mina he loves her too much to continue. A century later, Mina enacts his perverse desires; she forces Dracula to yield and he lets her drink from the wound on his chest. In an unusual reversal, the camera focuses on his pleasure. He is filmed in the way a woman is so often represented, the camera focusing on his face, head thrown back, an expression of ecstasy—of feminine jouissance—lighting his features. The male monster is the feminised, passive, bleeding lover; the woman is the active, assertive sexual predator. When the lovers are forced apart by the arrival of Van Helsing, he transforms into a body of phallic rats, which for a moment looks like the classical figure of Astarte the goddess whose body is made up of numerous breasts. Coppola represents this as a scene of extreme uncanniness because of the frightening way in which the human body is suddenly rendered unfamiliar. Dracula's body breaks apart as the rats—familiars of the witch— separate and escape through the window into the night.

Mina and Lucy are in need of a Dracula. Mina is sensible and modest; Lucy is voluptuous and immodest. As in the novel, Mina is represented as a New Woman; she is brave, intelligent, well read, skilled in the use of the new wonder the typewriter, and not happy when the men act as her protectors. In the novel,

Dr Seward says Mina has 'a man's brain'.[35] When the story begins, Mina is engaged to be married and Lucy, who has many suitors, is in search of the right man. The couple share secrets, talk about men and even read from a semi-pornographic illustrated volume of *The Arabian Nights*. They wonder whether the sexual poses illustrated in the book are even possible. Dracula is clearly the only one who is capable of fulfilling their erotic urges. In comparison with Dracula, the men hovering around the two women are immature and repressed. Dracula is very different; he has experienced the passions of love and is interested in women's sexual pleasure. The Count offers his female followers the opportunity of eternal sexual and sensual pleasure either with their victims or with each other.

In one erotically charged scene, Mina and Lucy kiss in a storm, suggesting a nascent lesbian desire echoing the erotic embraces of the three female vampires that live in Dracula's castle. As a creature of perversion, Dracula understands the attractions of animal sex, sadism, oral sex, biting, masochism, blood and satiety. These are of course the very reasons why the avenging, masculine and righteous figures, the fathers and brothers who signify law and order, must destroy Dracula. He scorns the sanctity of heterosexual penetrative coupling necessary for the perpetuation of civilised patriarchal society. Dracula's most monstrous crime is that he refuses to enforce the phallocentric order; he is on the side of the feminine. As film scholar David Pirie has written:

> *Dracula can be seen as the great submerged force of Victorian libido breaking out to punish the repressive society which had imprisoned it; one of the most appalling things that Dracula does to the matronly women of his Victorian enemies (in the novel as in the film) is to make them sensual.*[36]

The other boundary that Dracula erases is that between man and beast. Coppola makes the most of the King Vampire's powers of shape shifting, a factor that further enhances the film's atmosphere of confusion and disorientation. It is often difficult to determine which form Dracula has inhabited, what he is and where he is travelling. The camera frequently adopts a rapid travelling shot, filmed from Dracula's point of view. One minute we speed across the ground in the form of a swirling mist, the next in the shape of a running wolf. These sequences, which ask us to identify with Dracula in different shapes and forms, are particularly uncanny. According to the vampire myth, the creature can transform itself into a wolf, bat, rat, even into a mist, moonlight and dust. Coppola produces his Vampire through the commingling of familiar and unfamiliar: female and male, human and animal. Mladen Dolar argues that the dominant culture attempts to rob the uncanny of its power by making the unfamiliar familiar; but as cultural critic Ken Gelder reminds us, in terms of Freud's definition, 'the unfamiliar is *already* familiar'.[37]

In the film's most sexually confronting scene, Dracula metamorphoses into a beast, a strange ape creature that copulates with Lucy at night in the garden. This is the night of Dracula's arrival in London. There is a fierce storm at sea, the vampire's eyes appear again in the sky, animals at the zoo become agitated, and inmates at the asylum are unusually unruly. Lucy rushes into the night in her red nightgown. Mina runs after Lucy, who she finds stretched out on a grave, mating with Dracula who is transformed into a beast. As the two women run from the scene Lucy tries to explain what happened; she says her soul seemed to leave her body, which was filled with an agonising feeling, as she was pulled along, lured by great eyes. She still tastes his blood in her mouth. This scene leaves no doubt in the viewer's mind that the kind of sex that Dracula offers is bestial. Dracula tears away all vestiges of civilisation, forcing his partner into a primitive, animalistic sexual encounter. The puncture holes left by his two fangs testify to the fact that his sexual partner now not only bears the 'mark of the beast' but that she too has the power to transform into a beast. It is as if Dracula's fangs tear away at the thin fabric of civilisation, releasing the individual from the restrictive power of the law and conscience. Dracula might appear as a beautifully cultivated aristocrat, but beneath his civilised demeanour lurks the beast; bloodlust and the tearing of flesh replace proper civilised sex. Worse still, he makes it clear that woman is on the side of the animal.

Dracula's association with the primal uncanny is particularly evident in his attachment to the earth. Before he travels to London, he prepares a number of coffins filled with earth from the cellars of his castle. Jonathan observes his meticulous, strange behaviour. In a letter to Mina he writes that the Count has filled 'boxes with decrepit earth from the bowels of the castle'. In this film, Dracula, like an animal, sleeps in the damp soil of Mother Earth in order to replenish his deadly powers.

Dracula is monstrous because his oral sexuality threatens the very basis of phallic heterosexuality. His sexuality is feminised and animalised in relation to his acts of metamorphosis, orality, cannibalism and bestiality. He is the thing that lies beneath, rising into consciousness with the force of an erotic nightmare. His mythic and symbolic associations with woman's menstrual cycle, virginal blood and foetal blood make him the supreme blood monster of the cinema. His power over women is particularly threatening, as evidenced in the scene where the men savagely destroy Lucy. Not only do they drive a stake through her heart, they also decapitate her—their actions betraying a marked degree of sadomasochistic pleasure. With his attachment to Mother Earth, his association with woman's blood cycle, his power to transform into animal forms and his existence as an undead creature, Dracula is closely linked to the primal uncanny. Because Dracula gives birth through the act of vampirism, because he re-creates himself, his perverse sexuality threatens to continue. Cixous writes that the '*Unheimliche* has no end' and that this is the true source of its horror. Dracula's monstrousness resides in his knowingness; he understands all too well the uncanny appeal of the perverse, of being undead yet sexually alive 'forever', a state brought about by his alliance with the primal uncanny.

5

FREUD'S WOLF MAN, OR THE TALE OF GRANNY'S FURRY PHALLUS

Unheimliche ... *infiltrates the interstices of the narrative and points to the gaps we need to explain.*

HÉLÈNE CIXOUS[1]

Published in 1918 under the title 'From the History of an Infantile Neurosis', 'The Wolf Man' is Freud's most famous and fascinating case study. However, his interpretation of the Wolf Man's personal history has always been controversial. This is because Freud drew on his analysis to propose a number of psychoanalytic theories central to his own views, with which a number of theorists disagreed.[2] These included his theory of the primal scene—that is, the child's observation of parental intercourse, in which the child interprets the scene as an act of aggression by the father towards the mother. Freud argued that the child, ignorant of the anatomical differences between men and women, also interprets the primal scene as representing castration. He argued that a scene of parental sex, which the Wolf Man witnessed as an infant, traumatised him later in life—even though it actually occurred when he was eighteen months old and was unable to understand its significance at the time. Critics disagree as to whether the primal scene should be viewed as a memory of an actual event, witnessed by the child, or as phantasy.

Freud also used his analysis to support his theory that children are more frightened of the castrating father than the maternal figure whom Freud designated as uncanny in relation to her genital organs and womb.[3] Freud elevated the figure of the castrating father in causing the Wolf Man's neurosis while downplaying the role(s) of the incorporating/castrating woman and the terrifying wolf, both of which I argue constitute figures of the 'primal uncanny'. The Wolf Man might well have witnessed the scene of parental sex, but the origin of his wolf phobia lies, primarily, with his superstitious belief that he was marked out from birth to become a werewolf.

Freud's argument about the paternal castrator has exerted a profound influence on psychoanalytic and feminist film theory, particularly with the publication in 1975 of Laura Mulvey's ground-breaking article on male castration anxiety and film spectatorship.[4] Many theorists have drawn on Freud's theory to argue that castration and castration anxiety are central to horror, and other genres, although they propose different approaches.[5] Some define the male of the slasher film as essentially a castrating monster. There are two other frightening figures in the Wolf Man case history: the castrating/castrated woman, who Freud acknowledged but downplayed; and the savage wolf that Freud aligned with the castrating father, but ignored as a terrifying animal in its own right. Freud's neglect of these two figures, particularly the animal, is evident not only in the Wolf Man case history but also in his essay 'The Uncanny'. In turn, critical writings on the horror film which do theorise the male monster tend to focus on his identity as a castrating figure who fears/ attacks woman because she reminds him of his own possible castration. It is possible to re-read the Wolf Man case history in order to reinsert woman, but more importantly the animal, as a basis for discussion of the male monster, particularly the werewolf, of the horror film. The concept of the primal uncanny also enables us to interpret castrating male monsters, such as the Ripper and Freddy, the spectral monster of the *Elm Street* films, from a new perspective. By uncovering the primal uncanny, bringing it into the critical light of day, we are better able to analyse the representation of horror in popular cultural forms such as film and to understand the role of male monstrosity in the popular imagination. The uncanny, as an aesthetic device, is important because, as Rosemary Jackson argues, it has a radical potential to uncover those things that the dominant culture prefers to keep hidden.

The son of a rich Russian landowner, Sergius Konstanti-novitch Pankejeff (1887–1979), who was later known as the Wolf Man, grew up on a great estate in czarist Russia. Serge Pankejeff was a good-natured child who caused his parents no trouble. It was said that he should have been the girl, his sister the boy. His sister was 'lively, gifted, and precociously naughty' and she played 'an important part in his life'.[6] Inexplicably, he changed. One year, he recalled, his parents returned from their summer holidays to find he had become 'discontented, irritable and violent, took offence on every possible occasion, and then flew into a rage and screamed like a savage'.[7] Just before the age of four, he developed a wolf phobia, or an exaggerated fear of wolves. At the same age he also experienced a terrible nightmare about wolves that Freud interpreted as offering the key to his childhood and adult neuroses. According to Freud, his anxiety and hysteria changed into 'an obsessional neurosis with a reli-gious content, and lasted with its offshoots as far as into his tenth year'.[8] However, according to the Wolf Man, his fear of 'seeing something terrible' in his dreams lasted until his twelfth year.[9]

In February 1910, at twenty-four years of age, the Wolf Man came to Freud and started his analysis, which lasted until July 1914. Freud regarded it as possibly his most important case, par-ticularly because it provided him with material to support his criticisms of Jung and Adler who disagreed with his theories of infantile sexuality.[10] The key figures in the patient's life were his parents (with whom he had infrequent contact), his sister, his beloved Nanya, various governesses, servants and relatives. He believed initially that his own neurosis was a result of an hereditary flaw that had afflicted other family members, primarily on his father's side. His mother suffered from a range of illnesses, his father was diagnosed as a manic-depressive, and his paternal uncle was believed to suffer from obsessional neurosis. In addition, his grandmother and father were both thought to have committed suicide. His sister, Anna, committed suicide as a young woman by drinking mercury while travelling away from home.

The Wolf Man entered into therapy with Freud because of ill health, severe depression and an inability to function at all in daily life. Freud turned to the Wolf Man's childhood to explain the origins of his psychological problems, specifically his infantile neurosis which included a wolf phobia and his castration anxiety. Freud explained that his account would 'deal with an infantile neurosis which was analysed not while it actually existed, but only fifteen years after its termination'.[11] He argued that 'analyses of children's neuroses' are of 'high theoretical interest' because of the assistance they offer in coming to 'a proper understanding of the neuroses of adults'.[12]

THE WOLF MAN'S NIGHTMARE

Freud interpreted the little boy's wolf nightmare, which occurred when he was four years of age, as the boy's recollection or interpretation of the primal scene of parental sex. The Wolf Man's dream, which drew heavily on fairy tales, focused on the figure of the wolf—the creature whose image in a storybook had previously been used by his sister to terrify him. The Wolf Man was lying in bed at night and dreamt that it was a winter's night; suddenly 'the window opened of its own accord' and he became terrified to see that six or seven white wolves were sitting in the branches of a big walnut tree outside the window:

*The wolves were quite white, and looked more like foxes or
sheep-dogs, for they had big tails like foxes and they had their
ears pricked like dogs when they pay attention to something.
In great terror, evidently of being eaten up by the wolves, I
screamed and woke up.*[13]

The Wolf Man said the dream reminded him of a picture in
the storybook that his sister teased him with by holding it
upright before his eyes until he screamed. In both the picture
and the nightmare the boy says he is terrified of being 'eaten up'
by the wolves—a factor that, in my own view, plays an important role in his phantasy that he will be reborn as a wolf–man.
Freud analysed the little boy's wolf dream to mean that he
had witnessed a scene of parental sex at the age of eighteen
months when he was in his crib in his parent's room. This was
the primal scene that lay behind the terrifying dream. The boy
of course was too young to understand fully the scene before
him; he only came to a realisation of its true significance retroactively after he became aware of his own sexual desires that had
been shaped by his various sexual experiences. In other words,
no single event was alone responsible for the Wolf Man's infantile neurosis.

Freud interpreted the boy's wolf nightmare as signifying
a scene of parental sex. What the infant saw was a scene of
coitus *a tergo*—that is, 'intercourse from behind'. His father had
mounted his mother from behind and both appeared to be enjoying themselves as they made love like animals. He saw 'the man
upright, and the woman bent down like an animal'.[14] The young
Wolf Man witnessed 'a coitus *a tergo*, three times repeated; he
was able to see his mother's genitals as well as his father's organ;
and he understood the process [of their intercourse] as well as its
significance'.[15]

Upon watching the scene of parental intercourse, the boy
retroactively understood that in order for his father to make love
to him he would have to become like his mother—castrated.
This terrified him because his Nanya had threatened him with

castration if he did not cease his masturbatory practices. When he played with his penis in front of his Nanya she said that he would get a 'wound' in the place of his penis. When watching his parents, he had seen 'with his own eyes the wound of which his Nanya had spoken'.[16] He saw that his mother did not have a penis and mistakenly thought that in order to be loved by his father he would first have to be castrated. He saw his father, whom he loved and feared, as the castrating parent.

Freud interpreted the wolves of the Wolf Man's terrifying nightmare as his parents. Freud also interpreted the primal scene as one overlaid not just with castration anxiety but also with masochism. As a result of having witnessed the sexual act, the Wolf Man (who desired sex with his father) believed he, like his mother, would have to be mounted by his father from behind. In other words he would have to adopt what Freud defined as the feminine, masochistic position. In adult life, the Wolf Man was only interested in sex with servants and other women of lower station with whom he could only enjoy sex in the form of 'copulation from behind—*more ferarum* [in the fashion of animals]'.[17]

Freud had also established that the Wolf Man loved his father and sister but was jealous of their relationship. When he was about three and a quarter years of age his sister had rubbed his penis and given him satisfaction; as a consequence, Freud argued, he was predisposed to assuming a passive, feminine position. Ruth Mack Brunswick, who also analysed the Wolf Man, was able to add more information about the boy's anal erotic disposition. Because his Nanya had frequently given him anal pleasure when she taught him how to massage his anus when constipated, his preference throughout his life was for anal sex.[18] So while he wanted his father to love him and to give him sexual satisfaction through anal sex, his desires also terrified him.

In my view, Freud did not explore the Wolf Man's story in enough depth. This is primarily because he wanted to promote his theory of the father as the uncanny paternal castrator, the parent who—by extension—signified the threat of castration within all families. Freud argued that, as a result of his fear of the father, the boy relinquished his incestuous desire for the mother on the implicit understanding that one day he would have a wife and family of his own. Thus the threat of castration embodied by the father explains the formation and perpetuation of the family. In his attempt to reduce the Wolf Man's extremely complex set of childhood recollections, his animal phobia and nightmares, to one discrete problem—that of castration anxiety—Freud overlooked or omitted other possible interpretations. Existing alongside the primal scene of parental sex, with its overlay of masochism and castration, there are two other primal scenes. The key to understanding the Wolf Man's history revolves around these two scenes—one of which Freud considered only briefly, the other of which he did not refer to at all. The former relates to the Wolf Man's sister, Anna, and her account of having witnessed coitus *a tergo* between Nanya and the gardener; the latter was the Wolf Man's primal phantasy of origins—that is, his childhood belief that he was destined to become a wolf–man, which exerted a dominant influence on the shaping of his terrible nightmare of the white wolves. These two 'other' scenes do not relate to the father as castrator, but to woman and animal, and as such they invoke the horror of the primal uncanny which haunted the waking and sleeping hours of the young Wolf Man.

THE PRIMAL UNCANNY AND THE WOLF MAN

The Wolf Man story is filled with uncanny disturbances, coincidences and fears. He was particularly fearful of wolves that were in some way human, suggesting an uncanny merging of human and animal. Freud stated that actual fairy tales are not uncanny insofar as they describe events considered impossible, but where primitive beliefs are confirmed the uncanny feelings may arise. In his essay on the uncanny he argued that 'an uncanny experience occurs ... when primitive beliefs which have been accounted for seem once more to be confirmed'.[19] To the young

Wolf Man, the possibility of a human turning into a wolf was clearly a source of terror. He was particularly terrified of a picture of an upright wolf from a children's book of fairy stories. Everything that relates to the boy's wolf phobia is particularly uncanny in that he is only frightened of a tail-less wolf or a wolf that seems human—that is, the wolf that renders the familiar unfamiliar. As in the werewolf film, the upright wolf suggests that man and animal inhabit each other, that civilisation is not so 'human' after all.

In his analysis of the events that befell the Wolf Man, Freud painted a particularly uncanny picture. In his essay 'The Uncanny', many of those objects and events that Freud listed as uncanny appear also in the case history: castration, dismemberment, the female genital organ, intra-uterine existence, womb phantasies, doubles, oral incorporation, obsessive repetition of an act, magic, and erasure of a distinction between imagination and reality. In my view, the most uncanny of all is the upright wolf, the human beast. Despite the multiplication of uncanny signs, objects, sensations and events in the case history, Freud pays the notion of the uncanny hardly any attention at all. As Hélène Cixous states in the quotation at the beginning of this chapter, the uncanny in narrative points to 'gaps we need to explain'. In addition, Cixous has said that Freud's interpretation of the 'Sand-Man is also a surreptitious re-reading of the Wolf-Man'.[20] She draws parallels between repeated motifs: the maids of each story, the fathers, the father substitutes and the feminine attitudes of the two sons. 'The Wolf Man', written in 1914 and published in 1918, was completed before Freud's essay 'The Uncanny' (1919). The sandman may well offer a 'surreptitious re-reading' of the Wolf Man but the Wolf Man also represents Freud's neglect of the role of the uncanny in creating fear and dread and in bringing about phobias, particularly in relation to the animal and the collapse of boundaries between the human and animal. If we re-read the Wolf Man's story in the context of lycanthropy we can see that the animal is also a powerful source of uncanniness in Freud's famous case history.

The account of the primal scene itself is particularly uncanny in that it is subject to a marked degree of 'intellectual
uncertainty' or undecidability. Did the boy really see his parents
mating as if wolves? Or was his neurosis based on something else,
perhaps seeing animals copulating on the estate combined with
other related fears? Did his parents have coitus *a tergo* not once
but three times? If his mother was on all fours, how did he see
her 'wound'?[21] In disagreeing with Ernst Jentsch's claim that
the hallmark of the uncanny was intellectual uncertainty, Freud,
in his essay on the sandman, was able to assert with confidence
his argument that castration is the main cause of the uncanny in
Hoffman's story.

In the Wolf Man case history, Freud refers to the uncanny
directly in relation to the boy's fear of animals and women, yet
he does not develop this line of thought. The first reference is
to the Wolf Man's childhood 'fear and loathing' of butterflies,
beetles and caterpillars, 'horses, too, gave him an uncanny feeling', particularly if a horse was being beaten.[22] The 'opening and
shutting of the butterfly's wings while it was settled on the flower
had also given him an uncanny feeling. It had looked, so he said,
like a woman opening her legs, and the legs then made the shape
of a Roman V.'[23] Although he does not use the word uncanny,
the other two key events that fill the boy with fear and terror are
both connected with his wolf phobia. The first is the image of
the wolf standing upright in the book of fairytales; which, as I
have indicated, is uncanny because it renders the familiar (the
wolf) into the unfamiliar (the wolf–man). The second is his
nightmare of the window uncannily opening of its own accord
and the six or seven white wolves sitting in the old walnut tree
in front of his bedroom window, staring intently at him.

The central source of the primal uncanny is the boy's wolf
phobia. Fear of being incorporated into the wolf's tummy and
later rescued by the axeman invokes the phantasy of being
buried alive when not dead, which, according to Freud, is a particularly strong cause of the uncanny. Freud's account of the boy's

phobia invokes the uncanny at every turn of the narrative—yet he doesn't draw attention to it as such in the case history.

There are a number of key reasons that might help to explain the Wolf Man's phobia, apart from his supposedly having witnessed a scene of parental sex at the age of one and a half years. The first and most important is the fact that he—like Freud—was born with a caul—that is, a membrane attached to the head at birth. Folkloric belief held that anyone born with a caul would have the power to transform into a wolf–man or werewolf. Freud became aware of the Wolf Man's caul only at the end of the analysis when the Wolf Man recalled this distinguishing feature. The German word for 'caul', *Glückshaube*, literally means 'lucky hood' and as a result the Wolf Man had always felt he was 'a special child of fortune whom no ill could befall'.[24]

The lycanthropic superstitions associated with the caul were not discussed. According to Freud 'the caul was the veil which hid him from the world and hid the world from him'.[25] Significantly, Freud also argued in his famous essay that this was the function of the uncanny. The uncanny brings secret, hidden things into the light. The caul/veil is the gap that runs between the self and the world, shielding one from the other. If the caul is removed, the uncanny emerges. Freud interpreted this veil as signifying a desire to return to the womb; as a phantasy of re-birth: 'Thus, the caul ... was, in fact, a wishful fantasy of flight from the world'.[26] 'The necessary condition of his re-birth was that he should have an enema administered to him by a man.'[27] Freud interpreted this to mean that his re-birth was intimately related to his attaining sexual satisfaction with a man who was his father. He desired to return to the womb in order to copulate with his father and even bear him a child. Freud discusses the Wolf Man's re-birth phantasies, but only in the context of the father. In my view, the Wolf Man's phantasy of re-birth is also associated with his belief that he could become a werewolf, a transformation that first involved being reincorporated into the body of the devouring female wolf—a primitive and uncanny fear.

In Slavic folk traditions of lycanthropy, individuals born during the twelve days between Christmas and Epiphany also have the power to become werewolves. The Wolf Man therefore was doubly in danger of becoming a werewolf. Once a werewolf, the newly born creature had the power to travel to the land of the dead. He could also return to his human shape. However, a wolf–man always bears the wound of his metamorphosis—that is, the bite mark he suffered when first attacked by the wolf. This is the only way in which a werewolf can be detected—through his wound. The only difference between the werewolf and wolves is that the former is tail-less.

According to historian Carlo Ginzburg, Freud, although having written on the relationship between dreams and folklore, strangely did 'not recognise the element of folklore present in the wolf-man's dream'.[28] In Ginzburg's view, the young Wolf Man would have been fully aware of this connection primarily because of the influence of his beloved Nanya, whom he describes as a 'pious and superstitious woman' and an 'intermediary between the sphere of folkloric beliefs connected with werewolves and Freud's future patient' who was from the upper strata of Russian society.[29] Ginzburg interprets the Wolf Man's nightmare as 'a dream of initiatory character'.[30] In other words, the six or seven white wolves sitting silently and quite still on branches of the old walnut tree could be interpreted as calling to the young Wolf Man to leave his bed and join the pack outside in the snow. This is presumably why they stared at him so intently; they were beckoning to him to use his magical powers and become part of the wolf pack. Ginzburg does not apply his interpretation in any detail to the Wolf Man's case. Folkloric belief, however, sheds new light on the origin of the boy's wolf phobia and infantile neurosis. Ginzburg does point out that the cultural contents of the nightmare, which Freud ignores, 'integrate but do not confute Freud's interpretation' about the key significance of repression and the primal scene in the history of the individual subject.[31]

Lycanthropic folklore explains why, in the nightmare, the white wolves were sitting on a tree outside the window. As mentioned, the boy was doubly blessed with special powers of metamorphosis. Given this, Christmas must have been a source of both pleasure and anxiety for the little Wolf Man. At the age of four he dreamed that his birthday presents, which would have been hanging on the Christmas tree, had been replaced by wolves sitting motionless, suspended like presents, on the branches of a large walnut tree. They 'replace the Christmas presents hanging on the tree'.[32] Have the wolves in the tree come for him? How will his transformation occur? Will one of the wolves eat him up (as in fairy stories) and incorporate him inside its stomach from where he will be re-born as one of the pack? In analysis the Wolf Man agreed that the fairy story he had in mind, which seemed connected with his nightmare, was probably 'The Wolf and the Seven Little Goats' which refers to numbers six and seven—the number of wolves in the dream. In this story there is also a tree and a white wolf. As in 'Little Red Riding Hood', 'there is the eating up, the cutting open of the belly, the taking out of the people who have been eaten and their replacement by heavy stones, and finally in both of them the wicked wolf perishes'.[33]

Little Red Riding Hood also had a special hood. Perhaps the little Wolf Man identified her hood with his caul, there being only the one German word for both. The boy may have found the fairy tale disturbing because of its suggestion that the wolf was a she-wolf, which, like his mother (in the sex act), went on all fours and also had a wound. Perhaps he believed that, just like little Red Riding Hood, he too would be eaten up by the she-wolf, along with the grandmother, and that when the hunter cut open the wolf's stomach he would be re-born not as a boy but as a wolf. Little Red Riding Hood was cut out of the wolf's belly as if the wolf had been given a caesarean section. Thus the boy may well have drawn a connection between being 'eaten up' (pregnancy) and birth (cut from the stomach). The Wolf Man may have also found the fairy tale disturbing because of its portrayal of the father. The actual father is absent but nonetheless is present in the story in two forms: as the bad, sexual father (the upright wolf) and the good father (the woodsman). The bad father is a monstrous figure; he has big eyes, big ears, large hands and a horrible mouth with big teeth. Freud also referred to the possibility that the boy feared that his father might gobble him up—a threat adults often utter when playing games with their children. The wolf is an uncanny figure with male and female characteristics. Just as the fairy story suggests that Little Red Riding Hood is also attracted to the wolf (she gives him directions to granny's house), it is likely that the Wolf Man shared her ambivalence towards the animal father or mother.

Child psychiatrist Bruno Bettelheim writes that 'the wolf is not just the male seducer, he also represents all the asocial, animalistic tendencies within ourselves'.[34] The bad wolf is an attractive figure. Bettelheim argues that if 'there is a central theme to the wide variety of fairy tales, it is that of re-birth to a higher plane'.[35] Yet children may also relish the idea of being re-born as a potent animal. Bettelheim acknowledges the appeal of animality when he quotes Djuna Barnes: 'Children know something they can't tell; they like Red Riding Hood and the wolf in bed!'[36] Thus the little Wolf Man may have had a deeply ambivalent attitude to the wolf in the story. On the one hand, the wolf terrified him because he didn't want to be eaten up and re-born as a wolf. But on the other hand, at an unconscious level, the wolf may also have symbolised the seductive power of the father who had sexual access to his mother and his sister and possibly himself. Freud tells us that the Wolf Man held ambivalent feelings towards his own father, whom he adored yet of whom he was also very afraid. The true monster of the tale may well have been the Wolf Man's own uncanny father, a sexual predator who lured children into his bed. Granny is also sacrificed because Little Red Riding Hood gave the wolf detailed instructions to her house in the woods. The wolf knew how to find her home just as the six or seven wolves in the Wolf Man's nightmare knew where he lived. Perhaps the boy himself was responsible for the presence of the white wolves in the old walnut tree.

Otto Rank claimed that Freud overemphasised the young Wolf Man's castration anxiety, developed in relation to the father/wolf, while neglecting his fear of being incorporated, a fear associated with the mother/wolf.[37] It also is relevant to note that it was at the Christmas of his fourth birthday that his behaviour inexplicably changed. He became angry and threw tantrums. Was it around this time that he first learnt about his special uncanny powers from his Nanya, leading to his fear of incorporation and transformation? It was certainly when his sister first began to taunt him with the illustration of the wolf. It is worth re-reading the boy's nightmare in relation to the uncanny belief that those born with a caul and on Christmas day are to become wolf–men. The dream itself does not, on first hearing, seem particularly terrifying, but it certainly becomes so if interpreted in the light of the primal uncanny.

The boy's nightmare had particularly uncanny aspects. If we read the nightmare alongside the various things that Freud describes as uncanny in his essay we can see that the uncanny is ominously present. The six or seven white wolves/gifts on the branches of the walnut/Christmas tree rendered the whole scene both familiar and unfamiliar. Further, the white wolves stared intently at him as if they might do him harm—suggesting 'the evil eye', another indicator of the uncanny. There are other signs of the uncanny in the boy's life. The Wolf Man thought he possessed special powers because he was born with a caul—Freud lists a belief in special powers as a sign of the uncanny. The Wolf Man recounted another dream in which he was carving the bark of a walnut tree (the same tree as in his nightmare?) and cut off his finger with his pocket knife, but when he looked again it was whole. In re-telling the story on another occasion, he said he was cutting the walnut tree and blood came out of the tree. The Wolf Man said that the dream was brought on by hearing of a female relative who was born with six toes and the extra one was cut off with an axe. Freud focused on these events in terms of castration anxiety. As in the story of Tancred, the tree is female and bleeds because of the woman trapped inside. In addition, his mother suffered from haemorrhages, further reinforcing the uncanny idea that women are castrated and have a wound that bleeds. This wound, however, is associated not just with castration but also with being eaten by the wolves and the mark of the werewolf. Signs of the primal uncanny—woman, animal, death—run throughout the case history and constitute the central reason for the boy's infantile neurosis.

METAMORPHOSIS

Freud paid no attention to the motif of metamorphosis that runs through these narratives. Not even the image of the white wolves is stable. The Wolf Man states that they 'looked more like foxes or sheep-dogs'. One animal merges into the other. Freud did state that the wolves sitting in the tree represented the boy's Christmas presents hanging on the Christmas tree, but he does not comment further on the transformation of one into the other. If in the Wolf Man's dreams the Christmas gifts have changed into wolves, it is most likely this has happened because the wolves are about to bring the boy's own special gift to realisation. One gift becomes the other. The Wolf Man told Freud that he believed his lucky caul was a gift giving him special powers, yet Freud paid little attention to this new piece of information. This special power is one of transformation and metamorphosis. Because of his caul and his birth date he has the power to become a wolf–man.

It is also possible that the Wolf Man identified tail-lessness with woman's 'wound'. No doubt his Nanya informed him of the superstition that the wolf–man, who runs with the pack, is different in that he does not have a tail. She had already told him he would get a wound if he continued to masturbate. In the boy's mind tail-lessness and the wound may well have come together in an uncanny image signifying metamorphosis. Folkloric belief also held that, when the werewolf changed back into a man, the wound that initiated his metamorphosis would remain on his body. One way to discover a werewolf was to look for the wound. A number of fairy stories referred to a tail-less wolf. In other words, to become a werewolf he first must lose his tail—that is, suffer castration—which suggests he regarded a werewolf as a feminised creature, made this way through metamorphosis. When he is not a wolf his finger/tail/penis will return. His penis is also a furry phallus—both present and absent as in coition. Naturally the boy is terrified.

If Ginzburg is correct and the young Wolf Man believed he possessed the power to become a werewolf, then it is possible to advance a different interpretation of his fear of the wolf in the picture book. No doubt his sister, Anna, also shared knowledge of werewolves with her brother. She too was very close to their Nanya, who would have passed on a great deal of information along with fairy tales and folkloric beliefs to her two young charges. This would explain why Anna taunted her brother with the picture of the wolf from a book of fairy tales. The Wolf Man told Freud that his nightmare of the wolves in the tree reminded him of a picture of a wolf of which he was very fearful. His sister would hold this picture in front of him until he screamed. 'There was a particular picture book, in which a wolf was represented, standing upright and striding along. Whenever he caught sight of this picture he began to scream like a lunatic that he was afraid of the wolf coming and eating him up.'[38] The wolf in the picture 'was standing upright, striding out with one foot, with its claws stretched out and its ears pricked', and the Wolf Man thought that the picture must have been from the story of Little Red Riding Hood who also had a red hood/caul and was eaten by a wolf–man disguised as a granny, perhaps someone not unlike his own Nanya who had already threatened him with a wound.[39] Despite this, Freud ignored Nanya's role as a maternal castrator. Anna, who was a gifted child and exceeded her brother in all things, may have even been jealous of the fact that her brother —not herself—was born with special powers. She obviously went out of her way to torment him: 'His sister, however, always succeeded in arranging [things] so that he was obliged to see this picture, and was delighted at his terror'.[40]

In showing her young brother the terrifying wolf, Anna was no doubt mercilessly teasing him. Was this an image of the little boy as a future wolf? Or was this the wolf coming to eat him up? The fact that the wolf was walking along in an upright posture, instead of running on all fours, is very telling. The wolf was striding along as if he were a man; he had a purposeful air. Perhaps he was looking for someone—perhaps little Sergius. Freud stressed that the boy was only afraid of the upright wolf. The wolf is a very humanised figure; in the picture it is male but in the story it becomes female. The wolf dresses up in grandmother's nightclothes and bonnet before climbing into bed, pretending to be the old lady—a woman with a furry tail. The little Wolf Man found the wolf terrifying, not just because it was a ferocious animal that might 'eat him up', as his fairy tales suggested, but also because the wolves he encountered in his dreams, in his picture book and in fairy stories were all anthropomorphised figures—wolves behaving like men, wolves dressed as women. To the fertile and active imagination of a young boy, these uncanny creatures could only have been what he believed, in his darkest moments, he was destined to become: a wolf–man or werewolf.

It is relevant to note that later in life, and on important occasions, Sergius signed himself as the 'Wolf Man'. I am not suggesting that the Wolf Man adopted a wolf's identity because he actually believed he was a werewolf. He would have been referring, perhaps ironically, to the fact that psychoanalysis had created his new identity; it was Freud who gave him the title, and his years of analysis that transformed him into a 'wolf–man'. Perhaps he was also referring to his childhood belief that one day he would become a wolf–man. In the Wolf Man's own mind, the caul was of central importance. Significantly, he did not mention that he was born with a caul until the end of his treatment. Why did he offer this crucial information only when it was almost too late for Freud to explore its significance? Given their almost continuous discussions with reference to wolves, it is strange that he should have forgotten/repressed such a vital piece of information until the final meetings. Or perhaps not; perhaps he felt uneasy about his magical powers. Why then, did Freud fail to mention his own caul? Was it enough that the Wolf Man was wearing his caul for the two of them? In the end, he associated the 'caul' with the Wolf Man's problematic 'veil', which, according to Freud, the Wolf Man used as a way of bringing together his whole pathology, of 'summing up the troubles of which he complained'.[41] Freud acknowledged the central importance of the caul, but he interpreted it only in one context, ignoring its association with the animal and the fragile nature of civilisation.

THE FURRY PHALLUS

Freud states that everything seemed to confirm the possibility of castration although the Wolf Man did not yet fear it for himself. When he began to play with his penis in front of his Nanya she reprimanded him and said he would 'get a "wound" in the place' of his penis.[42] His Nanya, it appears, was (perversely) happy to touch his anus and show him how to manually evacuate his bowels but she was not at all happy with genital play. Not long after the threat from his Nanya, he observed his sister and a friend urinating. According to Freud: 'He rejected the idea that he saw before him a confirmation of the wound with which his Nanya had threatened him and explained to himself that this was the girls' "front bottom"'.[43]

Later, he discovered that farm animals were neutered. He learnt the names (stallion, gelding) by which horses were called, depending upon whether they still retained their sexual organs. He recalled that his father had once beaten a snake with a stick, which made the governess say that sugar sticks were 'pieces of chopped-up snakes'.[44] After his Nanya's rejection, he gave up masturbation but began to behave sadistically towards small animals as well as developing masochistic fantasies of being 'beaten on the penis'.[45] He had become preoccupied with the penis and its various functions.

Although Freud did not say so, it seems most likely that during this period the little Wolf Man found it increasingly difficult to distinguish between the human penis and animal tail. This confusion would have arisen in relation to castration and the fact that in humans the male lost his penis as a result of castration (a wound took the place of the penis), whereas in the fairy stories the wolf is punished by losing its bushy tail. Were the penis and the tail the same thing? In the story 'Reynard the Fox', the wolf used his tail as bait when fishing and his tail was 'broken off in the ice'.[46] In the story 'The Tailor and the Wolves', the tailor pulled off the wolf's tail and the tail-less creature ran away in terror. Perhaps he had to have a wound in order to become a wolf–man. Certainly the wolves' bushy tails play a dominant role in his nightmare. The Wolf Man describes the wolves as more like foxes or sheep dogs because they had 'big tails like foxes' and 'ears pricked like dogs'. Freud interpreted the fox tails of the wolves in the tree as a 'compensation' for the 'tail-lessness' of the wolves in the fairy story of the tailor and the wolves. The Wolf Man said the nightmare reminded him of this story. Yet these wolves have not had their tails docked. The tailfullness of the white wolves may have been just as terrifying to the little boy as tail-lessness. The nightmare in fact contains animal images associated with fullness—the 'big tails' and 'pricked ears'. Tailfullness suggests the full horror of the potent wolf. If the Wolf Man confused penis and tail, this would have affected his response to the primal scene—if this indeed was the origin of his neurosis.

The father's possible possession of an imaginary furry wolf phallus in the primal scene has a number of important consequences for understanding the little Wolf Man's anxieties. Firstly, it offers the boy further evidence for the existence of the werewolf. Perhaps the Wolf Man thought that his own father was also able to transform into an actual wolf. Freud does describe both the father and mother as wolves during the sex act: 'His mother took the part of the castrated wolf, which let the others climb upon it; his father took the part of the wolf that climbed.'[47] Secondly, it offers another reason as to why the little boy might have been terrified of the wolves of his nightmare. If his father was a wolf, then having sex with the father, which Freud argued he strongly desired, became a much more daunting prospect. It involved not only adopting a passive position but also becoming the recipient of an animal penis. He no doubt witnessed many scenes of animal mating on the estate; in fact the boy's first glimpse of animal mating (horses, dogs, sheep)—that is, his first sight of an (animal) primal scene—would have been coitus *a tergo*, as Freud points out. Throughout his life his sexual pleasure retained its anal character. According to Freud 'to copulate except from behind gave him scarcely any enjoyment'.[48]

It is possible that the boy's belief that he might change into a wolf–man was strengthened by a confusion, in his young mind, over the difference, if any, between the man's penis and the wolf's furry tail. He may even have thought women also possessed a furry wolf's tail. A puzzling comment made by his English governess may have confirmed for the young Wolf Man that men and women were the same. He recalled that once, when she was walking on the estate with the children and she was ahead of them, she called out: 'Do look at my little tail!'[49] The comment makes little sense on its own (perhaps she was wearing a fur of some kind) but Freud interprets it to signify castration. Equally, her comments could suggest that she has a 'tail' even if only a little one. When the wolf dressed as granny, 'she' also possessed a tail.

Finally, it is possible that the young Wolf Man had constructed a primal phantasy of origins in which the sex of the animal participants was not clearly delineated. As a child he was intrigued by this issue. When he heard the stories 'Little Red Riding Hood' and 'The Seven Little Goats' he learnt that the children who had been eaten by the wolf were later taken out of the wolf's body. This made him wonder whether the wolf was female. Or could men/male wolves have children in their stomachs? Freud states that at the time when the young man asked these questions he had not yet developed his wolf phobia.

As Austrian psychoanalyst Melanie Klein claimed, the young Wolf Man's wolf phobia, which Freud interpreted as a fear of his father, does not necessarily have to be read in terms of the boy's fear of being castrated but could be seen as part of primary anxiety.[50] As I have argued, his phobia may well have resulted from a culmination of uncanny events and superstitious beliefs about changing into a wolf combined with a fear of his father-as-wolf, brought about by a confusion over the animal phallus and penis, which could be male or female. Since in fairy stories the wolf's tail is castrated and in reality his Nanya said his penis would be castrated, the young boy may well have drawn an equation between the wolf's furry tail and the penis. This confusion would have led him to see his father as a wolf/animal, when engaged in coitus with his mother—an impression intensified by a real/imaginary scene of coitus *a tergo*. Hence the terror created by his nightmare of the wolves. His animal phobia was not restricted to wolves. He also recalled that one night he had dreamt that his new tutor had metamorphosed into a lion and that it 'came towards his bed roaring loudly and in the posture of the wolf in the picture' with which his sister had terrified him.[51] In addition his Latin teacher, of whom he had a 'paralysing fear', was called Wolf. It seems that he had a generalised fear of human-into-beast metamorphosis, with strong focus on transformation into a werewolf.

In agreement with Klein, Otto Rank has argued that Freud overemphasised the Wolf Man's castration anxiety, focusing on his father as wolf-father, while neglecting his fear of being devoured by the wolf-mother. Freud assumed that the wolves in the boy's nightmare were male, but they could equally have been female. Given that the young Wolf Man's earliest fears were fears of being devoured by wolves (as happened in his fairy stories), they may have stemmed from archaic anxieties about incorporation by the mother. The formative figures in his early years were primarily women—his sister, Nanya, mother and governess. He understood that female wolves could devour people and keep them in their stomachs. It is possible that for him the idea of being castrated might not have been as terrifying as the thought of being devoured. Perhaps as much as being eaten, he feared being kept a prisoner in the wolf's belly. Was this how his rebirth as a werewolf would take place?

I agree with Klein and Rank that, in the Wolf Man's history, Freud overestimated the boy's castration anxiety. This may well have been at the expense of his fear of being devoured, re-incorporated by the mother. In my view, Freud's interpretation was also at the expense of another interpretation: the young Wolf Man's fear of 'becoming animal', of being summoned by the wolf pack, being eaten by a she-wolf and re-born as a wolf–man. Fear of becoming animal is also related to fear of animal sex.

THE WOLF MAN'S SISTER

The other major influence on the Wolf Man was his sister, Anna. She was two years older than her brother and according to Freud she was 'boyish and unmanageable', intellectually 'brilliant', with a strong interest in the natural sciences as well as poetry.[52] She exerted a profound influence on her brother, who adored her. She was her father's favourite—a fact of which her brother was exceedingly jealous. She was 'mentally far superior' to her male admirers. When she reached her twenties her outlook and behaviour changed. She began to suffer depression, felt she was not pretty enough and withdrew from society. Her brother, according to his own writings, was devastated when she committed suicide by drinking mercury—although when he recounted the story to Freud, the Wolf Man said he did not express any such feelings at the 'loss of the most dearly loved member of his family'.[53] Freud claimed the brother was both jealous of his sister and experienced 'incestuous love for her'.[54] The Wolf Man claimed that his choice of women throughout his life was based on their resemblance to his beloved sister.

His love for Anna appeared to have been repressed in analysis, as is evident in relation to the episode of the poet's grave. Several months after Anna's death, the Wolf Man visited the countryside where she died. Once there he sought out the grave not of his sister but of a poet whose work he loved. Freud writes that he 'shed bitter tears upon his grave'.[55] Initially, the Wolf Man was puzzled by this as the poet had died a long time before; then he recalled that his father used to compare the poetry of his sister with that of the poet. In addition, he had adopted the practice of saying that his sister had shot herself. It was the poet who had been shot when fighting a duel. Gradually, the Wolf Man accepted that Anna had died of poison.

The Wolf Man recalls that when he was young (three and a quarter years) his sister seduced him by fondling his penis. Freud's account of this recollection is crucial to an understanding of Anna's own primal scene. His sister had taken hold of his penis and played with it, at the same time telling him incomprehensible stories about his Nanya, as though by way of explanation. His Nanya, she said, used to do the same thing with all kinds of people—for instance, with the gardener, whom she used to stand on his head before taking hold of his genitals.[56]

Freud argues that Anna's seduction of her brother was not a phantasy; this was made clear by the Wolf Man's memory of a later event in which a cousin who was ten years older told him that he 'very well remembered what a forward and sensual little thing she [his sister] had been: once, when she was a child of four or five, she had sat on his lap and opened his trousers to take hold of his penis'.[57] On the basis of the older cousin's recollections, it seems clear that Anna was sexually abused as a child. How would a child of about five years of age learn how to give an adult male pleasure? It would appear that a male, possibly her father, with whom she was very close, had taught her how to open a man's fly, take out his penis and play with it. Being naturally precocious for her age, as is evident in her educational achievements, she applied what she had been taught to other males—her brother and cousin. Sexual abuse in childhood—perhaps lasting into puberty in Anna's case—would also explain why she later experienced severe depression and committed suicide. Abuse is invariably accompanied by strong feelings of guilt and a sense of worthlessness.

The most puzzling aspect of Anna's behaviour is her reference to the fact that her Nanya used to 'stand the gardener on his head, and then take hold of his genitals'. The only explanation for this bizarre scene is that it is a phantasy covering over a primal scene—a fact that Freud did consider. Perhaps it is also a description of coitus *a tergo* as described by a young child who either was part of, or witnessed, such a scene. When Freud described what the infant Wolf Man was supposed to have witnessed at age eighteen months, he described a similar physical configuration between the father and mother: 'By the latter I mean the postures which he saw his parents adopt—the man upright, and the woman bent down like an animal'.[58] If the man is standing fully upright then the woman is forced downwards, her buttocks raised up high, her shoulders and head descending downwards to the ground. To a young girl this would appear as if she were 'standing on her head'. While she adopted this posture, the man was able to 'take hold of [her] genitals'. The only difference is that Anna changes the roles; she places Nanya in the role of the dominant partner and the gardener in the submissive role. This is perfectly understandable. It is Anna's way of imagining herself, as a woman, in the dominant position. If her father (or another male) was sexually abusing her, placing her in the role of passive victim, then she no doubt yearned to adopt the dominant role by identifying with her Nanya and subjecting the man to her power. Perhaps she played the game with her brother when she seduced him.

*We cannot fail to be struck by the idea that perhaps the sister,
at a similar tender age, also witnessed the same scene as was
observed by her brother later on and that it was this that had
suggested to her the notion about 'standing people on their
heads' during the sexual act.*[59]

Towards the end of the case history, Freud briefly considers the
possibility that Anna might have also witnessed her parents
engaged in scene of coitus *a tergo*. He recalls Anna's remark to
her brother that the old nurse stood the gardener on his head
and played with his genitals. Astonishingly, Freud then states
that this 'hypothesis would also give us a hint of the reason for
her own sexual precocity'. Nowhere does he raise the possibility
that Anna's precocity may have resulted from her own abuse in
childhood.

Freud's definition of the primal scene as one of parental
seduction does tie in with a study by Nicholas Abraham and
Maria Torok, who argue that a close analysis of the Wolf Man's
unconscious speech reveals that what the little boy actually witnessed was the father's seduction of his beloved sister: his 'sister
as seduced by the father and trying to repeat the same scene with
her brother'.[60] Nor does Freud reinterpret Anna's aggressive
behaviour towards her brother, when she frightened him with
the wolf picture, as an attempt to work through/replay her own
possible abuse. Perhaps she was also alluding to the belief that he
was destined to become a wolf himself. Perhaps she was referring
to the upright male wolf she had encountered, who had sex with
her in the way of animals. Instead Freud sees this episode only in
terms of its effects on her brother. In his view, the boy may well
have associated the postures of the wolf 'standing upright' with
the upright father, standing over the woman bent down. While
this may well be true, it is also most probable that Anna was
frightening her brother with the image of the upright phallic
wolf ('ears pricked', 'claws stretched') striding purposefully
towards the viewer. This is the wolf coming to seduce you. This

is the wolf coming to take you away, to gobble you up inside where you will be turned into a wolf.

It seems clear that the Wolf Man did associate his sister with the wolf. As I have mentioned, almost at the close of the analysis with Freud, the Wolf Man recalled that he had been born with a caul. In Freud's view the caul was associated with the veil of which the Wolf Man had spoken in relation to his enemas. The associations between caul, veil, butterflies and enemas are particularly uncanny. Freud stated that he referred to this veil in a manner that signified something 'elusive, as a feeling of twilight, "ténèbres", and of other impalpable things'.[61] Freud found that their attempts to interpret this veil 'progressed with as much difficulty as we met with in clearing up his fear of the butterfly'.[62] The boy described his fear of the butterfly as uncanny, which suggests something uncanny about the veil too. Anna wore a white nightdress which her brother described as veils that he tried to tear apart—presumably to see her sex. He related to Freud the content of some of his early dreams: 'It was as though ... after her bath ... he had tried ... to undress his sister ... to tear off her coverings ... or veils—and so on'.[63] The veil haunted him for the rest of his life. He had told Freud that 'the world ... was hidden from him by a veil' and that this veil was torn only in one situation—that is, 'when he passed a motion through his anus' administered by a man servant, after which he 'then felt well again and for a very short while he saw the world clearly'.[64] This event is essentially similar to an act of coitus a tergo that he may have enacted—even as a game—with his sister. Perhaps he saw the 'world clearly' through the torn veil because the ritual with his servant reawakened memories of Anna who wore a nightdress of veils.

Freud interpreted this phantasy as the boy's attempt to rescue his self-esteem (after his seduction) and play an aggressive role in relation to his sister by trying 'to see his sister undressed'.[65] Obviously he was also trying to see her body and her genitals in order to determine whether she was different, but it was like trying to look through a veil which he tried to 'tear off'. Perhaps he wanted to see whether she possessed a penis/tail. Given that he was confused about the distinction between penis and tail he may well have imagined that his sister had a penis/tail. Perhaps she was also destined to become a wolf. If woman was the one who stood upright (in Anna's primal phantasy) and man was bent over, then she may well have possessed the animal phallus. Is this why he, throughout his life, preferred coitus *a tergo*? This preference was determined not by having witnessed such a scene between his father and mother, with the father as the standing wolf, but by having imagined/experienced such a scene with his sister (or Nanya) in this role. The Wolf Man himself maintained in his own writings that it was seduction by his sister that was at the heart of his neurosis.[66] Or perhaps in his fantasy life, the sex of the upright wolf oscillated between male and female. He could become an upright wolf–man—except during sex when he was on all fours, like his mother. On some occasions, with servant girls, he could be upright just as his Nanya/Anna was when she 'stood the gardener on his head' and fondled his genitals. In fact throughout his life he could only fall in love with servant girls who resembled Anna and with whom he had coitus *a tergo*. When the veil was torn, the primal uncanny inserted itself into the Wolf Man's conscious mind, terrifying him with fears of becoming animal, becoming anal and becoming woman. These uncanny fears also appeared to offer a source of fantasy for his most unorthodox sex life.

Freud covered over, or 'veiled', these two important areas—woman and the animal—because they weakened his own theory that the paternal castrator is the key figure in the origin and evolution of civilisation. Freud downplayed or repressed the key roles played by woman and the wolf to construct a narrative about the paternal castrator. Repression of the feminine and natural worlds is also central to the perpetuation of patriarchal civilisation. However, the return of these repressed formations through the agency of the primal uncanny points to the potentially subversive nature of monstrosity and its uncanny representation in the cinema, an exceptionally popular vehicle for the representation of werewolf tales—as discussed in the following chapter. These tales are subversive in that they point to the fragile boundary between nature and civilisation, animal and human. They also point to the lure of the uncanny; the desire of the human to return to its primitive origins, which finds its strongest expression in folklore, popular culture, dreams and nightmares. Freud focused too much on his own phantasy of the castrating paternal figure and not enough on his fearful folkloric son, the wolf–man in sheep's clothing.

6

FEAR OF FUR:
BESTIALITY AND
THE UNCANNY
SKIN MONSTER

Freud proposes that 'anything that is uncanny ... becomes
subject to taboo' and goes on to inscribe cannibalism at the
origin of human history.

NICHOLAS ROYLE[1]

The wolf–man, or werewolf, is the uncanny skin monster
of myth and legend. He is a 'versipellous', that is a 'skin
changer', a creature who is able to turn his skin inside out as he
metamorphoses from human to animal. This is particularly
uncanny in that almost 'nothing'—the thinnest of membranes
—separates the inside from the outside of the body. The inside
is in fact its own outside, and vice versa; hence the familiar
human skin is suddenly rendered unfamiliar as the wolf–man
gives birth to himself, his animal hairs bursting through and
spreading over his entire body. Kristeva described the skin as 'a
fragile container' whose function is to preserve a border between
inside and outside in order to maintain a clean and proper body.[2]
The werewolf's body is too unstable to guarantee the classical,
coherent physicality required by the symbolic order. In pointing
to the boundary between human and animal, the werewolf
brings to light what should have remained hidden: the absolute
fragility of that border. The werewolf is monstrous precisely
because its skin can no longer guarantee the border between

inside and outside. In addition, once the man becomes wolf, he gives in to that desire which should have been surmounted—cannibalism.

Possibly the most ubiquitous of all human beasts, the werewolf is found in the majority of cultures of the world; its name exists in all Indo-European languages, from the Danish *var-ulf* and the German *Wahrwolffe* to the French *loup-garou*. The werewolf historically has always assumed both female and male forms. In her discussion of the history of the werewolf, Barbara Walker points out that the werewolf was a spirit–wolf originally associated with pagan religions.[3] Pagan belief held that metamorphosis into a werewolf took place on the full moon. The idea of shape-changing is probably as old as human consciousness and almost always involves an animal that is the totem of a particular area; the wolf is one of the most common animal forms assumed by the human. According to Walker, early peoples would have donned wolf skins to assume its magical powers and worn wolves' teeth for healing amulets. In some regions a newborn child would be symbolically passed through the skin of a wolf so it could be said the infant was born of a she-wolf. Walker refers to 'an old Russian charm, to be spoken by one who wished to invoke the Moon-goddess and become a werewolf'.[4] Belief in the werewolf was central to the classical world in which people worshipped gods in wolf form. Apollo Lycaeus or 'wolfish Apollo' gave his name to 'lycanthropy', the belief that a human can change into a wolf. The Lupercalia is an ancient Festival of Lupa, the she-wolf. Gradually the term 'werewolf' changed from denoting a spiritual or sacred creature to an outlaw. With the rise of Christianity and the banning of pagan religions, the term 'werewolf' was frequently used to describe opponents of Christianity. During the Inquisition, those accused of werewolfism, which included the eating of children, suffered terrible tortures until they had no choice but to admit to the most terrible crimes, including murder and cannibalism.

The pagan belief in the spirit–wolf is related to, but different from, the myth of the werewolf which was strengthened by the behaviour of men, known as lycanthropes, who actually believed they were able to transform into wolves, at which point they developed a craving for raw meat (not necessarily human), and even exhibited wolf-like behaviour such as running on all fours. Plato wrote about the lycanthrope and in the sixteenth century the German woodcut artist Lucus Cranach created an extremely vivid image of a lycanthrope running with a baby in its mouth. There are still people in this century who, according to psychological case studies, believe they are werewolves.[5] If the werewolf myth enjoyed something of a renaissance at the close of the nineteenth century in the pages of popular Gothic fiction, it came into its own in the next century in the cinema. The modern world may no longer believe in werewolves, but these fabulous creatures continue to excite the human imagination, finding expression in popular culture through fantasy fiction, song and film.

As ancient as the vampire, the werewolf myth similarly sets out certain defining characteristics. The creature stalks the earth at night, particularly on the full moon, and also spreads his contagion by biting. In certain instances the werewolf can change into a vampire. By night the werewolf runs with the pack; the only thing that marks him as different is that he is tail-less. By day the werewolf transforms back into human form but the wound remains. The creature can be killed by fire or a silver bullet. One of the main features of lycanthropy is that the creature is possessed by a terrible fury.

The film that established the werewolf genre was George Waggner's 1941 classic The Wolf Man. It also laid down the conventions that were to become central to the genre. One of the horror film's most brutal creatures, the wolf–man, like King Kong, at first inspires dread. Savage and snarling, the classic werewolf is almost always male, although post-modern werewolf films such as Ginger Snaps (John Fawcett, 2000) and Ginger Snaps Back (Grant Harvey, 2004) star a young female werewolf. Regardless of which film one considers—from The Wolf Man to An American Werewolf in London or Wolf—the wolf–man, like Kong, is both a source of horror and sympathy. This is because he has no desire to become a wolf; he is almost always an innocent figure who has been attacked and bitten by a werewolf. Werewolf films almost always represent the man about to metamorphose as a helpless victim of his own body. Because the creature's bite carries with it the inescapable taint of werewolfism, the new victim is similarly destined to become a werewolf. Under the light of the full moon, the werewolf is compelled to hunt his human prey and eat flesh in order to survive. When, by light of day, the wolf metamorphoses back into his human form, he remains cognisant of his evil deeds and bestial nature but is unable to do anything to change his fate. He clearly represents the modern view that man is a creature divided against himself. When returned to human form, however, he often retains signs of his alterations: his body is more hirsute or his teeth assume a canine shape. The boundary between human and animal becomes more blurred as the narrative progresses. He can only free himself from further killings through a ritualised death, which is almost always inflicted by a

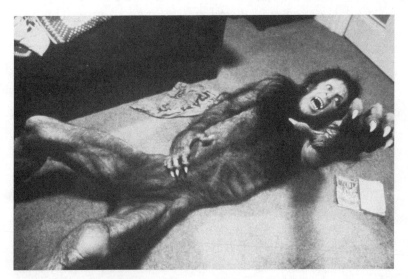

Man as helpless victim of his own body—An American Werewolf in London, *1981*
(*Polygram/Universal/The Kobal Collection*)

weapon made from silver, a knife or bullet. It is only through the sacrifice of his life that the tormented wolf–man of the classic films can achieve redemption.

In the early Hollywood versions of the werewolf story, such as *The Wolf Man* (1941), the creature was literally a wolf–man— that is, he stood upright and, because of censorship restrictions, continued to wear clothing. Forty years later the revolution in cinematic special effects and altered censorship laws changed this situation. In *An American Werewolf in London* (1981), the male victim transforms completely into a wolf. The film's most horrific and uncanny scene is where the audience sees for the first time, and in convincing and bone-crunching detail, the actual transformation of man into beast. The final instant before the complete transformation is the most uncanny; when the meta-morphosis is complete the tension between the familiar and unfamiliar dissipates—there is nothing uncanny about his wolverine form. Historically, the cinema has represented the werewolf as a sympathetic beast who is horrified by his fate; in more recent films, such as *The Howling* (Joe Dante, 1981) and *Wolf* (1994), the werewolf embraces his new identity. This new perspective points to a change in the meaning and function of the primal uncanny.

THE PRIMAL UNCANNY AND THE ANIMAL

The werewolf's versipellous nature is particularly confronting in representations of male monstrosity because the male body signifies and upholds the symbolic order. Unlike the feminine maternal body, the male has not been as closely assimilated through the workings of patriarchal ideology to nature and the animal. The male body does not secrete blood in menstruation, change shape in pregnancy or eject bodily matter during birth. The symbolic male body is discrete, firm, closed and classical. Woman's body, by contrast, is fluid, open and malleable. There is a union between mother and nature unknown to the male, who is meant to signify the clean and proper body of the symbolic order where shame and guilt come into play. According to Kristeva:

> *The abject confronts us, on the one hand, with those fragile states where man strays on the territories of animal. Thus, by way of abjection, primitive societies have marked out a precise area of their culture in order to remove it from the threatening world of animals or animalism, which were imagined as representatives of sex and murder.*[6]

The area of folklore that deals with the werewolf creates a familiar space in which to confront those territories where man and animal meet. The metamorphosis of man into wolf creates a strange, *unheimlich* creature, placing him on the side of woman and nature. Through the figure of the wolf–man, the irruption of the uncanny threatens identity and the familiar and known structures of the civilised male body and self. The wolf–man's transformations create an uncanny sense of otherness poised in the space between inside and outside. The wolf–man is no longer a speaking subject; he is a cannibalistic man/beast and his metamorphosis points to the frailty of the symbolic order. The wolf–man's association with the primal uncanny, the unstable feminine body, nature and death, renders his hybrid nature even more monstrous. His cannibalism makes him one of the most primitive and savage of male monsters. That such a creature is defined as a wolf–man rather than a wolf is crucial because the concept is intended to point to the intricate relationship that exists between man and nature, city and forest, life and death.

In 'Totem and Taboo' (1912–13) Freud states that 'anything that is uncanny ... becomes subject to taboo'.[7] In this essay, he locates cannibalism as the founding ritual of civilisation. Primitive belief systems held that by 'incorporating parts of the person's body through the act of eating, one at the same time acquires the qualities possessed by him'.[8] According to Freud, 'cannibal savages' killed and ate their father and 'in the act of devouring him they accomplished their identification with him, and each one of them acquired a portion of his strength'.[9] In Freud's view, 'The totem meal, which is perhaps mankind's earliest festival, would thus be a repetition of a commemoration of this memorable and criminal deed, which was the beginning of so many things of social organisation, of moral restrictions and of religion.'[10]

Freud's anthropological interpretation of the totem meal resonates with the cannibalistic desire of the wolf–man. In almost all werewolf films, the man who changes into a wolf acquires new powers. The genre seems to argue that humanity lost something important in the processes of evolution—that is, the wild and savage part of human nature. The individual who becomes a werewolf hunts and eats human flesh. The lost wildness is thus restored. At the same time, the wolf–man copulates with renewed vigour and in the manner of animals. It could be argued that the wolf–man's cannibalistic attacks represent a folkloric reworking of the totem meal; his metamorphosis and flesh-eating endow him with new animal powers. These are not attained through the eating of a powerful figure, as in the totem meal, but through the act of metamorphosis, of becoming animal. Through metamorphosis and cannibalism, the wolf–man points to 'the instability of the paternal metaphor'[11] and the failure of civilisation. Hence, in traditional film narratives the wolf–man is hunted down and killed. Thus the cannibal meal of the wolf–man myth symbolises a pact not with civilisation but with nature and wilderness.

As a being that ought to have remained secret and hidden but has come to light, the werewolf fulfils the basic condition of the uncanny. Its transformation—effectively an uncovering—challenges the symbolic order because it suggests that the animal is essential to the definition of what constitutes the human. The werewolf is man-as-animal and as such he is also a cannibal–perpetrator of an ancient totemistic ritual of incorporation. A primal brutal creature, he exhibits an *unheimlich* nature that can never be rendered *heimlich*.

Freud also associated cannibalism with sexual desire. In 'The Wolf Man' he writes: 'I have been driven to regard as the earliest recognisable sexual organisation the so-called "cannibalistic" or "oral phase"'.[12] Thus, cannibalism is characteristic of psycho-sexual development. German psychoanalyst Karl Abraham later divided the oral stage into two phases—'a preambivalent sucking phase and an ambivalent biting phase'—in which Abraham regarded the second as cannibalistic.[13] Insofar as biting signifies a sexually pleasurable activity, it is associated with cannibalism. In films such as *Wolf*, the wolf–man's bite when lavished on his female lover takes on these characteristics. The psycho-sexual dimensions of werewolfism may help to explain the almost universal existence of the myth and its popularity in contemporary cinema in relation to films such as *The Silence of the Lambs* (Jonathan Demme, 1991) and *Hannibal* (Ridley Scott, 2001), which star human cannibals, not wolf–men, as figures of monstrosity.

Nicholas Royle correctly points out that 'Nowhere in his essay, "The Uncanny", does Freud explicitly speak of the uncanniness of cannibalism'.[14] This does not mean, however, that the uncanny is not present. Royle directs our attention towards the image of the sandman, who robs children of their eyes, which he feeds to his own children. Freud interpreted the terror associated with the loss of one's eyes as a fear of castration. Royle refers to the passage where the sandman seizes the boy, Nathaniel, who is narrating this episode. The sandman, although monstrous, is still 'some sort of man'. Nathaniel's description is suggestive of cannibalism—there are references to Nathaniel as a 'little beast', the sandman's teeth, the hearth with its licking flames, the monster's desire to tear out the boy's eyes as food for his own children. Royle suggests that 'fear of blindness', which Freud located as central to his essay on the uncanny, may well have 'something to do with a cannibalistic terror and desire'. 'Doesn't the sandman evoke an uncanny trace or tang of cannibalism right from the start?'[15] The werewolf myth places cannibalism at its heart.

Italian philosopher Giorgio Agamben writes that the concept of the werewolf signifies 'a threshold of indistinction and of passage between animal and man, *physis* and *nomos*, exclusion and inclusion'. The wolf–man is an uncanny hybrid who 'is precisely neither man nor beast, and who dwells paradoxically within both while belonging to neither'.[16] He haunts what Cixous has termed 'the *between*' spaces of the uncanny. His cannibalism signifies an attack on the meaning of civilisation itself. In his discussion of the *homer sacer*, Agamben argues that the historical figures of the outlaw and exile (the man banned from the city) relates to the modern understanding of the werewolf.

> *What had to remain in the collective unconscious as a monstrous hybrid of human and animal, divided between the forest and the city—the werewolf—is, therefore, in its origin the figure of the man who has been banned from the city.*[17]

The modern view in turn raises the question of nature. The Hobbesian 'state of nature ... is not a real epoch chronologically prior to the foundation of the City but a principle internal to the city'.[18] The law has drawn upon this principle—the lack of distinction between man and animal—in its treatment of the outlaw. He refers to Edward the Confessor, who in the eleventh century defined a bandit as a '*wulfesheud*' (a wolf's head) and in assimilating him to the werewolf, decreed that he would bear 'a wolf's head from the day of his expulsion'.[19] In classic werewolf films such as *The Wolf Man*, however, narrative interest lies elsewhere. Although werewolf tales almost always end with the death/expulsion of the monster, the focus is on his existence within the city or town and on the nature of the threat he offers from within.

In my view, this 'principle', which is internal to the city, relates directly to the primal uncanny. The eruption of werewolfism is not a simple case of a return of the repressed—that is, man's desire to express his/her animal urges which have been worn down by the city—but, rather, the wolf–man signifies those indeterminate, uncanny animal spaces necessary to the creation and definition of their opposite: the familiar, civilised human city. The wolf–man does not leave the town or city to live in exile in the forest; he is compelled to live as an exile within the city where he commits the crime of cannibalism. Thus he engages in a modern reworking of murder and the totem meal which celebrates not the emergence of civilisation but its end.

In the cinema, the individual bitten by a werewolf has no choice but to become an outlaw. The mark of the wolf, the shedding of blood, initiates a transformation ritual whereby the insider becomes an outsider, released from the dictates of the law for the period of the transformation. The wolf–man is free to murder, eat flesh and spill human blood. A number of films about the wolf–man explore the relationship between these motifs: human and animal, city and forest, exclusion and inclusion. The re-telling of this narrative in the cinema has the mythic function of opening up to view the uncanny unfamiliar spaces of the city in order to re-establish and preserve the familiar city.

In contemporary versions of the werewolf film, such as Nichols's *Wolf*, the wolf–man in the end is not captured and killed; he is able to live 'in a state of nature' within the city. This suggests that the city is under threat from within; there is no suggestion that the threat will be brought under control or the city will be saved. Furthermore, the final image is of Lupa, the she-wolf, whose uncanny human/animal eyes glitter with possibilities while also pointing to woman as the new outlaw of the post-modern city. This has recently been reinforced by the popularity of the *Ginger Snaps* films in which Ginger metamorphoses into a wolf upon her menarche. The implication here is that the city depends on the free play of its savage uncanny energies in order to survive and that these energies are female and animal. If the origin of the werewolf is the outlaw, the exile, who was once banned from the city, it is relevant to pursue the contemporary image of the werewolf in order to determine what it is about this monstrous hybrid that threatens the modern city —its values and laws.

Intimately related to concepts of homely and unhomely, the uncanny has become, according to Anthony Vidler, 'a metaphor for a fundamentally unlivable modern condition'.[20] Vidler is particularly concerned with issues of war, dispossession and homelessness. 'Estrangement and unhomeliness have emerged as the intellectual watchword of our [the twentieth] century, given periodic material and political force by the resurgence of homelessness itself, a homelessness generated sometimes by war, sometimes by the unequal distribution of wealth.'[21] The werewolf lives within the city but its animal identity means it too is estranged from the city which, for the wolf, has become an uncanny space both *heimlich* yet *unheimlich*. The film *Wolfen* (Michael Wadleigh, 1981) portrays the wolves as having an uncannily close relationship to the American Indians. A native elder explains that the great hunters, Indian and wolf, were forced to flee into the depth of the cities. 'The smartest went underground into the new wilderness.' Represented as noble animals, the wolves exist in opposition to the modern city. 'In their eyes, you are the savage' says the elder. 'You got technology but have lost your senses.'

Werewolf films explore those things the city needs to draw from the primal uncanny in order to preserve itself. The fact that the city also replenishes itself through the uncanny signifies a change in the way in which the uncanny is viewed in the werewolf film. In almost all werewolf films, the creature's desire, its ravenous appetite for flesh and blood, also signifies animal sex, which is represented as uncanny in its representation of human desire as totemic and bestial.

BESTIALITY

All human cultures have myths and legends about beast men and beast women that explore the taboo subject of bestiality. The gods of the classical pantheon were forever changing into animal form in order to seduce unwitting maidens. Zeus metamorphosed into a bull to trap Europa, who instantly fell in love with him, and into a swan in order to mate with the beautiful Leda. The infant founders of Rome, Romulus and Remus, were suckled by a she-wolf. The medieval bestiary argued for an exceedingly close relationship between human and animal in its allocation of specific animals to match their human counterparts. Victorian literature, in particular, acknowledged the power of the beast. As well as Coleridge's reference to 'woman wailing for her demon lover' in his famous poem 'Kubla Khan', Catherine in Emily Bronte's *Wuthering Heights* describes Heathcliff, the passion of her life, as a 'fierce, pitiless, wolfish man'; and Robert Browning's 'The Ring and the Book' states the problem directly: 'Let me turn wolf, be whole, and state, for once/Wallow in what is now a wolfishness/Coerced too much by the humanity/That's half of me as well!'

By the turn of the century, with Freud's famous case study 'The Wolf Man', the beast man was well on its way to becoming an iconic figure. Since their inception at the beginning of the twentieth century, film narratives have explored bestial desires through a range of beast men including the wolf–man, Count Dracula, Tarzan, Dr Jekyll and Mr Hyde, King Kong and the beast people of the *Island of Dr Moreau* films. A number of other modern cult heroes such as Spiderman and Catwoman are a human/creature hybrid whose parentage is rarely raised, but nonetheless lends support to the ancient belief that an injection of the animal into the human provides extra strength and even magical powers. Tim Burton's recent remake of *The Planet of the Apes* (2001) breaks with the original of the same name, made in 1968, by suggesting a sexual attraction between a simian and a human male. Nagisa Oshima's *Max My Love* (1986) goes even further; in this surreal comedy of manners, the female star, Charlotte Rampling, has an affair with a chimpanzee, Max, who in many ways is more civilised than his bourgeois human counterparts.

The film that was possibly the first to openly explore the topic of bestiality was the 1933 classic *King Kong* (Merian C.

Cooper). The conventional interpretation of the movie is that it is a love story, a re-working of 'Beauty and the Beast', a fairy story much loved by the Surrealists and made into a film by Jean Cocteau. Fascinated by the theme of *l'amour fou*, or mad love, the Surrealists adored *King Kong*. Writing in 1962, Jean Ferry, in justifying the film's eroticism, said:

> in the last analysis why does King Kong carry off this white woman instead of devouring her, why does he tear off her clothes then sniff their perfume, why does he defend her against the other monsters, why does he pursue her when she is ravished by him … why does he let himself be gunned down by aeroplanes to keep her?[22]

The answer is, of course, that the beast has fallen in love with the woman and desires to mate with her and keep her to himself. The film suggests that a union between beauty and beast might be possible through the way it changes the scale and size of various images. 'One minute his hand is big enough to seize an underground train, the next it only goes around the torso of a woman we see waving her arms and legs about.'[23] The size of Kong's various limbs and appendages alters significantly throughout the narrative, suggesting a pattern of tumescence and detumescence which—at a conscious or unconscious level—may well convey to the audience the possibility of a mating between the diminutive beauty and the gigantic beast. Ferry was particularly drawn to the sense of the uncanny that pervaded *King Kong*. He said he loved its 'violent, oneiric power … its monstrous eroticism (the monster's unbridled love for the woman, cannibalism, human sacrifice) … the acute sensation of *unheimlich* with which the presence of automata and trickery imbues the whole film'.[24]

The most compelling source of the primal uncanny in *King Kong* is sexual in that the scene of passion is rendered unfamiliar by the replacement of man with animal, garden with jungle, skin with fur. The giant ape is then captured and brought into the city. It is as if the world's most modern city, New York, needed to conquer the world's most horrific and primal beast, King Kong, in order to confirm its dominance over nature. The city allows the beast to escape, thus ensuring that the city instead renews its contact with the horrifying primal uncanny, the hidden unfamiliar face of the city.

In terms of the concept of 'becoming animal' developed by French philosophers Gilles Deleuze and Felix Guattari, the wolf–man is continually in the process of transformation. 'What is real is the becoming itself.'[25] Metamorphosis is a persistent theme in myth, literature and the horror film, signifying a deep-seated anxiety over the definition of what it means to be male and human. In the twentieth century this anxiety focused on the rise and exponential growth of towns and cities and the concomitant destruction of nature. The definition of human is, more than ever, intimately bound up with the destruction of the natural and animal world. One interpretation is that the horror and fantasy film represents the wolf–man as a sympathetic monster precisely because he represents potent characteristics of the natural world that modern man is in danger of losing in his pursuit of progress. In the contemporary werewolf film these characteristics are represented in an excessive configuration of lust, potency and heightened sensual receptivity and sexual desire. While actual belief in werewolves and other creatures of the night might well have all but disappeared in the hard light of day, such beliefs continue to haunt the realm of popular culture, in particular the cinema. As with other beast men, the wolf–man signifies the ascendancy of nature and the ruin of classic patriarchal masculinity—a configuration that excludes woman, animal and nature. Hence the wolf–man is both ter-rifying yet immensely appealing. Yet, although the wolf–man remains the classic outlaw figure discussed earlier, he/she is now not forced to go into exile. Rather than forsake the city for the wilds and hiding out during the day, the wolf–man almost always remains close to towns or cities, where he unleashes his rein of terror from within. It is his urban nature that points to his symbolic function in setting out the uncanny spaces of the normally familiar town or city. If he is an exile he is in exile from *within* the city.

'THE WOLF MAN' (1941)

The Wolf Man is regarded as the definitive werewolf film; it achieved such remarkable box office success on its release that the wolf–man rapidly became an iconic figure wherever the film was screened.[26] So great was its success that Universal Studios immediately produced four follow-on versions, all starring Lon Chaney Jr as the doomed hero, Larry Talbot. Fully cognisant of censorship restrictions, scriptwriter Curt Siodmak tried to make it clear that the beast's attacks on women were not sexual, but there is no mistaking the wolf–man's inner animal passions. Siodmak's main achievement, however, was to humanise the legend, to make the werewolf a sympathetic figure. In this way he ensured that audiences would consciously or otherwise identify with the notion of the 'beast within', as they had with *King Kong*.

The story begins when Larry Talbot returns from America to his father's estate in Wales where he is to be trained by his dominating father, Sir John (Claude Rains), to eventually run Talbot Castle and its estates. Larry's brother, who was destined to take over the estate, has unexpectedly died. There is no mention throughout the film of Larry's mother. It soon becomes clear that Larry is particularly unsuited to the role—he is much more interested in his hobbies, such as looking at the stars, and in chasing pretty young girls. One of his first acts is to visit his father's astronomical observatory in the castle tower where he uses the telescope to seek out pretty women on the ground, not distant stars in the firmament. He is visibly stunned when he spies an attractive young woman (Evelyn Ankers) in the bedroom of her house in the village. Noticing her pretty earrings,

Larry later visits the village and discovers that the ground floor of her house is an antique shop. He meets the girl with the earrings, whose name is Gwen. She doesn't have a similar pair to sell, so Larry settles for a cane capped with a silver wolf's head carved inside a pentagram. Gwen explains to Larry that this is the mark of the werewolf who is able to see the sign of the pentagram imprinted on the palm of his next victim.

Larry is more interested in a date with Gwen than werewolf folklore, and he persuades her to accompany him to the nearby gypsy camp to have their fortunes read. She agrees but brings a girlfriend, Jenny, to keep Larry, the wolf, at bay. That night the fortune teller, Bela (Bela Lugosi), sees the sign of the pentagram in Jenny's hand and warns her of impending danger. She ignores his words and soon after is attacked by a werewolf. Dashing to the rescue, Larry attempts to beat off the wolf with his cane but is too late. In the ensuing struggle with the beast, Larry is bitten. Next morning Larry awakes to find the sign of the pentagram marked on his chest. Sir John tells him not to worry about the mark, adding that Bela's body has been discovered with Larry's silver-headed cane nearby. Larry's wound has by now mysteriously healed. From the opening scene, the narrative carefully delineates a series of spaces which increasingly become more and more unfamiliar and uncanny. These include the estate, the village, the gypsy camp and the woods. Having been bitten by the werewolf, Larry is to become the outlaw, the *unheimlich*, living within the *heimlich* civilised spaces of village and estate.

Larry decides to visit the renowned old gypsy lady, Queen Maleva (played by Madame Ouspenskaya of the Moscow Arts Theatre), who is the mother of Bela, the werewolf who bit Larry before Larry beat him to death with his silver-tipped cane. She inhabits the gypsy camp, which serves as a liminal space between the village and the woods. Queen Maleva is the female counterpart to Sir John: both are regal, both rule over their respective kingdoms, both have a dead son, and both call Larry their son. She knows the fate that awaits her new 'son'. She sends him on his way with the prophetic words: 'The way you walk is thorny through no fault of your own, but as the rain enters the soil, the river enters the sea, so tears run to a predestined end. Find peace for a moment my son'.

Maleva, understands fully the symbolism of the werewolf. The mark of the pentagram has an ancient history. The five-pointed star, a symbol of birth, appears to have been a central part of the female or pagan religions that pre-dated Christianity. It was worshipped by Pythagorean mystics who regarded it as the birth letter interwoven five times.[27] In Egypt the pentagram signified the underground womb.[28] The werewolf is a creature whose metamorphosis signifies birth and re-birth. The penta-gram is a birth symbol, as is the full moon. It is at the time of the full moon that man's blood undergoes the chemical changes necessary to transform him into the uncanny werewolf, com-pelling him to feast on the blood and flesh of humans.

Like the vampire, the werewolf is linked to the primal un-canny (woman, nature, death) through a web of ritual meanings. The wolf–man is a creature who literally gives birth to himself: his fur covers the inside of his skin. Thus, like woman, he carries the signs of nature within his body at all times. Like Dracula, the wolf–man is also associated with woman's menstrual cycle: the werewolf's transformations occur every twenty-eight days, according to the rhythms of the lunar calendar and the female menstrual cycle. Walter Evans also holds that the 'werewolf's blood attacks—which occur regularly every month—are certainly related to the menstrual cycle which suddenly and mysteriously commands the body of every adolescent girl.'[29] The werewolf is a feminised male monster, a queer creature aligned to the primal uncanny. Yet, strangely, the horror film almost always depicts the creature as male, despite the fact that myth and legend valourise the she-wolf, the beast who suckles Romulus and Remus and a number of infants, such as the wolf–boy, who are believed to have been nurtured by female wolves in the wild. The wolf–man is on the side of nature and woman, yet he is also a creature very much situated within the male symbolic. This is attested to by the horror with which he traditionally regards his metamorphoses. In some more recent examples of the genre (*The Howling, Wolf*), the male embraces his alignment with the primal uncanny.

The narrative of *The Wolf Man* has carefully drawn up a series of oppositions that separate the world of the father (Sir John) and the Mother (Queen Maleva). The former's domain is associated with man, civilisation, rationality, religion; the mother's world with woman, nature, superstition, paganism. Maleva is linked to the world of nature and the animal. Her son, Bela, is a werewolf and her new 'son', Larry, is also a werewolf. She rules over a world regulated by superstition, emotion, ritual and bloodshed. Significantly, Larry is drawn to her universe (stars, pentagrams, the gypsy camp, fortune-telling) rather than his father's world. The mysterious carnivalesque world of the gypsy camp signifies a place where rules are turned upside down and primitive, uncanny desires unleashed. This is a place of metamorphosis and change. The werewolf is a male monster whose animal desires seek liberation from repression through the feminised actions of bodily alteration and re-birth. He both resists yet is inevitably drawn to the world of animal transformations. Through these oppositions, the film depicts the normally hidden uncanny spaces that exist within the familiar, civilised world of village and estate. The male werewolf is the bearer of the forces of the primal uncanny that he carries between city and forest.

After leaving the gypsy camp and his new mother, Larry returns to his father's castle. That night his body undergoes a series of transformations: hair covers his face, his teeth change into fangs, his fingernails become claws, his nose changes to look like a wolf's muzzle, but unlike his 'brother', Bela, he does not drop to all fours or come to completely resemble a wolf. Larry is very much a wolf–man ready to hunt by the full moon. The next morning a set of incriminating wolf prints are found to lead from the castle to the body of a mutilated gravedigger and back to Larry's room. The following night the wolf–man is caught by a leg trap but rescued by Queen Maleva who strangely enough happened to be abroad in the dark hours. Next, Larry's worst fears are realised when he sees the sign of the pentagram on Gwen's hand. This is the prize the wolf–man seeks but the one that Larry cannot acknowledge. Larry entreats Sir John to tie him to a chair and lock him inside his bedroom. Whereas Larry believes in the reality of his metamorphosis, his father thinks that his son is suffering from the mental illness of lycanthropy. He tells Larry that all legends have some truth in them; the truth of the werewolf legend is that it offers an 'ancient explanation of the dual personality in all of us'. He says that lycanthropy explains 'the good and evil in everyman's soul. In this case evil takes the shape of an animal'. The doctor who attends Larry agrees: 'A man lost in the mazes of his mind may imagine he is anything'.

The representatives of the symbolic order (father, doctor) offer this as a rational 'explanation' of these irrational events, but the film (its emotional sympathies, narrative focus) suggests that Larry's metamorphosis is necessary to bring the rational civilised male world back in touch with the strange, interstitial, subversive workings of the primal uncanny. Rosemary Jackson argues: whatever is encountered in the uncanny realm, it is essentially an 'unconscious *projection*'.[30] Jackson defines this projection in relation to the self, the individual who refuses to recognise feelings and desires within him/herself. These are then projected onto something else, another person or an uncanny thing such as a ghost, a vampire or a werewolf. In addition, I would also argue that society or civilisation defines itself in relation to the primal uncanny, those *unheimlich* spaces submerged within the city whose existence is usually hidden but essential in order for the city to define itself as a friendly, *heimlich* place, a 'true' home and a refuge to its inhabitants. The function of the uncanny monster is to reveal that which is normally hidden, to bring the primal uncanny to light. The werewolf moves between human and animal, skin and fur, town and forest. As symbolised by its versipellous nature, the werewolf is an uncanny boundary monster that traverses borders, surfaces, limits and lines of demarcation.

The final scene takes place in woods that are engulfed by a thick swirling fog, suggesting the mysterious, barely understood workings of the unconscious mind. The fog also shrouds everything beneath within a heavy blanket, ensuring that the uncanny forest remains hidden from view. All of the key players are present: Sir John, who is searching for the wolf; Maleva, who has sensed the impending tragedy; Gwen, who—like all doomed heroines—is walking towards her fate; and Larry, who is following the dictates of his wild nature. Larry sees Gwen and rushes to her, but it is clear that his brutal embrace will tear her apart. Sir John leaps to her defence and savagely clubs the wolf–man, his son, to death. He dies in the arms of Maleva who says: 'Your suffering is over. You will find peace my son.' The policeman who arrives too late pronounces that Larry died while trying to protect Gwen from the wolf.

Werewolfism in the film is represented as a sign of man's direct lineage to nature and the uncanny primal animal. His versipellous powers point to the frailty of the symbolic order in the face of animal lust. While the censorship restrictions of the period would not permit direct expressions of an animalistic mating as we see in later werewolf films, the signs are there. Even the wolf's furry phallus is present through displacement. When Bela transforms into a wolf he becomes a werewolf complete with the animal's tail. When Larry transforms he becomes a wolf–man, without a visible tail, but nonetheless the association has already been made through the figure of Bela and the obvious symbolism of Larry's silver stick. What is most fascinating about the depiction of man as werewolf is that his transformation is represented in the context of feminine imagery and motifs (full moon, blood, re-birth) and in a feminised world (Queen Maleva's gypsy camp) as well as the feminine realm of Nature (Maleva rules over the forest) while his final shape as wolf is male. The father, Sir John, however, is helpless to save his son. In fact he is the one who kills his own son, perhaps unconsciously trying to re-establish his estate and its boundaries, the lines of his authority, which the wolf–man has eroded through his encounter with woman, the forest and the animal.

'AN AMERICAN WEREWOLF IN LONDON' (1981)

The versipellous nature of the wolf–man—that is, his amazing ability to change his skin and bring his furry inside to the outside—testifies to his close ties to the primal uncanny. The fact that his body lacks strong, discrete borders aligns him to woman and the abject and his animal self ties him to nature. Although werewolf films of the 1980s and 90s deviated from the structure of classic films such as *The Wolf Man* (1941), they still adhered to the basic conventions. Before the werewolf attack, there are signs that something is not quite right: a full moon, howling, a pentagram. Once the innocent man is bitten, it is only a matter of time—usually the morning after—before the first signs of his werewolfism appear.

In *An American Werewolf in London*, the mood is slightly teasing. A full-blooded horror film rather than a spoof, it has a stylish sense of wit. David Naughton plays David, an American student who is hiking with his friend Jack in northern England. The popular song 'Blue Moon' opens the film. A storm descends and they take refuge in a hotel, aptly called 'The Slaughtered Lamb', and notice a five-pointed star, or pentagram, on the wall. The locals send them on their way with a warning to 'beware of the moon, avoid the moors, and stick to the roads'. We know that an attack will occur that night—the signs are all there. Sure enough, the moors fill with the uncanny sound of howling and the full moon rises into the stormy sky.

The wolf attacks, killing Jack and wounding David, who wakes up in hospital. Sexually energised, he makes love to the nurse. He has terrible nightmares in which he sheds his clothes and hunts small animals in the forest where he devours them raw. Next, we see him urinating and he frightens another animal, a cat, which hisses and spits at him. The director, John Landis, introduces the first of a series of novel occurrences that upset the genre conventions. Jack appears as a ghost to warn David that the beast that attacked them was a werewolf and that he will become one on the next full moon. He will live in limbo until all werewolves are destroyed. With his skin hanging in pieces from his face and his skull bones on display, Jack presents a gruesome spectre. David's affair with the nurse blooms. Then, with the pop song 'Blue Moon' playing jauntily on the sound-track, the full moon rises and Jack's body begins its hideous transformation.

This is the first werewolf film to depict the transformation in such crystal clear, convincing detail. David's muscles seem to pop, his flesh pulsates into new shapes, bones crack and hair

Uncanny automata and monstrous eroticism in King Kong, *1933*
(RKO/The Kobal Collection)

sprouts. He develops a wolfish snout, terrible fangs and deadly claws. The film's makeup artist, Rick Baker, created a set of masks which were operated pneumatically, avoiding the need for stop-action filming or dissolves. Hence the metamorphosis appears seamless. The beast lying dormant just beneath the man's outer skin appears to burst forth in an uninterrupted motion and with terrible force. Man's skin can no longer guarantee the border between inside and outside. Abjection erupts from within. David then drops down on all fours and disappears into the night to hunt and kill. Eventually David, as werewolf, is killed by a rain of police bullets after he has engaged in an orgy of killings. In this film the werewolf also moves between carefully delineated geographical spaces: America and England, moors and towns, private and public spaces. The werewolf traverses these borders, bringing into the light the uncanny spaces of the familiar city.

The transformation scene is particularly uncanny. Landis's film has made visible the previously unseeable—in terms of the cinematic apparatus and in relation to the horrifying primal uncanniness of man changing into beast. The familiar landscape of the human body (smooth skin, erect body, even teeth, short nails) has become unfamiliar (rough, hair-covered skin, bent body, fangs and claws). Accompanying these changes are other alterations in relation to desire, sex, behaviour. With its sophis-ticated array of special effects technologies, film is perfectly suited to the production of the uncanny.

'THE HOWLING' (1981)

In *The Howling* werewolfism is also associated with perverse, erotic sexual desire. A major difference is that the wolf–man is no longer a lone killer; he is part of a group who live in the woods in a place known as The Colony. The narrative begins when a famous television reporter, Karen White (Dee Wallace-Stone), is sent by her psychiatrist, Dr Waggner (Patrick Macnee), to stay at The Colony to recover from trauma and memory loss. Karen is accompanied by her husband. She has became ill after being attacked by a man whom she had agreed to interview in an adult video store; she did not realise he was a werewolf. What she also does not know is that almost everyone at The Colony is a werewolf, including Dr Waggner who is named after the director of the 1941 classic *The Wolf Man*. (Almost all the characters have the names of werewolf film directors.) As with the other films discussed, *The Howling* also establishes carefully delineated boundaries between familiar and unfamiliar urban and rural spaces. This time they are between the safe and dangerous spaces of the city, forest and town into which the uncanny inserts itself.

Although *The Howling* is filled with werewolf jokes, it is still frightening—particularly the classic metamorphosis scene in which the werewolf, who has been wounded, is represented as an abject decaying body. Scenes of bodily abjection are alleviated by the fact that the entire narrative premise is based on a joke. The members of The Colony are into alternative therapies and are all being counselled by Dr Waggner in order to learn how to be less bestial and to live on animal rather than human flesh. Not all of the werewolves are happy with this arrangement. 'I want to bite somebody!' one of them screams. Although the werewolf is represented as a terrifying monster, the film argues that the real horrors are of an everyday kind: pornography, phoney New-Age therapies, media sensationalism and dishonest journalism. Television sets carefully placed in various scenes play material about werewolves: Disney Wolf cartoons, scenes from *The Wolf Man*, clips of Lon Chaney Jr, an interview with Dr Waggner who believes that 'we should never try to deny the animal in all of us'. In the terrifying climax, Karen is bitten. Her metamorphosis into a wolf is filmed live on television in order to warn people of the danger that stalks the city streets. The film cuts to the reactions of viewers whom the media has already made cynical—most think they are watching a hoax.

The frightening moments are those set in the eerie, moonlit woods with graphic scenes of metamorphosis. One in particular draws on the primal uncanny, aligning man with woman and nature. A female member of The Colony, Marsha, is portrayed as erotic and seductive. She sets out to seduce Karen's husband, who has already been bitten by a wolf. His relationship with Karen is also at a low ebb. The couple meet one night on the beach. We watch as each metamorphoses into a beast. As in *An American Werewolf in London*, muscles burst, flesh throbs, new shapes emerge, hair, fangs and claws sprout. The metamorphosis appears seamless. Once the change is complete, the camera focuses on the pair, each transformed into a wolf, mating on the beach. The scene of bestiality is particularly uncanny because it is almost always hidden in the werewolf film; here we see a perverse coupling between creatures who, because we have shared their metamorphoses, seem neither fully human nor animal. Furry sex is not a perversion, unless the fur has become a fetish object, a pleasurable substitute for the castrating female genital, frightening (to the fetishist) because of its wolfish look. No wonder granny ('My, what big teeth you have!) did not seem her old familiar self.

'WOLF' (1994)

In the 1990s, Jack Nicholson joined the pantheon of erotic celluloid beasts. In *Wolf* he plays Will Randall, a polite and courteous book editor (described as the 'last civilised man') who is transformed into a potent erotic werewolf. The opening scene depicts Randal driving at night through the snowy woods of Vermont. The moon is not only full but also closer to the Earth than it has been for at least one hundred years. While using his sleeve to wipe away condensation on the window, he suddenly hits something on the road; he stops his car to investigate and is bitten on the hand by a wolf. The signs of his werewolfism slowly emerge. Director Mike Nichols draws these out in order to emphasise the transformation of the polite, civilised Will into an aggressive competitive man. This change is just as significant as his eventual metamorphosis into a wolf.

No longer meek and retiring, he becomes 'wolfish' in the extreme. When visiting the new owner of the publishing company, Raymond Alden (Christopher Plummer), he meets his daughter, Laura (Michelle Pfeiffer), with whom he eventually falls in love. While visiting the Aldens' estate he frightens the horses, who react as if he were a dangerous animal. The details of Will's transformation, in which his familiar human habits become unfamiliar, are represented as more uncanny than his later transformation into a wolf. Hair sprouts from his wound. His sense of smell becomes so acute that he is able to detect the scent of another man on his wife's clothes, thus learning that she has been having an affair. His hearing becomes more acute and his sight improves so much that he is able to discard his glasses. His nostrils twitch and he sniffs at the air like a dog. His face grows more hair. He becomes aggressive at work.

Nicholas Royle argues that the uncanny is not simply bound up with aesthetics and psychological effects: 'its critical elaboration is necessarily bound up with analysing, questioning and even transforming what is called everyday life'.[31] *Wolf* certainly reinforces the view that the urban jungle is more ferocious than the actual world of nature. One of the film's most humorous scenes occurs when Will deliberately urinates on the expensive shoes of his colleague Stewart Swinton (James Spader), who is trying to take Will's job. The moment is strangely uncanny as we realise that Will's seemingly bizarre behaviour is not only entirely appropriate but, given Swinton's swinish behaviour, perfectly justifiable. At home he is filled with energy and makes savage love with his wife. He craves meat, preferably raw, and is forced to give up his vegetarianism. On the night of the next full moon, his eyes turn green and he develops fangs; after pursuing a deer through the nearby forest he tears ravenously at its bloody flesh. Next, he turns to humans as his prey. Will, 'the last civilised man', eventually murders his wife. Yet, despite his brutal acts, Will is never truly frightening.

Wolf marked a change of direction for the werewolf myth in that Will, who is portrayed as a sympathetic character throughout, does not perish in the end. In the final sequence Will and Stewart, who have metamorphosed into classic wolf–men, fight to the death. They stand upright, furry faces, sharp fangs and claws on view. The fight is savage and Laura is forced to shoot Stewart in order to save Will. Just before Will escapes into the night, she looks into his wolfish face for the first time and gasps in shock. Will speeds off into the night as the police and Laura's father arrive. He says remorsefully that none of this might have happened, if he had not been so 'dead set against Will Randall' because he was after his daughter. Laura tries to excuse her father's possessiveness: 'You were just trying to save me from a disastrous relationship, darling'. She concludes ironically: 'I would have left in a week. He was much too *tame* for me'.

As Laura departs she asks the police inspector if he would like a drink, perhaps another vodka and tonic. He is dumbfounded. 'How the hell did she know what we'd been drinking?' he asks his mate. 'I could smell it—smell it a mile away,' she retorts. Laura's acute sense of smell is our first hint that she is also now a werewolf. As she walks into the night the film cuts to a close-up of her face and blue eyes. The camera tracks rapidly into the forest, suggesting a wolf running, her face dissolves into a shot of a werewolf's head and its two piercing yellow eyes. The she-wolf throws back its head and howls. The camera tracks back out of the woods indicating that the wolf is leaving the forest. Her face reappears and her blue eyes become yellow; the camera moves into a tight close-up focusing on her large yellow eyes which fill the screen. The final shot creates an uncanny resemblance between the woman's eyes and a wolf's eyes, with a faint suggestion of their faces merging in the dark. The image is uncanny because, apart from the yellow eyes, there is no actual metamorphosis. The woman's face is the wolf's face. It is as if woman, depicted throughout the film as wild by nature, has always been the primal wolf. The film's main promotional image reinforces this: it depicts the man's distorted, screaming face caught in between an image of the full moon in the background and the woman's calm ethereal face in the foreground. The man's face is growing out of the woman's as if being re-born through her mind and body. She is Lupa, the primal she-wolf.

Wolf also delineates boundaries, this time between the city and the woods, the urban and the natural jungle. The film argues that the urban jungle that Will inhabits is a much more ferocious, terrifying place than the wilds of nature. Rather than resist, the male werewolf has freely aligned himself with the primal uncanny —woman and nature. The uncanny has not lost its power to unsettle, but the unfamiliar is rendered strange rather than horrific. The uncanny inserts itself into the gaps that run between these boundaries; in Cixous's terms 'it points to gaps we need to explain', denying the possibility of unity. *Wolf* argues that these gaps are now so wide that in order for a man to retain his dignity he must become animal. The werewolf film stages a collapse of proper symbolic masculinity through the deployment of the primal uncanny. It argues that the male subject, regardless of how civilised he appears, is always susceptible to becoming animal. His transformation, which uncovers what has been kept hidden, is disturbing because it suggests that the animal is essential to the definition of what constitutes the human. His uncanny transformations point to the frailty of the symbolic order and the possibility of re-birth through the agency of the primal uncanny. Is this what man wants? The ruin of the male symbolic order of law and language? A return to the animal? These questions, which undermine civilisation, generate an anxiety, a sense of phallic panic, that runs throughout the horror genre.

The male werewolf is assimilated to the primal uncanny in the latter's relation to woman, nature and death. Woman's boundaries are more permeable, fluid. Woman's body opens up wounds instead of smoothing them over. In werewolf films the male body is rendered feminine and uncanny—animal hair sprouts, flesh changes shape, the wolf's head and body insert themselves through the human shape, teeth become fangs and claws grow. The werewolf lives in the interstitial spaces between city and forest; it is able to negotiate the boundaries in order to render unfamiliar the familiar contours of nature and the city. The werewolf also points to gaps in desire; it speaks of bestial animal desires rather than the normal desires of the male symbolic order. It offers sex on all fours rather than an upright mating. The werewolf brings into the light all of these things which ought to have remained secret and hidden. Finally, it is uncanny in its relation to death: it makes apparent the reality of the death of the human subject. Cixous argues that the 'relationship to death reveals the highest degree of the *Unheimliche*', which presents us with a glimpse of what death might be like because death 'does not have any form in life'.[32] The werewolf film explores a different kind of death—the death of the human subject and its metamorphosis into the animal. It is as if the human is swallowed up, cannibalised, by the primal uncanny—in the manner of the threat presented by the wolf in the 'Little Red Riding Hood' tale. Angela Carter understood the appeal of the animal in her famous story, made into a film of the same name, *The Company of Wolves* (Neil Jordan, 1984). The heroine's grandmother warns her never to trust a man whose eyebrows meet in the middle and to avoid all men who are 'hairy on the inside'. Rosaleen, however, is emotionally drawn to the wilds and when she meets a huntsman whose eyebrows do meet in the middle she discards her human shape for that of the wolf. Werewolfism offers a perverse metamorphosis from human to animal, a rehearsal of the death of the proper subject and an intimation of the end of the civilised self. Rosaleen was more than happy to discard her hood for a hirsute hero, even if his ears were too big and his hands too hairy.

7

FREDDY'S FINGERNAILS:
CHILD ABUSE, GHOSTS
AND THE UNCANNY

*Many people experience the feeling [the uncanny] in the
highest degree in relation to death and dead bodies, to the
return of the dead, and to spirits and ghosts.*

SIGMUND FREUD[1]

Many films that explore our relationship to death through the ghost focus on teenagers and younger children, particularly the female child. The relationship between spirituality, ghosts and the feminine was explored by the surrealists in the 1920s.[2] They were fascinated by what they perceived as the dual (earthly/spirirtual) nature of the little girl, and her propensity for entering other worlds. This theme has also proven an enduring one in the history of the cinema and provided the basis for many acclaimed films, including *The Curse of the Cat People* (1944), *The Innocents* (1961), *The Haunting of Julia* (1976), *The Shining* (1980), *Poltergeist* (1982), and the various *Nightmare on Elm Street* films (1980s). In the majority of these the ghost is female or associated with the feminine. The ghost's connection to the feminine, combined with its close relationship to death, make the ghost a powerful figure of the primal uncanny. As Cixous has said, 'The Ghost is the fiction of our relationship to death' made concrete.[3] The ghost not only gives a 'shape' to death; perhaps more than any other monstrous figure, it evacuates the real of all meaning. Hence it is particularly threatening to the symbolic order of law and language, which attempts to endow all events with rational meaning. This may explain why the ghost of gothic literature and film often adopts an uncanny feminine form. The feminine is associated with qualities such as the ephemeral and the fleeting, which threaten characteristics such as solidity and stability that are valued by the male symbolic order.

The view of the female child as particularly close to the non-material world of fantasy and the imagination was central to the beliefs of the surrealists. They regarded childhood as 'the privileged age in which imaginative faculties were still *à l'état sauvage*—sensitive to all kinds of impressions and associations which education would systematically "correct"'.[4] 'Dissecting mystery is like violating a child,' Bunuel was fond of saying.[5] In the famous 1924 surrealist *Manifesto*, Breton claimed that 'The spirit which takes the plunge into Surrealism exultantly relives the best of its childhood.'[6]

The surrealists endowed the female child, whom they idealised as the *femme–enfant*, with a special ability to enter the realm of the marvellous. Through her, the surrealists hoped to return to a state of lost innocence and recapture that special state of childhood wonderment at the mysteries and magic of life. A famous Man Ray photograph shows a group of the photographer's colleagues listening in rapt attention to the young Gisèle Prassinos reading her poetry which, to them, was truly marvellous. For the surrealists the crucial aspect of the *femme–enfant* is her innocence. By virtue of her purity, she is able to make contact with the marvellous and enter the world of the surreal. Films like *The Curse of the Cat People* (Gunter von Fritsch, 1944) and *The Innocents* (Jack Clayton, 1961) explore the dark side of this experience. More recent films, such as *Poltergeist* (Tobe Hooper, 1982), take us right inside the surreal nightmarish world of the *femme–enfant*.

The surrealists, however, did not depict the *femme–enfant* only as an angel. Salvador Dalí endowed her with a dark side. When Dalí painted Shirley Temple, Hollywood's quintessential image of childhood innocence, he gave her a sphinx's body, coloured red and sporting long, dangerous claws. Hans Belmer's uncanny dolls—twisted into seductive poses of the nymphet—also point to the girl's potential for corruption. Lolita, the deadly woman/child, was terrifying because her innocent demeanour concealed what the audience knew, that she was already corrupt. Innocence invites corruption—the more pure and irreproachable, the greater the child's eventual fall from grace. Still not fully developed or formed, the girl child is malleable, capable of representing good as well as destructive archaic impulses. In a number of classic ghost films, haunting is associated directly with the feminine and the young girl, and in some instances with the theme of sexual disturbance, which is represented as a form of repressed spectral sexuality.

Robert Wise and Gunter von Fritsch's classic film noir *The Curse of the Cat People* (1944) might seem more of a fantasy than a horror film, but when one views it as a sequel to *Cat People* (Jacques Tourneur, 1942) and considers the meaning of the 'curse' of the title, it takes on an altogether sinister tone. *The Curse of the Cat People* tells the story of Amy, a six-year-old girl who leads a solitary existence. The film depicts Amy as particularly susceptible to communion with a spirit world. She lives with Oliver, her father, and her mother, in a small town next to Sleepy Hollow, the legendary forest which was the setting for the horrifying story of 'The Headless Horseman'. With its dark secret places, the forest is represented throughout as an extended metaphor for the unconscious. Amy lives in a fantasy world where she conjures up a ghostly playmate who is her father's first wife, Irena, the monstrous cat–woman. Although Amy seems innocent, and beyond all guile, she too is potentially monstrous, because she signifies excess—the threatening excess of the over-fertile feminine imagination that gives Amy a special ability to communicate with the spirit world. The 'curse' that haunts the story assumes a number of dimensions: it is the curse of the imagination that threatens to overwhelm Amy; and the curse that hangs over the house in the form of the ghost of Irena, the man killer. Irena is Amy's 'special friend'. Together they retreat into a world of fantasy, symbolised by the garden and by its extension —the forest in which dwells the headless horseman. Like Orpheus, Osiris, John the Baptist and Holofernes, the ghostly headless horseman belongs to a bloody tradition in which men are destroyed/decapitated by women.

Nicolas Roeg's *Don't Look Now* (1973) also plays on the association of women and the uncanny feminine with ghosts. In this film the apparent ghost of a dead daughter brings about the death of her father (Donald Sutherland). Overcome with grief at his young daughter's accidental death, the father catches a glimpse of 'her' on the canals of Venice, where he is restoring water-damaged churches. His dead 'daughter' appears to him as a small figure dressed in the red raincoat she was wearing the day she drowned. The mother (Julie Christie) becomes friends with two elderly sisters, one of whom claims to be a clairvoyant and in touch with her daughter. Through eerie images and sounds, the film suggests the sisters might be witches. When the father finally catches up with the little red figure, it turns out to be a homicidal female dwarf who severs his neck with a machette. What is most disturbing about *Don't Look Now* is its suggestion that all of the women—mother, daughter, the mysterious sisters, the dwarf—are in league with the spirit world and have joined forces to bring about the father's death, a death which he him- self foresaw in a vision of his own funeral. The red-capped dwarf is represented as the dead daughter's doppelgänger, a dark ghostly self that—like Amy and Irena from *The Curse of the Cat People*— wishes to lure the father into the underworld of the dead. The child's eerie cries, the imagery of dark uterine canals, water and the colour red—all converge to suggest the deadly aspect of a female ghost world.

The Haunting of Julia (Richard Loncraine, 1976) presents a mother–daughter bond as particularly conducive to ghosts and haunting. Julia (Mia Farrow) is forced to perform a fatal tracheo- tomy on her daughter when the young girl chokes on her food. In a desperate attempt to save her life, Julia cuts open her throat and the girl dies. Suffering from a nervous breakdown, Julia separates from her husband and moves by herself into a house that is haunted by the ghost of a young girl, who was murdered by her own mother because she savagely castrated a small boy. Julia is finally murdered by the mysterious girl (her own daughter or the killer daughter?) who materialises in the house and slits her throat—just as Julia cut her daughter's throat. We are left with the disturbing thought that Julia wished to kill her daughter and that the daughter, by returning as the ghost of another dead girl, wished also to murder her mother. The ghost world can be an uncanny female space.

The young girl of *Poltergeist* (Tobe Hooper, 1982) is able to 'pass' easily from one state of the spiritual divide to the other. She enters the spirit world, swept into the 'other side' via the family television set that sucks her into its uterine whirlpool. The source of the film's haunting is not clearly related to sexual repression, although the actual poltergeist adopts fluid feminine sexual forms. In *The Shining* (Stanley Kubrick, 1980) a young boy with the power to see the future is haunted by the ghosts of two sisters, identical twins who were murdered and dismembered by their father. The dead sisters reappear later in two different spectral forms: first as a beautiful young woman and second as the rotting ghost–corpses of two old women. The uncanny duo of ghostly female forms (young woman/hag) converges on the boy's father (Jack Nicholson) in an attempt to unsettle even further his already disturbed mind, leading him to try to dismember his own family with an axe.

Films such as *The Haunting* (Robert Wise, 1963) and *The Uninvited* (Lewis Allen, 1944) directly link the appearance of ghosts with sexual disturbance; each film suggests that the uncanny signs of haunting which dominate the respective narratives are associated with repressed lesbian desire. *The Haunting* is set in a house that has been haunted since the tragic and accidental death of its mistress. An anthropologist with an interest in the supernatural has invited two women with special psychic gifts to assist him in investigating the house in the hope of finding 'the key to another world'. Eleanor (Julie Harris) and Theodora (Claire Bloom), who call themselves 'Nell' and 'Theo', literally fall into each other's arms when they hear strange and terrible noises at night. Theo is comfortable with her lesbianism and constantly makes suggestive comments to Nell, a timid and insecure figure, who does not appear to understand the true nature of Theo's feelings for her. Nell narrates the events from her perspective in a voice-over that is distinctly eerie. Nell is terrified of Hill House and calls it a 'monster'. The doors all hang off-centre, none of the rooms is square and the doorknob to her bedroom room depicts the uncanny head of Medusa. Wise frames his scenes carefully, creating a sense of uncanny spaces in the house. The film argues that the signs of the terrifying ghost signify repressed sexual desire between the women, particularly in relation to Eleanor.

'THE INNOCENTS' (1961)

Jack Clayton's The Innocents, based on Henry James's famous novella The Turn of the Screw and scripted by Truman Capote, also offers a powerful and disturbing study of the uncanny ghost, possession and sexual disturbance. Two orphaned children, Miles and Flora, live on a vast country estate, provided for by a wealthy but absent uncle, who wants nothing to do with their world. When a new governess, Miss Giddens (Deborah Kerr), replaces the recently deceased governess, Miss Jessel, she becomes convinced that the children have been possessed by the spirits of Miss Jessel and her sinister partner, Quint, who also met an untimely death. Miss Giddens decides that the two former servants had attempted to corrupt the children and that their ghosts have returned to continue their unseemly work.

Sexually repressed and painfully sensitive, Miss Giddens tries to force the children to admit they are in mortal and moral danger, but only succeeds in terrifying them. They eventually appear to crack under the emotional strain, each one exhibiting all the signs of a breakdown. Or could it be possession? The question of whether or not the children are possessed by the transgressive ghosts of the dead couple, or by Miss Giddens's own unconscious desires, is left open. It is even possible that the ghostly figures which Miss Giddens thinks she sees might be creations of her own morbid imagination.

Although the central relationship is between Miss Giddens and Miles, with whom she appears to be in love, the film's theme of haunting and hysteria is played out more vividly in relation to Flora. Sensitive and pretty, Flora is also strangely self-possessed for a child. Through an accumulation of small details, Clayton suggests a dark, mysterious aspect to Flora's personality. On two separate occasions by the lake, Flora hums the song from Miss Jessel's music box: both times, a ghostly female figure uncannily appears in the reeds, as if in answer to Flora's music. The apparition communicates to Flora through song—the very song that Flora hummed one night over Miss Giddens's bed. After Miss Giddens verbally attacks Flora, trying to make her admit she can 'see' Miss Jessel, the girl becomes hysterical, voicing obscenities and yelling uncontrollably as if possessed by the ghost of Miss Jessel. 'To hear such filth from a child's mouth!' exclaims the horrified housekeeper after failing to subdue Flora, who screams throughout the night. Flora's cruel behaviour, night wanderings, eerie singing, lewd talk and apparent communion with Miss Jessel's spirit all suggest a mysterious uncanny side in Flora's make-up. The uncanniness stems from her special ability to seemingly inhabit the everyday world and the ghostly realm of the dead couple.

Under pressure from Miss Giddens to admit that he has been in communication with Quint, Miles also becomes hysterical. Before he collapses and dies, Miles, whose face becomes that of Quint's, screams at the distraught governess: 'You are a damned hussy, a damned dirty-minded hag'. The motif of the double adds to the already uncanny atmosphere. The scene is depicted with such ambiguity that it is impossible to determine whether Miles is possessed by Miss Giddens's hysteria or by Quint. His outburst, however, seems to expose Miss Giddens's repressed desire to shed her puritan values and embrace a life of sexual passion.

The Innocents represents Miss Giddens's relationship with, and effect on, each of the two children quite differently. While brother and sister both become channels for her repressed desires, Miles is the one with whom she is sexually obsessed. He treats her like a lover. He demands to know why she wants to be alone with him, offers no protest when she kisses him on the lips, and says to her, in the tone of an adult male: 'No, my dear! You don't think I'm like any other boy. Otherwise we wouldn't be having these conversations'. He responds to her kiss as if an adult, yet somehow seems to retain a degree of innocence. Miles's precocious sexuality is particularly uncanny. While his later death is portrayed largely as a consequence of Miss Giddens's hysteria, Flora's collapse is associated more with the girl's own propensity for cruelty and corruption. We are never certain whether or not the children have been possessed by the ghosts of Quint and Miss Jessel. Given the sexual knowingness of Flora and Miles, there is a clear suggestion that the pair may have been sexually abused by the dead couple.

In a fascinating article on uncanny trends in early nineteenth-century art, Stefan Germer discusses paintings of children by Théodore Géricault, with particular focus on a portrait of a young girl entitled 'Louise Vernet'. Germer points to her flirtatious, sexually aware stare. He is interested in the way this painting reverses the power relations between picture and spectator: 'This scenario alone is loaded enough to explode the frame of a simple male fantasy; thus it becomes downright uncanny because Louise appears to be aware of the desire directed at her, without making herself its object.'[7]

Germer argues that what 'Louise sets in motion brings about the disarming of phallic vision'; this occurs because Louise, who stares boldly at the spectator, 'ignores the boundary' between the world of children and adults.[8] By commingling these two worlds, Géricault captures 'the uncanniness of children whose bodies know more than they are actually allowed to'.[9]

Miles is particularly uncanny in this respect. His address to Miss Giddens ('No, my dear! You don't think I'm like any other boy.') reveals a precociousness beyond his years. He is fully aware of her repressed sexual yearnings. He looks like an innocent boy yet talks and behaves like a sexually aware man. Uncanniness is generated by his knowingness and by Miss Giddens's powerlessness to restore proper sexual boundaries. The transgressive function of the uncanny is clearly evident in the way the familiar is rendered unfamiliar and things normally kept out of sight rise to the surface. Does Miles speak for himself or is he possessed by Quint or even Miss Giddens? As literary historian and philosopher Rodolphe Gasche says in relation to the phantasm: 'The phantasmatic "structure" puts in play not the phantasm itself—there never could be one—but one of its figures … the phantasmatic is the space in which representation is fragmented'.[10]

The power of children to enter the realm of the phantasmatic space is central to the *Elm Street* films, which explore the uncanny in relation to sexual disturbance, dysfunctional parents and child abuse. Dysfunctional parenting is central to a number of the films discussed above. In *The Innocents*, the two children are orphans whose uncle is completely uninterested in their welfare; in *The Haunting of Julia*, the mothers of each family, through no fault of their own, have caused the deaths of their daughters; in *The Shining* the fathers of each family suffer a mental breakdown and try to murder their children; and the parents of *The Curse of the Cat People* simply do not understand their imaginative daughter and her fascination with the uncanny. *The Haunting* similarly explores this theme through the figure of two neglected daughters, one virtually abandoned after her mother dies and the other abused by her demanding invalid mother. In each of the films there is a pattern of impaired parenting which results in unintentional harm at one end of the scale and neglect, abuse and murder at the other. Into the phantasmatic space opened up in familial relations the ghost inserts itself. There are of course a number of horror films about abusive parents that do not produce spectral figures, such as David Cronenberg's

The Brood (1979) and Alfred Hitchcock's *Psycho* (1960) and *Marnie* (1964). The two do not always go together but when they do, the ghost points to the way in which dysfunctional family life gives rise to repression and uncanny disturbances.

THE 'UNHEIMLICH' GHOST OF ELM STREET

Freddy Krueger, the monstrous ghost of the *Elm Street* films, reveals the dysfunctional nature of the patriarchal family unit, exposing the myth that the family nurtures and protects children. Freddy represents the collective fears and anxieties of the children, mainly teenagers, of Elm Street. In particular he signifies the buried fears of the children who have been emotionally and/or sexually abused by parental figures. An abused child himself, Freddy Krueger knows exactly how to torment his victims before killing them and taking them with him to the dead zone. In particular, Freddy, forces his victims to confront the strangeness or uncanniness that dwells within. Freddy knows the secrets of family life—the loneliness of the young, their feelings of being unloved and unlovable, their estrangement from parents and longing for friends. He haunts the dark corners of the family home, waiting for the teenagers to fall asleep so that he can drag them into his nightmare world.

Although clearly a male spectre on the outside, Freddy's behaviour is also perversely maternal; his most uncanny characteristic is that he keeps the souls of his victims trapped inside his body like a collection of unborn babies. Many of the scenes in the *Elm Street* films suggest the workings of a surreal uterine landscape, a bizarre haunted house filled with the ghosts of those that Freddy has murdered and trapped . Death, spirits, haunted rooms, nightmares, a maternal spectre with a paternal face—all of these motifs associate Freddy with the primal uncanny. Freddy is a ghost, a figment of the imagination, a monster created in the minds of the children of Elm Street who project onto Freddy their darkest secrets and innermost fears. In all but one of the *Elm Street* films, Freddy's main adversary is female, a teenager with special abilities that enable her to enter Freddy's world and to try kill him. Insofar as Freddy represents her dark self, she cannot really destroy him without also killing off the stranger within. Freddy Krueger represents what Jacques Derrida defines as a key aspect of the uncanny. The uncanny, states Derrida, draws on a sense of 'a stranger who is already found within (*das Heimliche–Unheimliche*), more intimate with one than one is oneself'.[11] His association with death and the maternal body, the haunted house and the *femme–enfant* make him the spectral monster par excellence of the primal uncanny.

There are six films in the *Nightmare on Elm Street* series, all made between 1984 and 1991. In each, children are tortured, tormented and killed—in bizarre and bloody ways—by the ghost of Freddy Krueger. Freddy's special power is that he has the ability to murder the teenagers in their dreams. They must stay awake; once they fall asleep, they are Freddy's. The audience never knows when the teenagers will wake up from a nightmare, alive but filled with terror. They also have the power to pull their friends into their dreams. When alive, Freddy Krueger (Robert Englund) was a child murderer. The parents of the slain children discover the truth, form a lynch mob, capture Freddy Krueger and burn him alive in a disused boiler room. His empty and derelict house still stands, an eerie haunted house that terrifies on two accounts: it reminds the parents of their terrible deed and it terrifies the neighbourhood children. Years later Freddy reappears in the nightmares of the teenagers of Elm Street, although they at first do not know anything about Freddy Krueger. When the children enter his house—in actuality or in their nightmares—Freddy murders them. Although the *Elm Street* films contain marked evidence of a sadistic attitude to children, they are wildly popular with teenagers who seem to identify with Freddy and delight in his attacks on the children of Elm Street. Freddy draws them into his surreal nightmare world where they —like figures in a video game—are forced to pit their wits against a satanic monster. Despite his murderous intentions, Freddy also appeals because of his wisecracks, wicked intelligence and devious understanding of the best way to create fear. He is the contemporary anti-hero of horror. In 1994, ten years after he made the first *Elm Street* film, Wes Craven made a seventh film on the theme, *Wes Craven's New Nightmare*, about a group of 25 to 30 year olds who are parents; he wanted to explore the way in which they, as parents, saw Freddy.

In the *Elm Street* films, the 'unthinkable secret'[12] at the heart of the uncanny, that which should have remained hidden, is parental neglect and child sexual abuse—the latter rarely, if ever, commented on in detail in critical articles. Just as shocking as Freddy's attacks on the children is the secret of his own abuse, which is not revealed until the final film, *Freddy's Dead: The Final Nightmare* (Rachael Talalay, 1991). Although it might be argued, as does Nigel Floyd, that there is an 'exploitation of the subject of child abuse [which] has little to do with creative inspiration or genuine social concern',[13] this argument is not easy to sustain if we consider the dominant themes of the series as a whole. From the very beginning, the films explore the idea that abuse begets monsters; not only is Freddy depicted as a monstrous parental figure but actual parents are shown as abusive, enacting various deeds, including acts of neglect, dominance and sexual abuse, on the children of Elm Street. In *Freddy's Dead*, child psychologist Maggie Burroughs is able to enter Freddy's own dream world where she witnesses him being bullied by other children, being abused by his stepfather and engaging in acts of self-mutilation.

Freddy's trademark signs are a hideously scarred face, his infamous gloved hands, with sharp butter knives attached (to slice his victims), and his striped jumper and fedora. As with other classic male monsters discussed in this book, Freddy is also associated with two qualities attached to the primal uncanny: woman and death. Freddy's gender bending at first appears strange as he seems to be a very masculine monster. However, he is also a feminised, fluid and spectral monster. He regularly appears in his films disguised as a woman (nurse, teacher, pin-up girl) in order to put his victims off guard. In addition, he appears as a monstrous maternal body. In *The Dream Master* (Renny Harlin, 1988), film number four in the series, we see that Freddy has trapped the souls of the children he has murdered in his own body, where they appear as terrified disembodied faces. Freddy is literally pregnant with the victims he has incorporated into his being. Scenes such as this appear designed to rekindle infantile fears of re-incorporation and cannibalism. Male ghosts are not necessarily feminised to this degree, but they frequently assume qualities normally associated with the feminine. Freddy Krueger is associated with the primal uncanny—woman and death—through his identity as a maternal male, a feminised spectral figure and a harbinger of death. As the series progresses we learn that Freddy is only strong because he is able to feed off the energy of his victims. In a sense the teenagers of Elm Street create and keep Freddy alive. He is literally a monster of their dreams.

All but one of the *Elm Street* films appoint a teenage girl as the special avenger, the one who enters the nightmare world in

Freddy poses for his fans—The Dream Master, *1989*
(New Line/The Kobal Collection)

Freddy as 'Jaws' in A Nightmare on Elm Street, *1984*
(New Line/The Kobal Collection)

order to try to kill Freddy and free her friends whom he has taken captive. In *A Nightmare on Elm Street* (1984), the first in the series, her name is Nancy Thompson (Heather Langenkamp), a typical teenager with relationship problems and divorced parents. She lives in a middle-class Californian suburb with neat gardens and clean streets. Clever and courageous, Nancy sets a trap for Freddy. Nancy returns as the heroine of the third film in the series, *Dream Warriors* (Chuck Russell, 1987), in which the teenagers band together to fight Freddy as a group. The heroine of part four, *The Dream Master*, is Alice Johnson (Lisa Wilcox), a shy teenager who learns to control her dreams and outwit Freddy by absorbing the positive qualities of her friends. Alice is also the heroine of the next film, *The Dream Child* (Steven Hopkins, 1989), in which she is pregnant. She fights Freddy with help from her unborn child, Jacob, despite the fact that Freddy himself is trying to take control of Jacob while still in Alice's womb. In the last of the series, *Freddy's Dead: The Final*

Nightmare (1991), the heroine is Maggie Burroughs (Lisa Zane), a therapist who initially doesn't believe in Freddy's existence. Freddy returns to haunt the dreams of both the heroine and his own daughter before meeting his fate.

The female heroes of these films all have special abilities that enable them to fight Freddy. Each is able to outsmart Freddy in his own domain; the uncanny realm of 'the *between*'. In one sense, Freddy is the doppelgänger or dark self of his female adversaries. His special yet macabre relationship with the female hero is emphasised by the surreal image of a group of younger children, mainly girls, dressed in white who repeatedly sing 'Freddy's song' in each of the films. The repetition of the scenes of these children and the sounds of the eerie lyrics are particularly uncanny. The appearance of the ghostly singers always alerts us to the fact that Freddy is in the neighbourhood. These sequences also offer a compelling example of the use of sound to represent the uncanny.

In each film, Freddy creates elaborate death scenarios, phantasmatic primal scenes in which his young victims meet their end. In *The Dream Child* Freddy transports his victim, a comic book illustrator, into the setting of a black-and-white comic book where he transforms him into a two-dimensional cartoon character. Freddy himself then becomes a superhero and changes his victim into a cardboard cut-out; as Freddy slashes him to pieces the colour drains from his body and collects in a puddle at the victim's feet. In the climax of *Dream Warriors* Freddy masquerades as Nancy's dead father. As Nancy embraces her father's/Freddy's body and tells him she has always loved him she is torn apart by his finger-blades. The point is that it is dangerous for children to want the love of their parents—disappointment, even death, is the final result. Freddy inevitably traps his youthful victims because he knows what it is they most want; thus, he carefully sets out a mise en scène of desire that they cannot resist.

The *Nightmare on Elm Street* series explores what Cixous describes as the 'fiction' of death. 'The ghost is the fiction of our relationship to death' made concrete.[14] The ghost is the figure of uncanniness and death par excellence. Freud drew special attention to the ghost and its uncanny relationship to death, although he did not explore death itself in relation to either Hoffman's story 'The Sandman' or the uncanny in general. In her re-reading and elaboration of Freud's essay on the uncanny, Cixous stresses the relationship between representation and death. She emphasises the fact that we cannot represent death directly; it is without shape or form, known only through symbolic messengers such as the ghost.

> There is nothing more notorious and uncanny to our thought than mortality ... 'Death' does not have any form in life. Our unconscious makes no place for the representation of our mortality ... Death will recognise us, but we shall not recognise it.[15]

Death, however, can be presented in artistic practice in the form of a ghost who 'erases the limit which exists between two states, neither alive nor dead; passing through, the dead man returns in the manner of the Repressed ... In the end, death is never anything more than the disturbance of the limits'.[16] What we are most afraid of is being carried off by the ghost into his new existence: 'It is the *between* that is tainted with strangeness'.[17]

The ghost enjoys a unique relationship with the uncanny because of its association with mortality and the universal belief in spirits and the return of the dead. Ghost stories are no doubt as old as the human race, evolving through folklore, superstition, fairy stories, fiction and film. These stories have found a perfect medium of expression in the cinema, which through special-effects technologies, is able to represent uncanny spectral images and haunting scenarios. In addition, because the cinematic image itself is literally an apparition, images of ghosts on screen embody a double spectral meaning. Thus the ghost represents a strange figure of otherness, a spectral and textual other. Ghost stories constitute a special category of horror film in that they represent the return of the dead, not as the undead—such as the vampire and zombie—but as a spectral thing with the power to cross between the two realms, to enter 'the *between*' spaces referred to by Cixous.

Freddy Krueger, the terrifying ghost of the *Elm Street* films, not only merely haunts his victims but murders them and drags their tormented souls screaming into the 'the *between*' spaces of the next world. Because of the ability of film to represent the world of dream and fantasy with the same level of indexicality, or realism, as it portrays the actual world, the ghost can haunt both the actual and dream worlds with equal credibility. Freddy inhabits both domains. All of the films exploit the eerie slide between dreams and reality. Hence these '*between*' spaces terrify because they, like nightmares, are uncanny in that they have no boundaries. Sleep can be a terrifying state—a theme also explored in painting by surrealist artists such as Salvador Dalí. In the *Elm Street* films our relation to death is played out in nightmares via the logic of the dream. In Freddy's dream world anything is possible once the children fall asleep. *Dream Warriors* emphasises this point with an opening quote from Edgar Allen Poe: 'Sleep/Those little slices of Death/ How I loathe them'.

'A NIGHTMARE ON ELM STREET' (1984)

A Hitchcockian sense of suspense is created in the first *Nightmare on Elm Street* film as the heroine, Nancy, finds her peaceful existence shattered by a series of nightmares that involve a monstrous dream-stalker. When she describes her nightmares to her friends, she discovers that they have been experiencing the same dream about the same monster. When her friends begin to die in horrific ways, Nancy realises that they are being murdered in their sleep by the apparition she later identifies as Freddy Krueger. Nancy and her boyfriend Glen (Johnny Depp) try to stay awake long enough to drag Freddy back into the real world and kill him again and forever—if one can kill a ghost, that is. Eventually, Nancy's mother reveals that Freddy was a child murderer who was incinerated in a disused boiler room by a group of vigilante parents.

In a number of episodes Freddy is able to murder the teenagers by exploiting uneasy family relationships. The aggressive father of one of the boys causes his son's death by failing to give him a message from Nancy. Nancy's own mother might have prevented a number of deaths if she had been truthful about Freddy's identity. She tells Nancy that she only wanted to protect her because the truth was so unpalatable. Nancy's father risks his daughter's life by pretending he will carry out her wishes and return home at a certain time. In later versions, parents commit more serious acts against their own children. In *Freddy's Dead*, Tracy is sexually abused by her own father. Another child, Spencer, falls asleep in front of the television set and is sucked into a dream which appears as a video game; in the game he is killed by his father.

The most frightening aspect of *A Nightmare on Elm Street* is its uncanny dream logic; it argues that we do not own our dreams, that we cannot even control them and that at any moment the dream may become reality. In a classroom discussion on *Hamlet*, Nancy's teacher says, 'What is seen is not always what is real'. Craven encourages the spectator to think about the uncanny and uneasy relationship between dreams and reality by blurring the line between the two states. According to Freud:

> *an uncanny effect is often and easily produced when the distinction between imagination and reality is effaced, as when something we have hitherto regarded as imaginary appears before us in reality, or when a symbol takes over the full function of the thing it symbolizes, and so on.*[18]

Sometimes we are aware that the characters are in a dream world; at other times we think they are awake only to discover they are dreaming, and vice versa.

In the end, Nancy destroys Freddy (or appears to) not by refusing to sleep but by withdrawing her energy. Turning her

Freddy as the heroine's dark self—A Nightmare on Elm Street, *1984*
(New Line/The Kobal Collection)

back on him she says: 'I take back every bit of energy I gave you'. This statement is particularly significant because it points to the fact that Freddy represents the dark secret self of the heroine, emphasised by the way he is filmed as her shadow. His scarred face is an outer symbol of what happens to the children within familial structures that create loneliness and abuse. Freddy's finger-blades not only rip apart his victims; they also make Freddy himself untouchable—he cannot love or receive love. In the end Freddy forces the children to recognise the strangeness or un-canniness that dwells within all of them.

When Wes Craven portrayed Freddy Krueger as a mon-strous ghost, a frightening child killer, he did not anticipate the enormous success of the film and Freddy's future cult status. Media critic Jeffrey Sconce argues that the *Elm Street* series owes its appeal to 'the episodes of intense visual excitation' made pos-sible because 'a wise-cracking Freddy, much to the viewer's delight, has the absolute power to manipulate time, space, and matter'.[19] Sconce argues convincingly that the spectator iden-tifies with Freddy 'not so much as a character but as a facilitator, the dynamic "source" of the phantasmagoric imagery'.[20] I agree that Freddy's appeal as the source of phantasmagoric imagery is central; but Freddy also appeals because he can lure his victims into that '*between*' space where the border between dream and reality merge. As Žižek argues: 'reality is never directly "itself", it presents itself only via its incomplete-failed symbolization, and spectral apparitions emerge in this very gap that forever sep-arates reality from the real'.[21] It is here that those things that should have remained hidden—parental neglect, family violence and sexual abuse—are uncovered.

FREDDY AND THE PRIMAL UNCANNY

Wes Craven has described Freddy as a 'paradigm of the threat-ening adult: the savage side of male adulthood, the ultimate bad father'.[22] Freddy is much more than the 'ultimate bad father'; he is also a ghost who can change gender at will, even assuming the role of a womb father/mother who wants a child of his own. His castrating finger-blades, combined with his perverse maternal desires, make him a truly monstrous figure on the side of death and the primal uncanny. He is ghost and witch combined—the latter image represented in *Freddy's Dead: The Final Nightmare*, where we see Freddy flying on a broomstick in a scene that refers to the Wicked Witch of the West from *The Wizard of Oz* (Victor Fleming, 1939). Tony Williams describes this image as 'an appropriately dark maternal parallel to his patriarchal person'.[23]

The various films in the series also explore Freddy's status as an uncanny womb mother. Throughout the series, Freddy lures the children into the home in which he lived when he was alive; now it has become a monstrous place, a surreal dreamscape in which Freddy chases and torments his young victims. Freddy's haunted house, a stock image of the ghost film, is given a terrifyingly new face in the *Elm Street* films. In particular, the house takes on surreal uterine aspects. Freud also associated the family home with the maternal body when he argued that 'the female genital organ' is an *unheimlich* place because it is 'the entrance to the former *Heim* [home] of all human beings'. He drew particular attention to the uncanniness of the uterus in dreams: 'the *unheimlich* is what was once *heimish*, familiar; the prefix "*un*" ["un-"] is the token of repression'.[24] Given the close association between the *heimlich* and the homely, and the *unheimlich* and the unhomely, the haunted house becomes the uncanny domain par excellence.

Freddy's particular talent lies in transforming the *heimlich* into the *unheimlich*, which he brings about through his perversion of the dream. Freddy attacks in the place where his victims would normally feel most secure—their own bedrooms. His aim is to lure them into a familiar dreamscape that then becomes horrifyingly unfamiliar. His victims are constantly caught between the *heimlich* and *unheimlich*. In their dreams they at first think 'this place is familiar', but the homely rapidly transforms into the unhomely. This lack of clear distinction between the familiar and unfamiliar suggests the emotional experiences of those who might feel trapped in an abusive family situation in which the friendly spaces of the family home suddenly become alien and unfamiliar.

Freddy is also a womb monster. This is represented in a number of ways: his desire for a child of his own; the way he keeps the souls of the dead children trapped inside his own body; his propensity for luring his victims into womb-like traps. Freddy's image as a womb monster is vividly portrayed in a number of scenes which produce uncanny effects by transforming the *heimlich* into the *unheimlich*. In one episode we discover that, ironically, Freddy, who devotes himself to the murder of children, wants a child for himself. In *The Dream Child* he does battle with Alice for possession of her baby. He even has an eerie pram awaiting the unborn child. In the previous film, Alice believed she had killed Freddy. About to graduate from high school, she is increasingly disturbed by nightmares of Freddy Krueger. He begins murdering her friends when she is awake. She cannot understand how Freddy is able to gain access to her friends when she is not asleep. Gradually it dawns on her that Freddy is controlling the dreams of her unborn baby. Alice decides to have an ultra-sound examination in order to see whether she can detect anything unusual about her child. The doctor tells her that a foetus can spend up to seventy per cent of its time in a dream state.

During the examination Alice dreams she is sucked into her own uterus through a giant red twisting tube. The intra-uterine phantasy that follows is particularly uncanny. Inside her uterus, Alice encounters her unborn baby, which is floating peacefully in her ammiotic fluid. Suddenly, the idyllic mood is shattered as the menacing figure of Freddy appears alongside the embryo. Alice and Freddy then battle each other for control of Alice's future son, whom she has named Jacob. Alice learns that Freddy has been stealing the souls of the children he has murdered and feeding them to Jacob.

In another episode of *Dream Child* we see that Freddy is not always able to control his own uterine desires. Freddy emerges from the heroine's body only to be ripped open by the souls, or faces, of the dead children trapped inside his own body. In another scene of uterine imagery, an array of children's souls are pulled down an umbilical chord to encounter Freddy, who appears to be secreted inside the heroine's growing foetus. Freddy is a master at creating uterine imagery and uterine scenarios that are uncanny in the extreme; these scenes are familiar, signifying gestation and birth, yet unfamiliar because of their association with death. Freddy not only wants a living baby of his own, his body is uncannily alive with the souls of dead children, trapped inside his stomach, a monstrous womb and an abject place of torture and torment. In the climax, the souls escape, streaming away into the air like a torrent of fireflies.

Cixous points to the uncanny nature of the unborn child: 'You are on the return road which passes through the country of children in the maternal body'.[25] Her comment provides a very apt description of the main motifs of The Dream Child. However, Freddy's monstrous maternal body takes a different road—one that does not evoke the familiar, or feelings of homesickness. Freddy has transformed his own body into a substitute for the living womb; it is a ghostly grave teeming with the dead. These are the abused children of Elm Street—they are also Freddy himself.

The image of Freddy's body alive with the heads of the dead represents a bizarre spectral phantasy of death and torment. We see their terrified faces and open screaming mouths, a graveyard of unborn ghosts, a baroque image of children in limbo, caught between heaven and hell. They are haunted by what Freddy has done to them and they also haunt us, the spectators, taken aback as we are by their strange imprisonment. 'The souls of children give me strength,' Freddy explains. It is true—it is only the children who keep Freddy, the ghost, alive. Freddy's pregnant body, his alliance with death and his relationship to the haunted house/womb all signify his association with the primal uncanny.

There are a number of key parallels between Freddy Kreuger and the figure of the sandman. Both men are spectral figures repulsive to the beholder. In Hoffman's story, the terrified Nathaniel describes the sandman as a 'fearsome apparition', a 'dreadful spectre' and a 'repellent spectral monster'.[26] Freddy is also a repulsive figure, his face covered with hideous scars and sharp finger-blades attached to each hand. Both are also monsters of sleep.

In *The Dream Child* we learn that Freddy also succours his child in a gruesome manner, he is feeding the souls of the children to Alice's unborn child. Freddy Krueger also preys on children at bedtime, but he murders children who do fall asleep. He stabs them in their dreams with his finger-blades and takes their lives —not their eyes. It is essential that the children do not lose their sight because Freddy has the power to make them hallucinate— that is, to make them think they are still awake when they have actually fallen asleep. Both the sandman and Freddy desire to give birth to uncanny life forms: the sandman produces Olympia, the lifelike mechanical doll; Freddy attempts to become Jacob's surrogate father by infiltrating his mother's womb. The success of the series may partly be due to the way it draws on the mythic image of the sandman but in a contemporary setting.

FILM AND THE SPECTRAL

In her book *The Female Thermometer*, Terry Castle argues for a special relationship between the cinema and the spectral. She holds that pre-cinematic devices are linked to what she calls the 'spectralization of the mind', pointing out that historically ghost stories evolved from folk tales and entered Gothic fiction where they enjoyed great popularity through the writings of Horace Walpole, Ann Radcliffe and Mathew Lewis. In the Victorian period the popularity of ghost stories continued via a range of authors, notably Sheridan Le Fanu, Elizabeth Gaskell and Henry James. The late eighteenth and early nineteenth centuries also explored the popular fascination with ghosts through magic lantern or so-called ghost shows; the magic lantern was a device for constructing and projecting phantasmagorical shows or spectres for a public viewing audience. Terry Castle explores the way in which these ghost shows came to represent the workings of the imagination or the 'spectralization of the mind'. She argues that the term *phantasmagoria* has undergone an interesting change in meaning over the past two centuries:

> From an initial connection with something external and public (an artificially produced 'spectral' illusion), the word has now come to refer to something wholly internal or subjective: the phantasmic imagery of the mind. This metaphoric shift bespeaks … the spectralization or 'ghostifying' of mental space [that is] the absorption of ghosts into the world of thought.[27]

Castle analyses this shift in the way we now happily affirm that our minds are

> filled with ghostly shapes and images, that we 'see' figures and scenes in our minds, that we are 'haunted' by our thoughts, that our thoughts can, as it were, materialize before us, like phantoms, in moments of hallucination, waking dream, or reverie.[28]

Castle points to the connection between motion pictures and magic lantern shows now regarded as part of the prehistory of the cinema. 'In various ways the new medium of motion pictures continued to acknowledge and reflect on its "spectral" nature and origins.'[29] She refers to the pioneering work of George Méliès (1861–1938), who made hundreds of short films between 1896 and 1912 that exploited special-effects technology to create magical and spectral effects. In my view, the cinema—particularly through the horror and supernatural film—has continued to influence shifts in meaning of the phantasmagoric and the 'spectralization of the mind'. I am not referring just to the enormous number of films that have brought to life tales of the undead, the supernatural and spectral, but also to the unique way in which film is able to depict the uncanny as if it were part of the viewer's own reality. Film, as we have seen, creates an uncanny gaze.

This process takes on particular power in relation to film in that the spectator's illusion of mastery over the visual field, created by what film theorist Christian Metz described as the spectator's 'identification with the (invisible) seeing agency of the film itself'. Metz argued that the film, projected seamlessly from the rear of the theatre, appears to flow from the imagination of the spectator.

> We are not referring here to the spectator's identification with the characters of the film (which is secondary), but to his preliminary identification with the (invisible) seeing agency of the film itself as discourse, as the agency which puts forward the story and shows it to us.[30]

In other words, the source of the story, the flow of images, seems to emanate from within the viewing subject. Uncannily present yet absent, the spectator is the source of the phantasmagoria—a process that has been naturalised through a century of film viewing. Castle talks of thoughts that 'materialize before us': in the cinema images flow before our eyes—they literally 'materialize before us, like phantoms, in moments of hallucination, waking dream, or reverie'—to use Castle's words. Film has made concrete what Castle calls 'the spectralization of the mind'. The cinematic viewing experience makes the spectator feel as if he/she is the actual source of the flow of spectral images, of the phantasmagoria unfolding before his/her eyes. The unfolding tale is literally a 'waking dream', but one accompanied by actual images, phantoms and apparent hallucinations. This is particularly true of the *Elm Street* films, which draw seductively upon a surreal flow of images to create a waking dream. This dream is, of course, disrupted when the spectator actively engages with the text in order to interpret the material, to construct meanings from the material presented on the screen.

Freddy is both uncanny male monster and a perverse primal mother who brings to the children of Elm Street a fear of death, accompanied by revelations about their own strange and estranged identities. As an emissary of the primal uncanny, the monstrous ghost brings to light what should have remained hidden. The underlying themes of the *Elm Street* series hold that the family home can be a dangerous place; that parents can harbour murderous feelings towards their own children; that abuse creates monsters; and that all families have terrible secrets. The ghost's uncanny power to assume different guises and shapes makes it the perfect monster to 'embody' such secrets, and the nightmare its perfect medium. This attack on the integrity of the proper family creates a sense of phallic panic that Freddy himself knowingly exploits through his gender-bending antics and black jokes. He is like a thorn in the side of the symbolic order, puncturing its smooth surfaces with black holes.

The *Nightmare on Elm Street* films unleash a series of fears that are inextricably bound up with the primal uncanny—fear of the family and of the incorporating maternal body, fear of the dissolution of boundaries, and fear of death. The one substantial thing that Freddy communicates to all is that death is inevitable. 'One, two, Freddy's coming for you', the children sing outside Freddy's house, their eerie melody echoing along Elm Street. 'Nine, ten, never sleep again.' The opening sequence of *Freddy's Dead* makes this point very effectively. A quotation from Friedrich Nietzsche covers the black screen. 'Do you know the terror of he who falls asleep? To the very toes he is terrified. Because the ground gives way under him. And the dream begins.'

8

JACK THE RIPPER: MODERNITY AND THE UNCANNY MALE MONSTER

We can also speak of a living person as uncanny, and we do so when we ascribe evil intentions to him … in addition to this we must feel that his intentions to harm us are going to be carried out with the help of special powers.

SIGMUND FREUD[1]

One of the most uncanny things about Jack the Ripper was that he appeared to be superhuman. In 1888 he brutally murdered at least five prostitutes in London's East End, one of the most populated areas of the city. He slaughtered his victims in the streets under the very eyes of the police and public. He killed at night and removed sets of organs, including the uterus, with great care and precision and without the aid of lighting. He usually pulled out the intestines and other organs and laid them out on the ground; he took body parts away with him. He then disappeared without a trace. The Ripper was never apprehended. The first modern serial killer, he was never given a 'face'. The Ripper was able to commit his crimes in anonymity and seemingly without fear of apprehension. The terrible nature of his victims' deaths created widespread panic throughout White-chapel and beyond.

Although the identity of the infamous Ripper has not been conclusively determined, Patricia Cornwell, in her recent study

Portrait of a Killer: Jack the Ripper Case Closed, provides a well-documented argument about his identity. Drawing upon the most recent police and forensic techniques, she argues that the Ripper was the German-born 'thoroughly English' artist Walter Sickert. Not everyone agrees. Sickert himself was certainly interested in the Ripper as evidenced by his 1908 painting *Jack the Ripper's Bedroom*, which depicted a gloomy dark scene of his own room. In the same year he also painted *The Camden Town Murder* which depicted a scene of a killer (believed to be Jack the Ripper) with the body of Emily Dimmock, a prostitute who was murdered in Camden Town in 1907. Cornwell's recent study indicates the extent to which the mystery of the Ripper's identity continues to haunt the popular imagination. Other suspects included: the Queen's grandson, the Duke of Clarence; the Queen's surgeon, Sir William Gull; and the famous stage actor Richard Mansfield. Because the Ripper possessed an advanced knowledge of the female anatomy and the kind of surgical precision needed to dissect a body, it was widely believed he was educated and from the upper classes of society.

Jack the Ripper was a new kind of killer—one of the first modern, as distinct from Gothic, monsters. He was a cruel observer of modern life, a *flâneur* of death. He knew the city intimately—its back streets, doss houses and dark corners. Almost all of his victims were found in the streets. His prey was a new kind of woman, the urban prostitute, who came to the city hoping to earn a living by selling sex.

The Ripper craved publicity and when he felt that the press were not paying enough attention to him he would write a new spate of letters or give details of his next killing. Between 1888 and 1896, The Ripper wrote some 250 mocking, taunting letters to the police, which revealed that he saw himself as playing a 'game' in which he would never be caught. He even named himself, signing many of his letters 'Love, Jack the Ripper'. A number contained the exclamation 'Ha Ha Ha!'. Some appeared to be written by an illiterate hand, but Cornwell argues this was another of his ruses: 'He couldn't resist reminding people he was literate by an occasional letter with perfect spelling, neat or beautiful script, and an excellent vocabulary.'[2] He taunted the police ('donkeys', 'idiots and fools') for not being able to catch him, talked about the reason why he murdered women ('filthy whores' who do not deserve to live), discussed the body parts he had removed and in one case he claimed that he had cooked and eaten his victim's organs. The Ripper thrived on sensational crimes and he also supplied the reading public with shocking details of his latest murder. Cornwell argues that most of these letters are genuine and claims the watermark on paper used in the Ripper letters matches the watermark on paper used by Sickert. The Ripper was a very modern murderer who enjoyed celebrity status.

The Ripper is possibly the most uncanny modern murderer of all time, never being caught despite having committed terrible deeds almost under the eyes of the police. Nearly all of his killings took place outdoors, at night, in the foggy streets. He tore open women's bodies, yet left very little blood at the scene of the crime. He committed terrible deeds, earning the title of 'lust murderer', yet there were no signs that he raped any of his victims. He hated prostitutes (and doubtless all women), yet he stole their reproductive organs. His shocking acts conveyed the impression that he was a beast, scarcely human, yet he no doubt looked completely normal, just like any other man. Cornwell argues that he was a psychopath who must have possessed great strength, probably wore disguises, loved to play macabre games and always adopted the same modus operandi. She attributes to the Ripper many more deaths than the official number.[3] Although the police numbers were dramatically increased and some were on the streets in disguise, the Ripper could not be caught; he was everywhere and nowhere. Freud stated that a living person is uncanny when he appears to carry out his evil acts with the assistance of special powers. A number of Ripper commentators point to this very feature. The Ripper 'has a strange and almost supernatural power to commit his crimes with impunity and in anonymity'.[4] The many films about Jack the Ripper certainly represent him as possessing uncanny powers that enabled him to avoid detection.

Jack the Ripper has also been the subject of popular novels, films, plays and television dramas. There have been over twenty film versions, yet strangely these have received very little theoretical attention apart from critical reviews. The most recent, *From Hell* (Albert & Allen Hughes, 2001), was based on the award-winning graphic novel of the same title. It starred Johnny Depp as Inspector Abberline, the detective from Scotland Yard who was in charge of the case. The Ripper murders took place in the same year as *Dr Jekyll and Mr Hyde* was being performed at the Lyceum. Robert Louis Stevenson's famous play about man's divided nature caught the popular imagination and became linked in the public mind with Jack the Ripper. Richard Mansfield's performance as the brutish Mr Hyde was so powerful and convincing that the famous American actor came under suspicion of the murders. The idea that the Ripper was a modern-day Jekyll and Hyde helped fuel the huge publicity that surrounded the faceless killer from the very beginning.

In the famous thriller *The Lodger*, written by Laura Marcus in 1913, the Ripper is without any identity from the start. 'Mrs Bunting always visioned The Avenger as a black shadow in the centre of a bright blinding light—but the shadow had no form or definite substance.'[5] This is perhaps the most uncanny thing about filmic and literary representations of Jack the Ripper: his 'facelessness'. *The Lodger* was the first fictionalised account of the murderer; it proved so popular that it was made into a film four times, most famously by Alfred Hitchcock in 1926 and again in 1932. In the 1988 television movie *Jack the Ripper*, the director and co-writer, David Wickes, draws on his own research to unmask the killer or killers. Until the final disclosure, Wickes generates suspense by implying that almost any of the male protagonists could have been the killer. In the end, he argues Jack the Ripper was the Queen's surgeon, Sir William Gull, assisted by his coachman who is portrayed in the film as a figure of death, perched high on the coach, face masked, and dressed in black.

The tendency to represent the Ripper as a 'superman' who could not be caught has become part of the Ripper mythology. In the cinema, the Ripper has in recent decades been assimilated into other figures such as the 'slasher' and the 'stalker' and killers such as the psychopaths from the *Halloween* and *Friday the 13th* series of films. The slasher figures hunt their victims, who are almost always unknown to them, in the dead of night, striking fear into the community and exacting a terrible death using a knife or sharp blade of some kind. The slasher is not unlike a modern version of the medieval figure of death, the Grim Reaper with its bloody scythe. The slasher film, which is a contemporary re-working of the Ripper myth, operates as a cautionary tale. Films such as *Friday the 13th* and *Halloween*, and their many follow-up films, feature a killer who murders teenagers while they are away from the watchful eyes of parents and enjoying illicit sex. Invariably, these films focus more on the gruesome deaths of the female victims. The female heroine of the modern slasher film—described by Carol Clover as 'the Final Girl'—is a courageous masculinised heroine who fights back and is usually victorious.[6] In this context, the contemporary slasher/stalker films represent a female right of passage.

The Ripper films are very different; they are about the complete destruction of woman. The attack is a vicious onslaught in which the Ripper essentially destroys the female body. Cornwell points out that when Jack the Ripper killed Mary Kelly, he hacked off her facial features, amputated her breasts, mutilated her genitalia 'to a pulp' and removed every organ except her brain. Many of these he neatly arranged around what was left of her body.[7] The graphic details of these murders are laid out in Ripper films such as *Jack the Ripper* and *From Hell*. In other ripper-style films the male killers similarly attack the bodies of their female victims: the mad doctor of *Eyes without a Face* (Georges Franju, 1959) removes the faces of his female victims;

the killer of *The Silence of the Lambs* (Jonathan Demme, 1991) flayed his victims to make a 'suit' of women's skins that he could wear; the killer from Hitchcock's *Psycho* inflicted a welter of deep knife cuts in the woman's stomach and uterus. The Ripper figure wants to destroy woman through her body.

THE PRIMAL UNCANNY AND DEATH

The Ripper is related to the primal uncanny through non-being and death. In psychoanalytic writings, the uncanny signifies an obscure, unfamiliar area which brushes up against the familiar. Rosemary Jackson points out that the term has been used 'philosophically as well as in psychoanalytic writing, to indicate a disturbing, vacuous area'. She refers to the philosopher Heidegger, who described the uncanny as an 'empty' space brought about by a loss of faith in the divine: 'The place which, metaphysically speaking, belongs to God ... can remain empty. Instead of it another, that is, a metaphysically corresponding place can appear, which is neither identical with God's sphere of being nor with that of man.'[8] According to Jackson the 'emergence of modern fantasy coincides with a recognition of this uncanny region'. This region is uncanny because it is familiar, in a metaphysical sense, but unfamiliar because it is occupied by neither God nor man.

The notion of the uncanny signifying not just an unfamiliar region but also an empty region is of particular relevance to an understanding of the representation of Jack the Ripper, whose identity is anonymous, and who occupies an empty region, identical with neither God's sphere nor man's sphere. Nothing is known about Jack the Ripper. He signifies a non-self, a lack-of-being, not only through his own anonymity but also because he brings about a lack-of-being in others. In completely destroying the bodies of his female victims, removing their organs, and cutting up the bodies, Jack the Ripper disassembles his victims as if to wipe out, to obliterate, their feminine and sexual identities. Their bodies become monstrous and uncanny in that each corpse signifies simultaneously a whole body (the woman that was) and a body in bits and pieces (the woman that is).

Freud wrote: 'the uncanny is that class of the frightening which leads back to what is known of old and long familiar'.[9] The Ripper brings to light what is hidden; he opens up his female victims and puts their internal organs (some he kept for himself) on display, arranged around the body, often in the darkened street. Those who stumbled unaware across these terrible scenes were filled with horror. The murder scene obliterates the well-preserved division between interiority and exteriority, thus invoking the uncanniness associated with indeterminate or blurred boundaries. The Ripper brought to light those things that should have remained hidden. He literally opened up woman's body and her internal organs to his own gaze and the gaze of others. According to Freud: 'It often happens that neurotic men declare that they feel there is something uncanny about the female genital organs',[10] 'this *unheimlich* place' that Freud finds familiar yet unfamiliar. Clearly, for Jack the Ripper the uncanniness of the female genitals overwhelms any feelings of familiarity; he sets out to destroy this 'first home' where he began life. In ripping out the womb from the body of the woman, transforming the *heimlich* into the *unheimlich*, he embraces death—but not for himself, only vicariously through the woman.

According to Freud, the uncanny also refers to 'dismembered limbs, a severed head, a hand cut off at the wrist … this kind of uncanniness spring[ing] from its proximity to the castration complex'.[11] Thus, Jack the Ripper created two uncanny scenes: one in which he brings to light woman's genitals and womb, the first home that should have remained hidden; and the other in relation to her dismembered body, a scene that directly invokes castration. He castrates the woman in order to assure himself that only woman can be castrated, to stave off recognition of the possibility of his own loss.

Eventually the name Jack the Ripper became synonymous with death and facelessness. The Ripper's identity is known only through what he did; it is closely associated with murder, dismemberment and non-identity. In a sense the name 'Ripper' —like that of 'Grim Reaper'—is synonymous with death itself. According to Cixous, the 'relationship to death reveals *the highest degree* of the *Unheimlich*'.[12]

> *'Death' does not have any form in life. Our unconscious makes no place for the representation of our mortality. As an impossible representation, death is that which mines, by this very impossibility, the reality of death. It goes even further. That which signifies without that which is signified ... Death will recognize us, but we shall not recognize it.*[13]

Because Jack the Ripper lacks an identity—apart from his identity as death—his name points only to the horror and formlessness of death. Precisely because he has no identity/face, he can signify the horrific face of the primal uncanny—death itself—but only vicariously. The killer of *Peeping Tom* (Michael Powell, 1960) is similarly obsessed with prostitutes and the vicarious experience of death. Once he is alone with his female victim, he brings out his movie camera; as he releases a knife hidden in the tripod leg and plunges it into her body, he films the expression of horror on her face. This enables him to capture on film the look of death as it flickers across his victim's face. He later projects the film onto the wall of his darkroom, masturbating himself into life as he watches the woman die. Woman, who is aligned with death, must die on his behalf. Fearful of embracing the primal uncanny (in the manner of the vampire or werewolf), the Ripper attempts to experience it vicariously through the destruction of woman, the one who, for him, signifies death. Like a medieval *memento mori*, she assumes the form of death in life because death has no *adequate* signifier. Thus the Ripper attempts to signify death through repetition—that is, through the repeated annihilation of woman.

The notion of fragmentation is central in the representation of the monster. The many forms of the monster, from werewolf and vampire to ghost and slasher, violates a universally dominant belief in the unity of the self—that is, the self as a discrete coherent whole. The horror film focuses almost exclusively on motifs associated with the self as divided, fractured, multiple. The monster, in his many faces, represents an attack on the notion of the unified rational self. Jack the Ripper is a monster of fragmentation; the threat he represents is displaced onto the cut and dismembered bodies of his female victims. The fragmentation of the female body in *Jack the Ripper* films points to the concomitant idea of the fragmented self, thus undermining one of society's most sacred beliefs: that the self is unified, whole and coherent.

Jacques Lacan's theory of the fragmented self is relevant to this discussion.[14] Lacan opposed the traditional view that human subjectivity was whole and coherent. He argued that subjectivity itself was a construct and that just as it was 'constructed' it could also be deconstructed. An individual could lose his or her sense of self, as happens in certain psychological conditions. According to Lacan the subject's sense of self is formed in infancy, between the ages of six months and eighteen months, in what he described as 'the mirror phase'. During this period the infant does not initially have a sense of itself as an entity that is separate from its parents, particularly the mother. It continues to feel a part of her body, a feeling reinforced through breast-feeding. It is at this point, however, that the infant experiences for the first time the thrill of recognising itself as separate and independent. This occurs when it sees the image of itself reflected back through the eyes of the mother or through a mirror. In other words, the infant's sense of self is given to it, confirmed by, the other. This has important consequences for the remainder of the child's life. When the infant first recognises itself as a separate entity it is filled with joy. The child also thinks it is just like its parents, fully formed, an adult, complete and perfect. Only gradually does the child learn it must 'walk before it can run'. This moment, according to Lacan, is a moment of recognition and misrecognition. Thus the self is split, always yearning to be a more perfect self than it ever can be.

In order for the subject to preserve its sense of self as complete and unified, it must preserve boundaries between itself and those things that threaten the self, such as fragmentation and death. The uncanny, which dissolves boundaries, must be kept at bay. Mladen Dolar points out that, because the French language does not have a term for the uncanny, 'Lacan had to invent one, *extimité*.'[15] This term blurs the line between interior and exterior, a line that traditional thought, from religion to philosophy, has attempted to keep in place. As Ken Gelder explains: 'the uncanny is always "at stake" in ideology, which ceaselessly tries to integrate it, to make it familiar to itself in order to be rid of it'.[16] Dolar writes:

> *Now the dimension of* extimité *blurs this line. It points neither to the interior nor to the exterior, but is located there where the most intimate interiority coincides with the exterior and becomes threatening, provoking horror and anxiety. The extimate [*extimité*] is simultaneously the intimate kernel and the foreign body; in a word, it is* unheimlich.[17]

In her discussion of the vampire, Joan Copjec states that we can experience an uncanny feeling 'when we too closely approach the extimate object in ourselves'—that is, when we fail to keep the appropriate boundaries in place.[18] In order to constitute ourselves as subjects we must reject that part of ourselves that we are not, that which signifies our lack-of-being, such as death. We define ourselves in relation to what we are not, we carry the uncanny, the familiar/unfamiliar self within us. It is as if Jack the Ripper signifies only a lack of being, a non-self, which threatens to overwhelm him. Thus he displaces onto woman what he can no longer tolerate within himself: his own mortality, his own fragmentation, his own death as a man. The Ripper is an uncanny monster who collapses into woman all distinctions between life and death, self and other. His female victims represent the primal uncanny—the scene of his violent desires. The horror of their dismembered and opened bodies correlates to the horror that lives within his own being. To the Ripper the woman is nothing in and of herself; she exists only to be destroyed. To the female (and male) viewer, the plight of the female victim encourages us to identify, misogynistically, with our 'lack of being' or non-being. The slasher himself signifies a monster with no sense of identity, a creature without an inner core who is only truly alive when taking the life of others. Cixous's comment on death is equally applicable to Jack the Ripper: 'The strange power of death moves in the realm of life as the *Unheimliche* in the *Heimliche*, as the void fills up the lack.'[19]

'JACK THE RIPPER' (1988)

David Wickes's television movie *Jack the Ripper*, through its deliberate play on identity and non-identity, portrays the Ripper as an uncanny monster. The film is at pains to enforce the view that almost any man in London, from any walk of life, might have been Jack the Ripper. Inspector Abberline, played by Michael Caine, suspects almost all of the men with whom he comes into contact during his investigation: the Duke of Clarence, next-in-line to the throne; Sir William Gull, the Queen's surgeon; Dr Llewellyn, the police surgeon; Richard Mansfield; and Mr Lees, the Queen's clairvoyant. In addition, he investigates a large number of potential suspects on the basis of their profession. The terrible precision with which the women's organs are removed indicates that the Ripper must have an excellent knowledge of anatomy. Abberline calls for a list of all doctors, surgeons, vets, butchers and artists; the latter on the grounds that some operate on corpses in order to study the human body. 'It could be half the men in London,' one police-man announces. The murders also gave rise to racial prejudice. The reporter from *The Star* describes the East End as 'a jungle', with 'Poles, Frenchmen, Jews pouring in from everywhere'. 'It is a wonder there hasn't been a killing every day,' he adds with a hint of opportunism. In his first article on the killings, he is reprimanded by the editor for sensationalism: 'Eighty thousand prostitutes. A disgrace to the Nation. Crime is now a way of life'. Although, in the end, the film does produce a killer (Sir William Gull), there is no evidence to support this conclusion in actuality. In another sense, the film's narrative logic indicates that the identity of the killer will never be known, which of course is the actual truth. The fact that Jack the Ripper's identity has always remained an enigma is what drives the film's narrative and shapes its visual patterns.

The facelessness of Jack the Ripper creates a gap in the narrative, undermining any sense that the self is by definition a unified coherent whole with a history and identity. The mutilated bodies of his female victims also create—or mirror—such a gap. The women must bear man's wound. This is one of the most transgressive functions of the uncanny. In a film like *Jack the Ripper*, however, the price of confronting such transgression is the dehumanising toll exacted by the workings of misogyny and murder. The Ripper finds women uncanny; they signify for him disunity, the gap, which is why he must destroy them totally, attempt to fragment their entire bodies into an absence, leaving only 'a pulp'.

The Ripper's anonymity is suggested through four interrelated motifs: the clairvoyant's visions, the artist's drawing, the police department's identikit and the actor's performance as the monster in *Dr Jekyll and Mr Hyde*. In all four instances, the face of the monster is represented as a blank. This recurring motif creates an uncanny disturbance throughout the film. Eventually, the film attempts to make this 'lack' concrete by suggesting that perhaps the Ripper has a divided personality; that he is normal one minute and insane the next, a human being and a primitive beast.

The artist Miss Emma Prentiss draws Jack the Ripper as a man with two faces: one is normal and the other has the look of someone deranged and brutish. She is attempting to draw what Mr Lees, the clairvoyant, has seen in a 'vision'. He tells the Inspector that he has seen the killer's face, but not clearly. 'My visions are symbolic, intuitive, not like a photograph.' The Inspector is incredulous. Lees continues: 'Imagine two windmills turning like two wheels and each a face together and apart like the wheels of a coach. Two wheels, not two faces'. Lees is a lean, dark man with a mesmerising stare. As he describes his vision the camera focuses on his hands, which imitate the action of turning wheels. He tells the Inspector to look for 'one killer with two faces—look for a man with two faces!' As Emma makes changes to the drawing, she says that the normal face reminds her of someone. It is the American actor Richard Mansfield, who is currently playing in *Dr Jekyll and Mr Hyde* at the Lyceum. The group decides to see the play. Mansfield is on stage, about to transform into Mr Hyde. As he drinks a special potion from a flask, his face begins to change and we hear eerie, uncanny laughter fill the theatre. The clairvoyant is so disturbed that he runs from the theatre and collapses. He is overwhelmed by another vision: the camera focuses on a close-up of his eyes; two coach wheels emerge, one from each eye; they spin in unison until they collide in the middle forming one large wheel. The latter transforms into a man's featureless, blank face. In a particularly uncanny moment the face metamorphoses into the face of a beast with open, snarling jaws. The effect is momentary and the beast transforms into the clairvoyant's eyes.

The clairvoyant's vision is disturbing and eerie. It is designed to capture an image of man as half beast; a new, heretical idea (to some) which had received wide public exposure in the late nineteenth century due to the popularisation of the ideas of Charles Darwin. The film returns repeatedly to this concept in order to stress the fact it was at the time a controversial, disturbing notion. The Inspector decides to visit the leading expert on madness, Sir William Gull, who has written books on 'Diseases of the Brain' and 'Cretinoid Women'. When he enters Gull's rooms, he recognises a bust of Darwin. He asks if this was the one who said: 'all our ancestors were monkeys'. He asks the Inspector if it is possible for someone to be 'normal one minute, insane the next'. Sir William replies with a short speech:

The concept of the multi-faceted mind is too radical for the medical profession to cope with. In years to come it will be accepted as a matter of course ... in the meantime we lump such phenomena under the rather vague title of dementia praecox. *Take Darwin. He was perfectly right. Yet millions of educated men still believe that the human race began with two naked lovers frolicking in the garden of Eden.*

During this period, Freud's controversial theories about the human mind were also finding public expression. *Fin-de-siècle* culture was opening up to embrace radically new ideas about human nature. The appearance of the Ripper at this moment in history was symbolic of a new age and new ideas about civilisation and repression. The Inspector then asks whether a man could have two minds, one good and one evil. Sir William replies: 'Yes, I don't see why not. I don't see why not.' The film then cuts to the Lyceum where Richard Mansfield is changing from Dr Jekyll into Mr Hyde. Again the uncanny laughter begins as we see the right and left sides of his cranium begin to bulge and pulsate. Members of the audience leave in horror.

The film suggests that Stevenson's play provided the police and public with a way of understanding the insane behaviour of the Ripper; he was a man with a split personality, someone who outwardly appeared just like a respectable member of the Victorian public, possibly even someone from the upper reaches of society. Yet inwardly he was a beast. The film *From Hell* depicts him as a silhouette with a top hat to convey his anonymity and his upper class identity. Just like Jekyll, he felt none of the constraints imposed by civilisation. Whereas Stevenson was deliberately vague about the exact nature of Hyde's terrible crimes, leaving the details to the imaginations of the reader/spectator, Jack the Ripper's unspeakable acts left nothing to the imagination. Although the newspapers shrouded the details of the murders in abstract descriptions ('he took certain organs'), the film describes each atrocity in detail. In one macabre scene, Dr Llewellyn, who carried out the autopsy on the

The anonymous, terrifying Ripper in top hat—From Hell, 2001
(*20th Century Fox/The Kobal Collection/Vollmer, Jurgen*)

first victim, Mary Ann Nichols, stated that the killer had 'severed the throat right back to the vertebrae and removed the uterus, the kidneys'. 'Your poor woman wasn't just murdered, she was plundered,' he added. The film gives prominence to one Ripper letter in particular as the victim's cut ear plays a key role in the narrative:

> *Dear Boss, I keep hearing the police have caught me. And that joke about the leather apron gave me a real fit. I'm down on all fours and I shall keep ripping them … The next job I do I shall clip the ladies ears off just for jolly wouldn't you, Yours truly jack the Ripper. They say I'm a doctor now. Ha! Ha!*

Martin Tropp argues that the Ripper set out to create 'a literature of fear unprotected by the mask of fiction'. He cites another letter in which the Ripper included part of a kidney from Catherine Eddowes: 'From hell, Mr Lusk, sir, I send you half the kidne I took from one woman, prasarved it for you, tother piece I fried and ate it; was very nice'. His macabre joke was echoed in the recent film *The Silence of the Lambs*, in which the cannibal killer, Hannibal Lecter, talks about eating the liver of one of his victims.

> The Ripper speaks directly to his readers, implying by his words and literacy (despite the [possibly intentional] misspellings) that he is one of them, acting out the grotesque fantasies that made popular fiction from Gothic romance to penny dreadfuls part of the imaginative life of a mass audience.[20]

THE 'UNHEIMLICH' CITY

As a result of the Ripper murders, women became afraid to leave their houses at night. Cultural historian Judith R. Walkowitz argues that the way in which the popular press reported his murders was a warning to women.

> The Ripper's London was presented as a city of 'light' and of 'darkness,' of pockets of civility surrounded by a menacing obscurity. A seasoned urban traveler, the Ripper could move effortlessly and invisibly through these spaces, transgressing all boundaries; committing his murderous acts in the open, under the cover of darkness; exposing the private parts of women to public view. These themes helped to construct the Ripper story as a cautionary tale for women: a warning that the city was a dangerous place when they transgressed the narrow boundaries of hearth and home and entered public space.[21]

The dangers of the London street for young women are emphasised in two other early films which portray the Ripper: Alfred Hitchcock's *The Lodger* (1926), in which the streets are always swathed in fog, and G. W. Pabst's *Pandora's Box* (1929), in which Lulu the free-spirited prostitute meets Jack the Ripper on the street at night. One of the most memorable images from early silent cinema is of Louise Brooks, in *Pandora's Box*, rushing out into the night, a childlike look of innocence on her face, to encounter the silent stranger, the figure of menace, who turns out to be the man who will murder her. In Lulu's death scene, the Ripper is represented as a handsome, almost sympathetic figure who struggles with his own conscience before murdering Lulu. In the stairway sequence, the camera cuts between Lulu's innocent smile and the Ripper's grip on his knife in order to highlight his internal conflict. Mary Ann Doane sees the portrayal of Jack as symptomatic of the view that, in modernity, man has experienced a crisis of identity and developed a new attitude of cynicism towards women and their new freedoms. She argues that the representation of Lulu, her image as woman, 'only magnifies an exploitative desire and calls forth the modern anxieties of male consciousness'.[22] Given the terrible cruelty of the Ripper's crimes against women, it is difficult to understand how Pabst could whitewash his deeds, let alone portray him as even slightly sympathetic. His unexpected presence at the end of *Pandora's Box* suggests that his narrative function is to punish Lulu for her immoral lifestyle.

The recent Ripper film, *From Hell*, directed by the Hughes brothers, places greater emphasis on the group of prostitutes whom the Ripper murdered than does the Wickes film. Based on the award-winning graphic novel, the eponymous *From Hell*, it offers a much more fictionalised account of the Ripper's murders. Inspector Abberline is portrayed as an opium addict who falls in love with one of the victims, Mary Kelly. Filmed from a subjective point of view, his surreal opium dreams anticipate the murders, even depicting the horrified faces of the victims. The film adopts a detached surreal vision combined with a graphic edgy style. The fog-bound streets of London are shrouded in a clammy uncanny atmosphere; scenes of the Ripper's butchery convey a visceral sense of gore.

From Hell endows each of the women with presence and character. Mary Kelly (Heather Graham), who in reality met the most gruesome death of all, is depicted as being intelligent and

Woman at the mercy of the unheimlich *caped monster*—From Hell, *2001*
(20th Century Fox/The Kobal Collection/Vollmer, Jurgen)

protective of her sisters. Ironically, the women are represented as possessing greater strength of character and resilience than members of the law and government. The film indicates that the Ripper is a member of upper-class society through a motif of fruit. He entices the women to accompany him by offering each one a bunch of grapes, which at that time were an expensive item. Emphasis is placed on the fact that corruption is strongest at the upper levels of government and society. *From Hell* opens with a statement by Jack the Ripper dated 1888—the year of the murders: 'One day men will look back and say I gave birth to the twentieth century.' With its graphic scenes of butchery, *From Hell* depicts the twentieth century as a charnel house in which women are at the mercy of a ubiquitous male sadism. At one point the Ripper says to his sadistic coachman: 'We are in the most extreme and utter region of the human mind—an abyss where men meet themselves. Hell, Netley, we are in Hell!'

With modernity there emerges what we might describe as a master narrative of male cruelty—that is, the narrative of the psychopath, the slasher. From the inaugural Jack the Ripper case in the late nineteenth century to the present, the cinema has demonstrated a fascination with the slasher, the male monster who murders women. The Ripper was possibly the first human monster of the cinema; his crimes represented as an inevitable part of modernity. He is the monster of the city par excellence, transforming into the slasher and stalker of the modern horror film.

Time After Time (Nicolas Meyer, 1979) draws a narrative connection between the Ripper of the late nineteenth century and the slasher of the later twentieth century. It begins with the Ripper (David Warner) escaping in H. G. Wells's time machine into the future. Wells (Malcolm McDowell) pursues the Ripper from Victorian England to find himself in America in the year 1979. There is no attempt to make a mystery out of the Ripper's identity. What is uncanny about *Time After Time* is that one century seems to mirror the other: very little has changed. Adopting a sardonic tone, the film suggests that the Ripper is much more at home in San Francisco in 1979. Women have become liber-ated and the nightclubs and streets offer many more potential victims. Wells himself is horrified to discover that the world has not improved over the previous century. If anything, it has regressed: the culture appears to be saturated in violence. Cultural critic Mark Seltzer's study of the serial killer in American culture, which he describes as a 'wound culture', argues that public culture has become 'one of the crucial sites where private desire and public fantasy cross'.[23]

Compared with rural existence, city life at the beginning of the twentieth century was characterised by new modes of work, the assembly line, glitzy entertainment, a fast pace of living, ease of transport, the emergence of the bustling anonymous crowd, stimulation and a growing fear of crime and of the stranger on the streets. Jack the Ripper was one of these strangers: a mon-strous man who stalked women as if they were animal prey. Aspects of modernity which helped to shape this fear were numerous: the new forms of transport (cars, trains), which gave individuals greater freedom of movement and opportunities for illicit sexual encounters; the growth of new urban centres of entertainment such as vaudeville, cinemas, nightclubs and bars, which encouraged a relaxation of morals; the growth of urban prostitution; a desire for novelty, thrills and eventually the taboo. The new cinema was quick to represent perverse forms of sexual desire. The Ripper terrorised London in the late nineteenth cen-tury; by the early twentieth century the cinema was already telling his story and has continued to re-tell it to the present day. Many of these films play on the Ripper's anonymity, suggesting that the Ripper dwells in all men. This possibility undermines the notion that the male subject is rational and just. The male monster also renders the dominant, familiar patriarchal order strange and unfamiliar, creating a sense of dread and panic. The narrative of the Ripper is a dark rite of passage about the hidden horrors of the *unheimlich* city.

Central to the modernist impulse that links sex and excite-ment, eroticism and death, is the figure of new woman. Cultural historian Patrice Petro refers to the image of the new woman that sparked ambivalence and anxiety in the writings of the cultural theorist Walter Benjamin: she was an erotic, aggressive, and therefore profoundly masculinised female figure linked to the prostitute and lesbian. This image of woman was personified by Louise Brooks in *Pandora's Box* and by Marlene Dietrich in her cycle of early 1930s films directed by Joseph von Sternberg. In these, the erotic scenarios are imbued with images of lesbianism, prostitution, bisexuality and woman as a masculinised threat. Louise Brooks embodies all of the traits of the new woman (sexual, desirable, in control of her sexuality, free to walk the streets) for which she is remorselessly punished. In the cinema, it has been woman's body that has visibly represented the changes associated with modernity; changes in work, family, fashion, sexuality. When the prosecutor in *Pandora's Box* condemns Lulu because she is a woman, he needs no further evidence than the myth of Pandora. As a woman she is, by nature, guilty. Lulu's fate at the hands of Jack the Ripper epitomises the fate of all women who signify modernity, the women who are independent, who live alone, walk the streets, smoke, drink and enjoy sex.

Films about Jack the Ripper draw upon the horrified uncanny gaze that was created by the cinema and remained central to the nature of cinematic looking throughout the twentieth century. Deployed in relation to scenarios that traverse moral and bodily boundaries and invoke the threat of the uncanny, this gaze is central to the formation of the horror genre. As Hélène Cixous states, the 'relationship to death reveals *the highest degree of the* Unheimliche'.[24] Death dissolves all boundaries. Death itself cannot be represented directly, except through symbolic references such as the dead body or through empty space. The secret that the uncanny Ripper films uncover is man's fear of death and woman, his sense of phallic panic brought on by this fear. Films about Jack the Ripper have always utilised scenes of 'empty space' to emphasise the impossibility of giving a face either to this most uncanny male monster or to the mutilated bodies of his female victims. The Ripper was obsessed with the primal uncanny yet terrified of entering its domain.

In contrast to the other monsters discussed in the preceding chapters, the Ripper is not finally put on display in order to show his grotesque or horrific features. Other male monsters are known by trademark motifs associated with the nature of the threat they offer: Dracula's bloody fanged mouth; the wolf–man's furry human/animal body; Freddy's scarred face and finger blades; the mad scientist's monstrous creations; the Mummy's decaying shroud. In contrast, the horror associated with the Ripper is displaced onto the bodies of his female victims. Unlike the other monstrous creatures, he does not transform from the familiar into the unfamiliar—rather his victims undergo metamorphosis, their familiar and reassuring female bodies/selves becoming unfamiliar and grotesque. In a sense the only face we have of the Ripper is that of the animal. The bloody, dismembered and mutilated bodies of his victims look as if they have been ripped apart by a primeval beast. The Ripper (and contemporary slasher) brings together the three aspects of the primal uncanny—woman, death and the animal—into a truly horrific scene that points to the dark misogynistic desires of this particular male monster. What he shares with the other classic male monsters is that through his monstrous desires and deeds he too uncovers gaps and contradictions at the heart of the symbolic order.

In drawing on the primal uncanny, the horror film questions phallic power and qualities associated with the male symbolic, such as identity, rationality, ascendancy and control. In particular it undermines the notion of a coherent, stable, civilised self. Instead it gives rise to a sense of disquiet, unease and fear. Through its depiction of the male monster as creature, the horror film addresses the issue of the animal in a more direct way than possibly any other film genre. It collapses the boundary between human and animal and in so doing raises the possibility of the end of civilisation. Like woman, the animal is defined as 'other' in relation to the symbolic order of law and language and as such signifies the ruin of representation. The uncanny alliance of woman, death and the animal is captured perfectly in the ancient figure of the Sphinx—the female monster with a dragon's tail and body of a winged lion. The male hero who failed to answer her riddle immediately met his end. In a sense, by aligning the male monster with the primal uncanny, the horror film creates man as Sphinx, creating a narrative space in which man is able to question the symbolic order, to ask himself: 'What does man want?'

NOTES

Introduction

1 Dika, 'The Stalker Film', pp. 86–101; Heath, p. 92; Lurie, pp. 159–73; Mulvey, pp. 6–18; Neale, pp. 41–5.
2 Critics and theorists are divided over whether or not one can assign a general definition to monstrosity, let alone male monstrosity. See Noel Carroll's *The Philosophy of Horror* and Judith Halberstam's *Skin Shows*.
3 Halberstam, p. 8.
4 ibid., p. 6.
5 Schelling, quoted in Freud, 'The Uncanny', p. 345.
6 Some critics argue that it is difficult to define monsters even as a group. For an excellent discussion of these issues see Schneider, 'Monsters as (Uncanny) Metaphors'.
7 Aristotle, book IV, p. 401.
8 ibid., book II, p. 175.
9 Kramer & Sprenger, pp. viii–ix.
10 ibid., p. 43.
11 ibid., p. 44.
12 Huet, *Monstrous Imagination*, p. 73.
13 ibid., p. 21.
14 Warner, 'Beauty & The Beast', p. 7.
15 ibid., p. 11.
16 Cixous, p. 536.
17 Fiedler, p. 38.
18 Warner, 'Beauty & The Beast', p. 11.
19 Kristeva, *Powers of Horror*, p. 4.
20 Žižek, 'Grimaces of the Real', p. 64.
21 There are many individual essays on film and the uncanny as well as on film, horror and the uncanny. An excellent collection is *The Return of the Uncanny*, a special edition of *Paradoxa: Studies in World Literary Genres*, vol. 3, no. 3–4, 1997. See also Schneider, *Horror Film and Psychoanalysis*, which contains a section, 'Theorizing the Uncanny', with four excellent essays.

1 Film, Horror and the Primal Uncanny

1 Freud, 'The Uncanny', pp. 366–8.
2 ibid., p. 339.
3 Important books and essays on the uncanny from various disciplines include: Arnzen, *The Return of the Uncanny*; Castle, *The Female Thermometer: Eighteenth Century Culture and the Invention of the Uncanny*; Stern, 'I think Sebastian, Therefore I … Somersault'; Gelder, 'Vampires and the Uncanny'; McQuire, 'The Uncanny Home'; Mellencamp, 'Uncanny Feminism'; Rank, *The Double: A Psychoanalytic Study*; Vidler, *The Architectural Uncanny*;

Wright, 'The Uncanny and Surrealism'; Yingling, 'Homosexuality and the Uncanny'.

4 Freud, 'The Uncanny', p. 351.
5 ibid., p. 349.
6 ibid., p. 354.
7 ibid., p. 339.
8 ibid., pp. 339–40.
9 ibid., p. 339.
10 ibid.
11 ibid., p. 340.
12 ibid.
13 ibid., p. 341.
14 Jackson, p. 69.
15 Freud, 'The Uncanny', p. 345.
16 ibid., p. 346.
17 ibid., p. 347.
18 ibid., p. 345.
19 ibid., p. 346.
20 ibid., p. 372.
21 ibid., pp. 371–2.
22 ibid., p. 372.
23 ibid., p. 374.
24 Royle, p. 2.
25 Todd, p. 526.
26 Cixous, p. 532.
27 ibid., p. 533.
28 McCaffrey, p. 96.
29 Freud, 'The Uncanny', p. 353.
30 ibid., p. 351.
31 Hoffman, pp. 90–1.
32 ibid., p. 88.
33 ibid., p. 89.
34 ibid., pp. 90–1.
35 ibid., p. 87.
36 Royle, p. 211.
37 ibid., p. 2.
38 ibid., p. 3.
39 ibid., p. 27.
40 Jackson, pp. 69–70.
41 Creed, *The Monstrous-Feminine*, ch. 1.
42 Linda Williams has presented a different but related argument. She argues that woman and the monster have a surprising affinity through their status as 'other' and that this has implications for the female spectator. See her important article 'When the Woman Looks'.
43 Freud, 'The Uncanny', p. 368.
44 ibid., p. 340.

45 ibid., pp. 363–4.
46 ibid., p. 364.
47 Cixous, p. 543.
48 Jackson, p. 68.
49 ibid.
50 Royle, p. 88.
51 Hoffman, pp. 114–15.
52 Hoffman, p. 105.
53 Williams, 'When the Woman Looks', p. 15.
54 Clover, p. 103.
55 Tudor, *Monsters and Mad Scientists*, p. 69.
56 Freud, *Art and Literature*, p. 224.
57 Freud, *The Interpretation of Dreams*, pp. 295–6.
58 Bronfen, p. 53.
59 ibid., p. 53.
60 ibid., p. 56.
61 Walker, p. 629.
62 ibid.
63 Dijkstra, p. 294.
64 Derrida, p. 375.
65 ibid., p. 375.
66 Wright, 'The Uncanny and Surrealism', pp. 265–82.

2 Film and the Uncanny Gaze

1 Royle, p. 76.
2 Freud, 'The Uncanny', p. 345.
3 ibid., p. 347.
4 Royle, p. 2.
5 Freud, 'The Uncanny', p. 345.
6 ibid.
7 ibid., p. 346.
8 Royle, p. 16.
9 Freud, 'The Uncanny', p. 371, footnote 1.
10 ibid., p. 371.
11 Derrida quoted in Royle, p. 68.
12 Kristeva, *Strangers to Ourselves*, p. 170.
13 Royle, p. 44.
14 Creed, *The Monstrous-Feminine*, p. 29.
15 Kristeva, *Powers of Horror*, p. 5.
16 Copjec, p. 59.
17 Hoffman, p. 124.
18 ibid., p. 87.
19 ibid.
20 ibid., p. 99.
21 ibid., pp. 114–15.

22 ibid., p. 105.
23 ibid., p. 120.
24 Freud, 'The Uncanny', p. 374.
25 ibid.
26 ibid.
27 ibid., p. 375.
28 Royle, p. 76.
29 Castle, p. 8.
30 Dolar, p. 7.
31 Stephen Schneider presents an interesting argument about the uncanny in modern horror. See Schneider, 'Uncanny Realism'.
32 Stern, p. 354.
33 Kittler, p. 96.
34 Stern, p. 354.
35 Freud, 'The Uncanny', p. 339.
36 See Creed, *The Monstrous-Feminine*, for a discussion of the female monster.
37 Castle, p. 16.

3 Man as Womb Monster: Frankenstein, Couvade and the Post-human

1 Cixous, 'Fiction and its Phantoms', p. 544.
2 Freud, 'The Uncanny', pp. 366–7.
3 Walker, p. 106.
4 Freud, 'Preface to the Translation of Charcot's Lectures', p. 11.
5 Showalter, p. 130.
6 Bullough, 'Medieval, Medical and Scientific Views of Women', pp. 485–501.
7 Showalter, p. 130.
8 Freud, 'Observation of a Severe Case of Hemi-anaesthesia in a Hysterical Male', p. 31.
9 Freud, 'Analysis of a Phobia in a Five Year Old Boy', p. 93.
10 Freud, 'From the History of an Infantile Neurosis', p. 230.
11 Kahane, p. 285.
12 Freud, 'The Uncanny', p. 368.
13 ibid.
14 ibid., p. 366–7.
15 Creed, *The Monstrous-Feminine*, ch. 1.
16 Hogan, p. 4.
17 Twitchell, p. 180.
18 Freud, 'The Uncanny', p. 369.
19 Shelley, p. 137.
20 ibid., p. 158.
21 ibid., p. 159.
22 For an excellent discussion of *Alien Resurrection* and the ethics of cloning see Stacey, pp. 251–76.

23 See Stacey for a detailed description and excellent discussion of each of these monsters.
24 Braidotti, p. 181.
25 Kristeva, *Powers of Horror*, p. 9.
26 Rank, p. 6.
27 ibid.
28 This discussion is based on a longer article. See Creed, 'Phallic Panic'.
29 For an analysis of the film in relation to womb envy see Robbins.

4 Man as Menstrual Monster: Dracula and His Uncanny Brides

1   Cixous, 'Fiction and Its Phantoms', p. 545.
2   Stoker, p. 28.
3   ibid., p. 47.
4   ibid., p. 51.
5   ibid., p. 52.
6   Taubin, 'Bloody Tales', p. 10.
7   Moretti, p. 84.
8   ibid., p. 85.
9   Halberstam, p. 29.
10 ibid., p. 29.
11 Twitchell, pp. 106–9.
12 Lacan, *Écrits*; and 'Wish (Desire)' in Laplanche & Pontalis, pp. 481–3.
13 Twitchell, p. 115.
14 ibid., p. 121–2.
15 Stoker, p. 336.
16 ibid., p. 339.
17 Tropp, p. 133.
18 Freud, 'The Taboo of Virginity', p. 204.
19 Dadoun, pp. 52–3.
20 Creed, *The Monstrous-Feminine*, p. 59.
21 Shuttle & Redgrove, pp. 267–8.
22 ibid.
23 Kristeva, *Powers of Horror*, p. 96.
24 Huet, *Monstrous Imagination*, p. 126.
25 Freud, 'The Uncanny', p. 366.
26 Moretti, p. 98.
27 ibid., p. 103.
28 ibid.
29 ibid., p. 101.
30 ibid.
31 ibid., p. 104.
32 Cited in ibid., p. 100.
33 Cook, p. 43.
34 Stoker, p. 343.

35 ibid., p. 404.
36 Pirie, p. 84.
37 Gelder, p. 53.

5 *Freud's Wolf Man, or the Tale of Granny's Furry Phallus*

1 Cixous, p. 543.
2 Freud's two main critics were Carl Gustav Jung and Alfred Adler, who disagreed with Freud's emphasis on the role of phantasy in early childhood. Freud refers to their criticism on pp. 287–8 of 'From the History of an Infantile Neurosis'.
3 Freud, 'The Uncanny', p. 368.
4 Mulvey, pp. 6–18.
5 Dika, 'The Stalker Film', pp. 86–101; Heath, p. 92; Lurie, pp. 159–73; Neale, pp. 41–5.
6 Freud, 'From the History of an Infantile Neurosis', p. 241.
7 ibid., p. 242.
8 ibid., p. 234.
9 ibid., p. 259.
10 ibid., p. 229.
11 ibid., p. 325.
12 ibid., p. 235.
13 ibid., p. 259.
14 ibid., p. 270.
15 ibid., p. 269.
16 ibid., p. 278.
17 ibid., p. 273.
18 Brunswick, Appendix in Davis, p. 218.
19 Freud, 'The Uncanny', p. 372.
20 Cixous, p. 537.
21 Møller, p. 75.
22 Freud, 'From the History of an Infantile Neurosis', p. 244.
23 ibid., p. 329.
24 ibid., p. 340.
25 ibid.
26 ibid.
27 ibid., p. 341.
28 Ginzburg, p. 149. Ginzburg argues that this explanation does not refute Freud's interpretation of the dream as a primal scene, but that it does complicate the issue if one considers Freud's earlier definition of the primal scene not as 'coitus between parents' but as 'acts of seduction perpetrated on children by adults (frequently parents)', a theory that he subsequently abandoned.
29 ibid., p. 148.
30 ibid.
31 ibid., p. 149.

32 Freud, 'From the History of an Infantile Neurosis', p. 275.
33 ibid., p. 262.
34 Bettelheim, p. 172.
35 ibid., p. 179.
36 Quoted in Bettelheim, p. 176.
37 Rank, cited in Davis, p. 186.
38 Freud, 'From the History of an Infantile Neurosis', p. 243.
39 ibid., p. 260.
40 ibid., p. 243.
41 ibid., p. 339.
42 ibid., p. 253.
43 ibid., p. 254.
44 ibid.
45 ibid., p. 255.
46 ibid., p. 254.
47 ibid., p. 280.
48 ibid., p. 273.
49 ibid., p. 247.
50 Klein, p. 223.
51 Freud, 'From the History of an Infantile Neurosis', p. 271.
52 ibid., p. 249.
53 ibid., p. 252.
54 ibid.
55 ibid.
56 ibid., p. 248.
57 ibid., p. 249.
58 ibid., p. 270.
59 ibid., p. 291.
60 Abraham & Torok, p. xv.
61 Freud, 'From the History of an Infantile Neurosis', p. 340.
62 ibid.
63 ibid., p. 247.
64 ibid., pp. 339–40.
65 ibid., p. 248.
66 Wolf-Man, 'The Memoirs of The Wolf–Man', in Gardiner, pp. 3–132.

6 Fear of Fur: Bestiality and the Uncanny Skin Monster

1 Royle, p. 207.
2 Kristeva, Powers of Horror, p. 53.
3 Walker, pp. 1068–72.
4 ibid., p. 1070.
5 Lawrence, p. 103.
6 Kristeva, pp. 12–13.
7 Freud, 'Totem and Taboo', p. 203.
8 ibid., p. 139.

9 ibid., p. 203.
10 ibid.
11 ibid., p. 48.
12 Freud, 'From the History of an Infantile Neurosis', p. 347.
13 Abraham quoted in Laplanche & Pontalis, p. 55.
14 Royle, p. 210.
15 ibid., p. 211.
16 Agamben, p. 105
17 ibid.
18 ibid.
19 ibid.
20 Vidler, p. x.
21 ibid., p. 9.
22 Ferry, p. 107.
23 ibid., p. 106.
24 ibid., p. 107.
25 Deleuze & Guattari, p. 238.
26 This discussion expands on an earlier article on the Wolf Man, Creed, 'Dark Desires', pp. 118–33.
27 Hornung, p. 212.
28 Walker, p. 782.
29 Evans, p. 56.
30 Jackson, p. 66.
31 Royle, p. 23.
32 ibid., pp. 542–3.

7 Freddy's Fingernails: Child Abuse, Ghosts and the Uncanny

1 Freud, 'The Uncanny', p. 364.
2 This following discussion of the surrealists and the female child in film is based on Creed, 'Baby Bitches from Hell: Monstrous Little Women in Film', <http://www.cinema.ucla.edu/women/creed/creed1.html>.
3 Cixous, p. 542.
4 Webb & Short, p. 42.
5 Bunuel, cited in Carrière, p. 92.
6 Webb & Short, p. 47.
7 Germer, p. 178.
8 ibid., pp. 179–80.
9 ibid., p. 181.
10 Gasché, in Wolfreys, p. 6.
11 Derrida quoted in Royle, p. 68.
12 Cixous, p. 536.
13 Floyd, p. 46.
14 Cixous, p. 542.
15 Cixous, pp. 542–3.

16 ibid., p. 543.
17 ibid.
18 Freud, 'The Uncanny', p. 367.
19 Sconce, p. 113.
20 ibid., p. 114.
21 Žižek, 'The Spectre of Ideology', p. 21.
22 Craven quoted in Williams, 'Trying to Survive in the Darker Side', p. 175.
23 ibid., p. 172.
24 Freud, 'The Uncanny', p. 368.
25 Cixous, p. 544.
26 Hoffman, pp. 87 and 90.
27 Castle, pp. 141–2.
28 ibid., p. 143.
29 ibid., p. 154.
30 Metz, p. 49.

8 Jack the Ripper: Modernity and the Uncanny Male Monster

1 Freud, 'The Uncanny', p. 365.
2 Cornwell, pp. 346–7.
3 ibid., p. 67.
4 Tropp, p. 111.
5 Lowndes, quote on back cover.
6 Clover, pp. 106–10.
7 Cornwell, p. 429.
8 Jackson, p. 63; Heidegger quoted in Jackson, ibid.
9 Freud, 'The Uncanny', p. 340.
10 ibid., p. 368.
11 ibid., p. 366.
12 Cixous, p. 542.
13 ibid., p. 543.
14 See Grosz, pp. 31–47, for an excellent discussion of the mirror phase.
15 Dolar, p. 6.
16 Gelder, p. 52.
17 Dolar, p. 6.
18 Copjec, p. 59.
19 Cixous, p. 543.
20 Tropp, p. 113.
21 Walkowitz, p. 3.
22 Doane, p. 162.
23 Seltzer, *Serial Killers*, p. 1.
24 Cixous, p. 542.

FILMOGRAPHY

Alien (Ridley Scott, 1979)

Alien Resurrection (Jean-Pierre Jeunet, 1997)

Aliens (James Cameron, 1986)

Alien 3 (David Fincher, 1992)

Altered States (Ken Russell, 1980)

An American Werewolf in London (John Landis, 1981)

Basic Instinct (Paul Verhoeven, 1992)

Beauty and the Beast (Jean Cocteau, 1946)

Beauty and the Beast (Gary Trousdale and Kirk Wise, 1991)

Blacula (William Crain, 1972)

Blade (Stephen Norrington, 1998)

The Boys from Brazil (Franklin J. Schaffner, 1978)

Bram Stoker's Dracula (Francis Ford Coppola, 1992)

The Bride of Frankenstein (James Whale, 1935)

· *The Brood* (David Cronenberg, 1979)

The Cabinet of Dr Caligari (Robert Weine, 1919)

Carrie (Brian De Palma, 1976)

Cat People (Jacques Tourneur, 1942)

The Company of Wolves (Neil Jordan, 1984)

Count Dracula (Jess Franco, 1970)

The Curse of the Cat People (Robert Wise, Gunter von Fritsch, 1944)

Dead Ringers (David Cronenberg, 1988)

Demon Seed (Donald Cammell, 1977)

Dracula (Tod Browning, 1931)

Dracula (Terence Fisher, 1958; also known as *Horror of Dracula*)

Dracula AD 1972 (Alan Gibson, 1972)

Dragonwyck (Joseph L. Mankiewicz, 1946)

Don't Look Now (Nicolas Roeg, 1973)

Dr Jekyll and Mr Hyde (John S. Robertson, 1920)

Dr Jekyll and Mr Hyde (Rouben Mamoulian, 1932)

Dr Jekyll and Mr Hyde (Victor Fleming, 1941)

Dr Jekyll and Sister Hyde (Roy Ward Baker, 1972)

Evil Dead II (Sam Raimi, 1987)

The Evil of Frankenstein (Freddie Francis, 1964)

Eyes without a Face (Georges Franju, 1959)

The Fly (Kurt Neumann, 1958)

The Fly (David Cronenberg, 1986)

Frankenstein (James Whale, 1931)

Freddy's Dead: The Final Nightmare (Rachael Talalay, 1991)

Friday the 13th (Sean S. Cunningham, 1980)

Fright Night (Tom Holland, 1985)

From Hell (Albert and Allen Hughes, 2001)

Gaslight (George Cukor, 1944)

Gattaca (Andrew Niccol, 1997)

Ginger Snaps (John Fawcett, 2000)

Ginger Snaps Back: The Beginning (Grant Harvey, 2004)

Gods and Monsters (Bill Condon, 1998)

Halloween (John Carpenter, 1978)

Hannibal (Ridley Scott, 2001)

The Haunting (Robert Wise, 1963)

The Haunting (Jan De Bont, 1999)

The Haunting of Julia (Richard Loncraine, 1976)

The Howling (Joe Dante, 1981)

The Hunger (Tony Scott, 1983)

The Innocents (Jack Clayton, 1961)

The Island of Dr Moreau (Don Taylor, 1977)

The Island of Dr Moreau (John Frankenheimer, 1996)

Interview with the Vampire: The Vampire Chronicles (Neil Jordan, 1994)

It's Alive! (Larry Cohen, 1974)

I Spit on Your Grave (Meir Zarchi, 1978)

Jack the Ripper (David Wickes, 1988)

Jaws (Steven Spielberg, 1975)

Junior (Ivan Reitman, 1994)

King Kong (Merian C. Cooper, 1933)

The Lodger (Alfred Hitchcock, 1926 & 1932)

The Manitou (William Girdler, 1978)

Marnie (Alfred Hitchcock, 1964)

Max My Love (Nagisa Oshima, 1986)

Metropolis (Fritz Lang, 1921)

A *Nightmare on Elm Street* (Wes Craven, 1984)

A *Nightmare on Elm Street Part 2: Freddy's Revenge* (Jack Sholder, 1985)

A *Nightmare on Elm Street 3: Dream Warriors* (Chuck Russell, 1987)

A *Nightmare on Elm Street 4: The Dream Master* (Renny Harlin, 1988)

A *Nightmare on Elm Street 5: The Dream Child* (Steven Hopkins, 1989)

Nosferatu (F. W. Murnau, 1922)

The Others (Alejandro Amenábar, 2001)

Pandora's Box (G. W. Pabst, 1929)

Peeping Tom (Michael Powell, 1960)

The Planet of the Apes (Tim Burton, 2001)

Poltergeist (Tobe Hooper, 1982)

Psycho (Alfred Hitchcock, 1960)

Rabid (David Cronenberg, 1977)

RoboCop (Paul Verhoeven, 1987)

Secret beyond the Door (Fritz Lang, 1948)

The Shining (Stanley Kubrick, 1980)

The Silence of the Lambs (Jonathan Demme, 1991)

Sleepy Hollow (Tim Burton, 1999)

Species (Roger Donaldson, 1995)

The Stepford Wives (Bryan Forbes, 1975)

The Student of Prague (Hans Ewers, 1913)

Tarzan the Ape Man (W. S. Van Dyke, 1932)

Time After Time (Nicolas Meyer, 1979)

Total Recall (Paul Verhoeven, 1990)

The Uninvited (Lewis Allen, 1944)

The Vampire Lovers (Roy Ward Baker, 1970)

Wes Craven's New Nightmare (Wes Craven, 1994)

What Ever Happened to Baby Jane? (Robert Aldrich, 1962)

The Wizard of Oz (Victor Fleming, 1939)

Wolf (Mike Nichols, 1994)

The Wolf Man (George Waggner, 1941)

Wolfen (Michael Wadleigh, 1981)

BIBLIOGRAPHY

Abraham, Nicholas, and Maria Torok, *The Wolf Man's Magic Word:*
A Cryptonymy, University of Minnesota Press, USA, 1986.

Agamben, Giorgio, *Homo Sacer*, Stanford University Press, California, 1998.

Aichele, George, 'Postmodern Fantasy, Ideology, and the Uncanny', in *The*
Return of the Uncanny, special issue of *Paradoxa: Studies in World*
Literary Genres, vol. 3, no. 3–4, 1997.

Apter, Terry E., *Fantasy Literature: An Approach to Reality*, Macmillan,
London, 1982.

Aristotle, *Generation of Animals*, Harvard University Press, Cambridge,
Massachusetts, William Heinemann Ltd, London, 1963.

Armstrong, Phillip, 'Uncanny Spectacles: Psychoanalysis and the Texts of
King Lear', *Textual Practice*, vol. 8, no. 2, pp. 414–34.

Arnzen, Michael, 'The Return of the Uncanny', in *The Return of the*
Uncanny, special issue of *Paradoxa: Studies in World Literary Genres*,
vol. 3, no. 3–4, 1997, pp. 315–320.

——, 'Supermarketing the Uncanny: Anxiety at the Point-of-sale', in *The*
Return of the Uncanny, special issue of *Paradoxa: Studies in World*
Literary Genres, vol. 3, no. 3–4, 1997, pp. 571–93.

Batty, Nancy, 'America's Worst Nightmare … Roseanne!', in *The Return of*
the Uncanny, special issue of *Paradoxa: Studies in World Literary*
Genres, vol. 3, no. 3–4, 1997, pp. 539–55.

Bettelheim, Bruno, *The Uses of Enchantment: The Meaning and Importance of*
Fairy Tales, Vintage Books, New York, 1977.

Braidotti, Rosi, *Metamorphoses: Towards a Materialist Theory of Becoming*,
Polity, Cambridge, 2002.

Bresnick, Adam, 'Prosopoetic Compulsion: Reading the Uncanny in Freud
and Hoffmann', *Germanic Review*, vol. 71, no. 2, pp. 114–32.

Bronfen, Elizabeth, 'The Death Drive (Freud)', in E. Wright (ed.), *Feminism*
and Psychoanalysis: A Critical Dictionary, Blackwell, USA, 1992,
pp. 52–7.

Bullough, Vern L., 'Medieval, Medical and Scientific Views of Women',
Medieval and Renaissance Studies, no. 4, 1973, pp. 485–501.

Carrière, Jean-Claude, *The Secret Language of Film*, Faber & Faber, London,
1994.

Carroll, Noel, *The Philosophy of Horror; or Paradoxes of the Heart*, Routledge,
New York, 1990.

Castle, Terry, *The Female Thermometer: Eighteenth Century Culture and the Invention of the Uncanny*, Oxford University Press, Oxford, 1995.

Chisolm, Dianne, 'The Uncanny', in E. Wright (ed.), *Feminism and Psychoanalysis: A Critical Dictionary*, Blackwell, USA, 1992, pp. 436–40.

Cixous, Hélène, 'Fiction and Its Phantoms: A Reading of Freud's *Das Unheimliche* (The "Uncanny")', *New Literary History*, vol. 7, 1976, pp. 525–48.

Clover, Carol, 'Her Body, Himself: Gender in the Slasher Film', in J. Donald (ed.), *Fantasy and the Cinema*, British Film Institute Publishing, London, 1989, pp. 91–133.

Coffman, Elizabeth, 'Uncanny Performances in Colonial Narratives: Josephine Baker in *Princess Tam Tam*', in *The Return of the Uncanny*, special issue of *Paradoxa: Studies in World Literary Genres*, vol. 3, no. 3–4, 1997, pp. 379–94.

Cook, Pam, 'Dracula', *Sight and Sound*, vol. 3, no. 2, 1993, pp. 42–3.

Copjec, Joan, 'Vampires, Breast-Feeding, and Anxiety', in K. Gelder (ed.), *The Horror Reader*, Routledge, London, pp. 52–63.

Cornwell, Patricia, *Portrait of a Killer: Jack the Ripper Case Closed*, Time Warner, United States, 2002.

Creed, Barbara, 'Phallic Panic: Male Hysteria and *Dead Ringers*', *Screen*, vol. 21, no. 2, Summer 1990, pp. 125–46.

——, 'Dark Desires: Male Masochism in the Horror Film', in S. Cohan and I. R. Hark (eds), *Screening the Male*, Routledge, London, 1993, pp. 118–33.

——, *The Monstrous-Feminine: Film, Feminism, Psychoanalysis*, Routledge, London, 1993.

——, 'Baby Bitches from Hell: Monstrous Little Women in Film', <http://www.cinema.ucla.edu/women/creed/creed1.html>, 1995.

Dadoun, Roger, 'Fetishism in the Horror Film', in J. Donald (ed.), *Fantasy and the Cinema*, BFI Publishing, London, 1991, pp. 39–62.

Davis, Whitney, *Drawing The Dream of the Wolves: Homosexuality, Interpretation and Freud's 'Wolf Man'*, Indiana University Press, Bloomington and Indianapolis, 1995.

Deleuze, G., and F. Guattari, *A Thousand Plateaus*, The University of Minnesota Press, Minneapolis, 1987.

Derrida, Jacques, 'The Animal That Therefore I Am', *Critical Inquiry*, Winter, 2002, vol. 28, pp. 369–419.

Dijkstra, Bram, *Idols of Perversity: Fantasies of Feminine Evil in Fin de Siècle Culture*, Oxford University Press, New York, 1986.

Dika, Vera, 'The Stalker Film: 1978–81', in G. A. Waller (ed.), *American Horrors: Essays on the Modern American Horror Film*, University of Illinois Press, Urbana, 1988, pp. 86–101.

——, 'From Dracula—with Love', in B. K. Grant (ed.), *The Dread of Difference: Gender and the Horror Film*, University of Texas Press, Austin, 1996, pp. 388–400.

Doane, Mary Ann, *Femmes Fatales*, Routledge, New York, 1991.

Doherty, Thomas, 'Genre, Gender, and the *Aliens* Trilogy', in B. K. Grant (ed.), *The Dread of Difference: Gender and the Horror Film*, University of Texas Press, Austin, 1996, pp. 181–99.

Dolar, Mladen, '"I Shall Be With You On Your Wedding-night": Lacan and the Uncanny', *October*, no. 58, 1991, pp. 5–23.

Evans, Walter, 'Monster Movies: A Sexual Theory', in B. K. Grant (ed.), *Planks of Reason: Essays on the Horror Film*, The Scarecrow Press, Inc. Metuchen, N.J., and London, 1984, pp. 53–64.

Ferreira, Maria Aline, 'The Uncanny (M)other: Angela Carter's *The Passion of New Eve*', in *The Return of the Uncanny*, special issue of *Paradoxa: Studies in World Literary Genres*, vol. 3, no. 3–4, 1997, pp. 471–88.

Ferry, Jean, 'Concerning King Kong', in P. Hammond (ed.), *The Shadow and Its Shadow: Surrealist Writings on Cinema*, British Film Institute, London, 1978.

Fiedler, Leslie, *The Stranger in Shakespeare*, Paladin, Frogmore St. Albans, 1974.

Floyd, Nigel, 'Freddy's Dead: The Final Nightmare' *Sight & Sound*, vol. 1, no. 10, 1992.

Foster, Hal, *Compulsive Beauty*, MIT Press, Cambridge, Mass., 1993.

Freud, Sigmund, 'Analysis of a Phobia in a Five Year Old Boy', in J. Strachey (ed.), *The Standard Edition of the Complete Psychological Works of Sigmund Freud*, vol. 10, The Hogarth Press, London, 1953–66.

——, 'Observation of a Severe Case of Hemi-anaesthesia in a Hysterical Male', in J. Strachey (ed.), *The Standard Edition of the Complete Psychological Works of Sigmund Freud*, vol. 1, The Hogarth Press, London, 1953–66.

——, 'Preface to the Translation of Charcot's Lectures on the Diseases of the Nervous System' (1886), in J. Strachey (ed.), *The Standard Edition of the Complete Psychological Works of Sigmund Freud*, vol. 1, The Hogarth Press, London, 1953–66.

——, 'The Taboo of Virginity', in J. Strachey (ed.), *The Standard Edition of the Complete Psychological Works of Sigmund Freud*, vol. 11, pp. 191–208, The Hogarth Press, London, 1953–66.

——, *Art and Literature*, The Pelican Freud Library, vol. 14, Penguin, Ringwood, Australia, 1975.

——, *The Interpretation of Dreams*, Pelican Freud Library, vol. 14, Penguin, Ringwood, Australia, 1975.

——, 'Totem and Taboo', The Pelican Freud Library, vol. 13, Penguin, Ringwood, Australia, 1975.

——, 'The Uncanny', *Pelican Freud Library*, vol. 14, Penguin, Ringwood, Australia, 1975.

——, 'From the History of an Infantile Neurosis (The "Wolf Man")', in *The Pelican Freud Library*, vol. 9, Penguin, England, 1979, pp. 227–345.

Gardiner, Muriel (ed.), *The Wolf-Man and Sigmund Freud*, Penguin, Harmondsworth, 1973.

Gelder, Ken, 'Vampires and the Uncanny: Le Fanu's "Carmilla"', in *Reading the Vampire*, Routledge, London and New York, 1994, pp. 42–64.

——and Jane M. Jacobs, *Uncanny Australia: Sacredness and Identity in a Postcolonial Nation*, Melbourne University Press, Carlton, 1998.

Germer, Stephan, 'Pleasurable Fear: Géricault and the Uncanny Trends at the Opening of the Nineteenth Century', *Art History*, vol. 22, no. 2, June 1999, pp. 159–83.

Ginsburg, Ruth, 'A Primal Scene of Reading: Freud and Hoffmann', in *Literature and Psychology*, vol. 38, no. 3, 1992, pp. 24–46.

Ginzburg, Carlo, *Clues, Myths and the Historical Method*, Johns Hopkins University Press, Baltimore and London, 1986.

Grant, Barry Keith, 'Interview with Barry Keith Grant', in *The Return of the Uncanny*, special issue of *Paradoxa: Studies in World Literary Genres*, vol. 3, no. 3–4, 1997, 429–37.

——(ed.), *The Dread of Difference*, University of Texas Press, Austin, USA, 1996.

Grosz, Elizabeth, *Jacques Lacan, A Feminist Introduction*, Allen & Unwin, Sydney, 1990.

Gunning, Tom, 'Phantom Images and Modern Manifestations: Spirit Photography, Magic Theatre, Trick Films, and Photography's Uncanny', in P. Petro (ed.), *Fugitive Images: From Photography to Video*, Indiana University Press, Bloomington, 1995, pp. 42–71.

Halberstam, Judith, *Skin Shows: Gothic Horror and the Technology of Monsters*, Duke University Press, London, 1995.

Heath, Stephen, 'Difference', *Screen*, vol. 19, no. 3, 1978, pp. 51–112.

Hertz, Neil, 'Freud and the Sandman', in *The End of the Line: Essays in Psychoanalysis and the Sublime*, Columbia University Press, New York, 1985, pp. 97–121.

Hoffman, E. T. A., 'The Sandman', in R. J. Hollingdale (trans.), *Tales of Hoffman*, Harmondsworth, Middlesex, 1982.

Hogan, David J., *Dark Romance: Sexuality in the Horror Film*, McFarland & Company, London, 1986.

Hornung, Clarence P., *Hornung's Handbook of Designs and Devices: 1836 Basic Designs and Their Variations*, Dover Publications, New York, 1959.

Huet, Marie-Hélène, 'Living Images: Monstrosity and Representation', *Representations*, 4, 1983, pp. 73–87.

——, *Monstrous Imagination*, Harvard University Press, London, 1993.

Jackson, Rosemary, *Fantasy: The Literature of Subversion*, Methuen, London and New York, 1981.

Jentsch, Ernst, 'On the Psychology of the Uncanny', trans. R. Sellars, in *Angelaki*, vol. 2, no. 1, 1906, pp. 7–16.

Kahane, Claire, 'Object-relations Theory', in E. Wright (ed.), *Feminism and Psychoanalysis: A Critical Dictionary*, Blackwell, Oxford, 1992.

Kelso, Sylvia, 'The Postmodern Uncanny: or Establishing Uncertainty', in *The Return of the Uncanny*, special issue of *Paradoxa: Studies in World Literary Genres*, vol. 3, no. 3–4, 1997, pp. 456–70.

Kittler, Friedrich A., 'Romanticism—Psychoanalysis—Film: A History of the Double' in J. Johnston (ed.), *Literature, Media, Information Systems*, G + B Arts International, Amsterdam, 1997, pp. 85–100.

Klein, Melanie, *The Psychoanalysis of Children*, The Hogarth Press, London, 1932.

Koffman, Sarah, *Freud and Fiction*, trans. S. Wykes, Polity Press, Cambridge, 1991.

Kramer, Heinrich, and James Sprenger, *The Malleus Maleficarum*, Dover Publications, New York, 1971.

Krell, David Farrell, '*Das Unheimliche*: Architectural Sections of Heidegger and Freud', *Research in Phenomenology*, vol. 22, 1991, pp. 43–61.

Kristeva, Julia, *Powers of Horror: An Essay on Abjection*, Columbia University Press, New York, 1982.

——, *Strangers to Ourselves*, trans. Leon S. Roudiez, Columbia University Press, New York, 1991.

Kunkle, Sheila, 'The Uncanny Effects of Cruelty', in *The Return of the Uncanny*, special issue of *Paradoxa: Studies in World Literary Genres*, vol. 3, no. 3–4, 1997, pp. 556–70.

Lacan, Jacques, *The Language of the Self*, A Delta Book, Dell Publishing, New York, 1968.

——, *Écrits: A Selection*, Tavistock Publications, London, 1977.

Laplanche, J., and J-B. Pontalis, *The Language of Psycho-Analysis*, The Hogarth Press, London, 1985.

Lapsley, Robert, and Michael Westlake, *Film Theory: An Introduction*, Manchester University Press, Manchester, 1988.

Lawrence, Elizabeth A., 'Werewolves in Psyche and Cinema: Man–Beast Transformation and Paradox', *Journal of American Culture*, vol. 19, 3, 1996, pp. 103–12.

Lowndes, Marie Belloc, *The Lodger*, Oxford University Press, New York, 1996.

Lurie, Susan, 'Pornography and the Dread of Women: The Male Sexual Dilemma', in L. Lederer (ed), *Take Back the Night: Women on Pornography*, Morrow, New York, 1980, pp. 159–73.

Lyndenberg, Robin, 'Freud's Uncanny Narratives', *PMLA*, 112, 1997, pp. 1072–86.

Masschelein, Anneleen, 'Double Reading / Reading Double: Psychoanalytical Poets at Work', in *The Return of the Uncanny*, special issue of *Paradoxa: Studies in World Literary Genres*, vol. 3, no. 3–4, 1997, pp. 395–406.

McCaffrey, Phillip, 'Freud's Uncanny Woman', in S. L. Gilman (ed.), *Reading Freud's Reading*, New York University, New York, 1994, pp. 91–108.

McNally, Raymond T., *Dracula Was a Woman: In Search of the Blood Countess of Transylvania*, Hamlyn, London, 1984.

McQuire, Scott, 'The Uncanny Home', in *The Return of the Uncanny*, special issue of *Paradoxa: Studies in World Literary Genres*, vol. 3, no. 3–4, 1997, pp. 527–38.

Medovoi, Leerom, 'Theorizing Historicity, or the Many Meanings of *Blacula*', *Screen*, vol. 39, no. 1, 1998, pp. 1–23.

Mellencamp, Patricia, 'Uncanny Feminism: The Exquisite Corpses of Cecelia Condit', *Framework*, vol. 32, no. 3, 1986, pp. 269–85.

Metz, Christian, *The Imaginary Signifier*, Indiana University Press, Bloomington, 1982.

Møller, Lis, *The Freudian Reading: Analytical and Fictional Constructions*, University of Pennsylvania Press, Philadelphia, 1991.

Moretti, Franco, *Signs Taken for Wonders: Essays in the Sociology of Literary Forms*, Verso Editions and NLB, London, 1983.

Morlock, Forbes, 'Double Uncanny', in S. Wood, *Home and Family*, special issue of *Angelaki*, vol. 2, no. 1, 1995, pp. 17–21.

Mulvey, Laura, 'Visual Pleasure and Narrative Cinema', *Screen*, vol. 16, no. 3, Autumn 1975, pp. 6–18.

Neale, Stephen, *Genre*, British Film Institute, London, 1980.

Norden, Martin, 'The Uncanny Film Image of the Obsessive Avenger', in *The Return of the Uncanny*, special issue of *Paradoxa: Studies in World Literary Genres*, vol. 3, no. 3–4, 1997, pp. 367–78.

Paradoxa: Studies in World Literary Genres, special issue, *The Return of the Uncanny*, vol. 3, no. 3–4, 1997.

Paul, William, 'Uncanny Theatre: The Twin Inheritances of the Movies', in *The Return of the Uncanny*, special issue of *Paradoxa: Studies in World Literary Genres*, vol. 3, no. 3–4, 1997, 321–47.

Petro, Patrice, *Joyless Streets, Women and Melodramatic Representation in Weimar Germany*, Princeton University Press, Princeton, 1989.

Phelan, Lyn, 'Artificial Women and Male Subjectivity in *42nd Street* and *Bride of Frankenstein*', *Screen*, vol. 41, no. 2, Summer 2000, pp. 161–82.

Pinedo, Isabel, 'Wet Death and the Uncanny', in *The Return of the Uncanny*, special issue of *Paradoxa: Studies in World Literary Genres*, vol. 3, no. 3–4, 1997, pp. 407–16.

Pirie, David, *A Heritage of Horror: The English Gothic Cinema 1947–1972*, Gordon Fraser, London, 1973.

Polidori, John, 'The Vampyre', in E. F. Bleiler (ed.), *Three Gothic Novels*, Dover, New York 1966.

Punter, David, 'Shape and Shadow: On Poetry and the Uncanny', in D. Punter (ed.), *A Companion to the Gothic*, Blackwell, Oxford, 2000, pp. 193–205.

Rand, Nicholas, and Maria Torok, '*The Sandman* Looks at "The Uncanny": The Return of the Repressed or of the Secret; Hoffmann's Question to Freud', in S. Shamdasani and M. Munchow (eds), *Speculations After Freud: Psychoanalysis, Philosophy and Culture*, Routledge, London, 1994, pp. 185–203.

Rank, Otto, *The Double: A Psychoanalytic Study* [1914], The University of North Carolina Press, Chapel Hill, 1971.

Robbins, Helen W., '"More Human Than I am Alone": Womb Envy in *The Fly* and *Dead Ringers*', in Steve Cohan and Ina Rae Hark (eds), *Screening the Male: Exploring Masculinities in Hollywood Cinema*, Routledge, London and New York, 1993, pp. 134–47.

Royle, Nicholas, *The Uncanny*, Manchester University Press, Manchester and New York, 2003.

Rushton, Ricrad, 'Cinema's Double: Some Reflections on Metz', *Screen*, vol. 43, no. 2, 2002, pp. 107–18.

Schneider, Steven, 'Uncanny Realism and the Decline of the Modern Horror Film', in *The Return of the Uncanny*, special issue of *Paradoxa: Studies in World Literary Genres*, vol. 3, no. 3–4, 1997, pp. 417–28.

——, 'Monsters as Uncanny Metaphors: Freud, Lakoff, and the Representation of Monstrosity in Cinematic Horror', *Other Voices*, vol. 1, no. 3, January 1999, pp. 1–20.

—— (ed.), *Horror Film and Psychoanalysis: Freud's Worst Nightmare*, Cambridge University Press, Cambridge and New York, 2004.

Sconce, Jeffrey, 'Spectacles of Death: Identification, Reflexivity, and Contemporary Horror', in J. Collins, H. Radner, and A. Preacher Collins (eds), *Film Theory Goes to the Movies*, Routledge, New York and London, 1993.

Seltzer, Mark, *Serial Killers: Death and Life in America's Wound Culture*, Routledge, New York, 1998.

——, *Wound Culture: Death and Life in America's Wound Culture*, Routledge, New York, 1998.

Shelley, Mary, *Frankenstein*, Signet, New York and Scarborough, Ontario, 1965.

Showalter, Elaine, *The Female Malady: Women, Madness and English Culture 1830–1980*, Virago Press, London, 1987.

Shuttle, Penelope, and Peter Redgrove, *The Wise Wound: Eve's Curse and Everywoman*, Richard Marek, New York, 1978.

Simms, Eva-Maria, 'Uncanny Dolls: Images of Death in Rilke and Freud', *New Literary History*, vol. 27, 1996, pp. 663–77.

Stacey, Jackie, 'She is Not Herself: The Deviant Relations of *Alien Resurrection*', *Screen*, vol. 44, no. 3, Autumn 2003, pp. 251–76.

Stern, Lesley, 'I Think Sebastian, Therefore I … Somersault: Film and the Uncanny', in *The Return of the Uncanny*, special issue of *Paradoxa: Studies in World Literary Genres*, vol. 3, no. 3–4, 1997, pp. 348–66.

Stoker, Bram, *Dracula*, Penguin, Melbourne, 1985.

Taubin, Amy, 'Bloody Tales', *Sight and Sound*, vol. 5, no. 1, January 1995, pp. 8–11.

Todd, Jane Marie, 'The Veiled Woman in Freud's "Das Unheimliche"', *Signs*, 2/3, 1986, pp. 519–28.

Tropp, Martin, *Images of Fear: How Horror Stories Helped Shape Modern Culture (1818–1918)*, McFarland, London, 1990.

Tudor, Andrew, *Monsters and Mad Scientists: A Cultural History of the Horror Movie*, Blackwell Publishers, Oxford, 1989.

——, 'Why Horror? The Peculiar Pleasures of a Popular Genre', *Cultural Studies*, 11, no. 3, 1997, pp. 443–63.

Twitchell, James, B., *Dreadful Pleasures: An Anatomy of Modern Horror*, Oxford University Press, New York and Oxford, 1985.

Vidler, Anthony, *The Architectural Uncanny: Essays in the Modern Unhomely*, MIT, Cambridge, Mass., 1992.

Walker, Barbara, *The Woman's Encyclopedia of Myths and Secrets*, Harper & Row, San Francisco, 1983.

Walkowitz, Judith R., 'Science and Séance: Transgressions of Gender and Genre in Late Victorian London', *Representations*, 22, 1988, pp. 3–29.

Warner, Marina, 'Beauty & The Beast', *Sight & Sound*, vol. 2., issue 6, 1992, pp. 6–11.

——, *From the Beast to the Blonde*, Vintage, London, 1994.

Webb, Peter, with Robert Short, *Hans Bellmer*, Quartet Books, London, 1985.

Weber, Samuel, 'The Sideshow, or: Remarks on a Canny Moment', *Modern Language Notes*, vol. 88, 1973, pp. 1102–33.

Williams, Linda, 'When the Woman Looks', in M. A. Doane, P. Mellencamp and L. Williams (eds), *Re-Vision*, The American Film Institute, Los Angeles, 1984, pp. 83–99.

——, *Critical Desire: Psychoanalysis and the Literary Subject*, Edward Arnold, London, 1995.

——, 'Trying to Survive in the Darker Side: 1980s Family Horror', in B. Grant (ed.), *The Dread of Difference: Gender and the Horror Film*, University of Texas Press, Austin, 1996, pp 164–80.

Winchell, James, 'Century of the Uncanny: The Modest Terror of Theory', in *The Return of the Uncanny*, special issue of *Paradoxa: Studies in World Literary Genres*, vol. 3, no. 3–4, 1997, pp. 515–20.

Wolfreys, Julian, *Victorian Hauntings: Spectrality, Gothic, the Uncanny and Literature*, Palgrave, Basingstoke and New York, 2002.

Wood, Robin, 'Burying the Undead: The Use and Obsolescence of Count Dracula', in B. K. Grant (ed.), *The Dread of Difference: Gender and the Horror Film*, University of Texas Press, Austin, 1996, pp. 364–78.

Wood, Sarah (ed.), *Home and Family*, special issue of *Angelaki*, vol. 2, no. 1, 1995.

Wright, Elizabeth, 'The Uncanny and Surrealism', in P. Collier and J. Davies (eds), *Modernism and the European Unconscious*, Polity Press, Cambridge, 1989, pp. 265–82.

——, *Psychoanalytic Criticism: A Reappraisal*, Polity Press, Cambridge, 1998.

——, *Speaking Desires Can Be Dangerous: The Poetics of the Unconscious*, Polity Press, Cambridge, 1999.

Yingling, Thomas, 'Homosexuality and the Uncanny: What's Fishy in Lacan', in T. Foster, C. Siegel and E. Berry (eds), *The Gay Nineties*, New York University Press, New York, 1997.

Young, Elizabeth, 'Here Comes the Bride: Wedding Gender and Race in *Bride of Frankenstein*', in B. K. Grant (ed.), *The Dread of Difference: Gender and the Horror Film*, University of Texas Press, Austin, 1996, pp. 309–37.

Young, Robert, 'Psychoanalytic Criticism: Has It Got Beyond a Joke?', *Paragraph*, vol. 4, 1984, pp. 87–114.

Žižek, Slavoj, 'Grimaces of the Real, or When the Phallus Appears', October, 58, 1991, pp. 44–8.

——, 'The Spectre of Ideology', in S. Zizek (ed.), *Mapping Ideologies*, Verso, London, 1994, pp. 1–33.

INDEX

Pages marked in **bold** indicate a photograph.

Dr Jekyll and Sister Hyde 50
Dracula (1931) 70, 75, **77**, **80**
Dracula (1958) 72
Dracula (Stoker) 69, 70, 74–6, 87
Dracula AD 1972 **73**,
Dracula xii, xiii, xv, xvi, 68–95, 201
Dracula Was a Woman (McNally) 75
Dream Child, The 166, 174–5, 176
Dream Master, The **165**
Dream Warriors 166, 167, 169
dreams xiii, 21, 48, 56, 80, 196; *Elm
Street* films and 162, 163, 169, 170,
173–4, 179; nightmares 45, 62, 65,
144; Wolf Man and 98, 99–102, 104,
106–107, 109–117, 121, 123

earth, vampires and the 79, 94
Eddowes, Catherine 194
Edward the Confessor 132
Elm Street film series. *See Nightmare on
Elm Street* film series
eroticism: bestiality and 136; female
eroticism, Dracula and 90–2, 94;
vampires and 81–2
Evil Dead II 7–8, **9**
Evil of Frankenstein, The 43, **44**
Ewers, Hans: *The Student of Prague* 62
extimité 189
eyes, uncanny and 7–8, 9, 59
Eyes without a Face 184

facelessness 184, 186–7, 191, 192
family relationships, Freddy Krueger and
167, 170
Farrow, Mia 156
father: Freddy Krueger as 172; monster
107–8
Fawcett, John: *Ginger Snaps* 126, 133
fear, uncanny and 2
female hero: *Elm Street* films and 165–7,
172; slasher films and 184
Female Thermometer, The (Castle) 176–8
feminine: destruction of 184, 187,
189–90, 191; Freddy Krueger and
164–5; ghosts and 153–4, 157; horror
and vii; masculinised 200; vampire
and 89
feminism, Dracula and 91–2

femme–enfant 154–5, 163
Ferry, Jean 136
Fiedler, Leslie xvii
Fincher, David: *Alien 3* 57, 62
Fisher, Terence: *Dracula* 72
Fleming, Victor: *The Wizard of Oz* 173
Fly, The (1958) 46, **47**
Fly, The (1986) xii, xiii, 17, 42, 43, **44**,
46, 63
Forbes, Bryan: *The Stepford Wives* 42, 50
forest, uncanny and 155–6
fragmented self 187–9
Francis, Freddie: *The Evil of Frankenstein*
43, **44**
Franju, Georges: *Eyes without a Face* 184
Frankenstein (1931) 42, 43, 50–6, 59, 66
Frankenstein, Dr xiii, 12, 41–67, 70
Frankenstein, or The Modern Prometheus
(Shelley) xi, 46, 50–1, 54, 73
Frankenstein's monster xii, xv, 11, 12,
41–67
Freddy's Dead: The Final Nightmare 164,
166–7, 170, 173
Freud, Sigmund vii, viii, xv, 1–2, 5–6, 8,
10–14, 17, 18, 25, 27, 28–9, 30, 34,
36–7, 41, 45, 46, 49, 52, 80, 84, 170,
180, 186, 193; 'From the History of an
Infantile Neurosis' 96–123; 'The
Taboo of Virginity' 79; 'The Theme of
the Three Caskets' 21; 'The Three
Fates' 21; 'Totem and Taboo' 129;
'The Uncanny' 1–2, 5, 8–14, 19, 28–9,
34–7, 49, 80, 97, 103, 131
Friday the 13th film series 184
Fright Night **xiv**
From Hell 183, 184, 193, **194**, 196,
197, 198
'From the History of an Infantile
Neurosis' (Freud) 96–123
fur fetishism 148

Gattaca 42
gaze, uncanny 27–40, 178, 200
Gelder, Ken 93, 189
genitals, female: fear of 7, 11; uncanny
and 15. *See also vagina dentata*
Géricault, Théodore 160
Germer, Stefan 160